Blinking, Eric  away from soft pink was pretty, and not in the way most L.A. women were. She was nice too. As simple and unceremonious as that sounded, Angel, the girl who was really Jenna, was nice, a sweet girl way out of his league. He wished she would turn and walk away before he did something stupid, like kiss her again.

Gingerly, she reached into her purse. "Here, I hope this covers it."

Eric stared at the two crisp, hundred-dollar bills she held in her hand. He tried to tell her he didn't want them, but a sudden shock of embarrassment tightened his throat. Her offer was like a sucker punch. He didn't see it coming and he almost snapped his head back from the force.

"I don't need your money, the clothes were a gift." He covered her hand and crushed the bills within it. He grabbed an empty beer keg from the top of the bar and walked away.

"Wait! I-I was just trying to pay you back for the favor," she shouted to his back.

Turning, he rested the keg on the floor. "I wasn't keeping score."

Dedication

To my husband Mike and daughters Kara and Jamie who believed in me more than I did myself. To the girls of the Silk Purse writer's group who served up great insight as well as great meals. And finally to my friend Tricia Neary who always lent an ear and encouraged me to "put myself out there."

Prologue

Cromline, NY, 2011

The sounds of morning in a suburban *cul-de-sac* were predictable, especially so in spring—a neighbor's car starting, a dog barking, and the barely audible whisper of a breeze fanning through an open window. It was that light kiss of air that made Jenna Black stir. Clinging to the last remnants of sleep, she pressed into her pillow and reached across to the other side of her bed. Nothing was there but the cool emptiness of sheets that hadn't known the weight or warmth of another body. Even after nine years, she wasn't used to sleeping alone.

Sitting up, she stretched to loosen the stiffness gripping her shoulders. Her jaw was also tight, a sign she'd been grinding her teeth again. A ripple of anxiety teased the back of her neck and was gone as quickly as it came. She stretched more and in lazy and resistant steps padded to the bathroom where she glanced longingly at the tub. A good long soak would have eased all the tension from her body but there was no time; cartoon voices sounding from the living room meant Janie was up and dawdling instead of getting ready for school.

"I'm going to take quick shower. Turn off that TV and get dressed," Jenna shouted while looking down from the top of the stairs.

"Okay," the child called back, though she continued staring mindlessly at the screen.

"Seriously, Janie. We're going to be late." Jenna rushed back into her bathroom and jumped into the shower even though the water had barely heated up.

****

The next forty minutes sped by in a harried labor of wolfing down breakfast and making lunches. Last minute homework was signed, keys were lost and then found, and finally mother and daughter sprinted through the front door of their neat little cape and hopped into the car. The Cromline Central School bus, its air brakes hissing, rolled to a stop, but Jenna waved it away. Though Janie Black had never been a passenger, it stopped every day, right on schedule—something else predictable about mornings in a suburban *cul-de-sac*.

"Why can't I ever take the bus like other kids?" Janie asked for the third time that week.

"Because I pass right by the school on my way to the shop," Jenna answered.

"No you don't. The shop is on the other side of town."

Lucky me, Jenna thought as she slipped her key into the ignition, *I have the only eight-year-old on the planet with a sense of direction.*

She latched her seatbelt and started the car to tune out more of her daughter's complaints. Driving Janie to school every day was the safety overkill of a single mother whose life revolved around her only child. Jenna would have driven miles out of her way for that oh-so-elusive peace of mind.

Continuing through town, they passed modest bilevels and ranch style houses, then into the pricier neighborhoods where Georgetown Colonials and Tudors reigned over sprawling yards. Weeping cherries and ornamental maples dotted lawns as lush as an Irish hillside.

In less than ten minutes, she pulled into the school parking lot, dropped Janie off, and in another ten she was at her shop. A discarded wrapper with the store's logo lay crumpled on the sidewalk. Litter desecrating the pavement was the one drawback to owning a business that catered to adolescent girls. *They were slobs.*

Neon signs, oversized window graphics, and refuse on the walkway were capital offenses on the pristine thoroughfare. Jenna bent to pick up the wrapper. As she straightened, she looked first right and then left before unlocking the door to the shop, an arbitrary an unnecessary habit since the area was monitored by private security and a burglary unlikely.

Cromline was a safe haven, a secure and perfect place to live.

****

The day plodded on as most of her days did. Jenna counted out bills and change for the cash register, restocked shelves, made a few early sales and more after the schools let out. By four thirty, she'd sold enough sunglasses, handbags, and bejeweled cell phone covers to clear a day's rent, so she closed up and went home to throw something together for dinner before picking Janie up from her Brownie meeting.

After making a casserole from a recipe glorified on the back of a soup can, she filled the kettle to make a cup of herbal tea and unwind. *Unwind.* That particular irony was not lost on Jenna. Her life was on a permanent cycle of wash, rinse, repeat. And while it was the ordinary lifestyle she'd sought, it often locked arms with dull.

Settling into a chair she turned on the television, and scrolled through the channels absently clicking past commercials, talk shows, and reruns—another part of her daily routine. It was hearing the name Eric Laine and the word "divorce" that made her suddenly stop.

As she slowly sat up, her back parted from the comfort of the brushed velvet cushions. Gripping the chair's arms, she stared at the TV. She swallowed what should have been saliva, but the inside of her mouth had withered to dust, and she gulped nothing but air. Her pulse became an insistent thump in her ears. She strained to listen as a reporter announced that after six years of marriage, the A-List actor and his style-icon wife were "calling it quits."

Jenna felt oddly weightless, no longer grounded or connected to her surroundings. Everything around her seemed to blur except for the television beaming bright and clear above her mantle. Lightheaded and breathless, she watched a montage of pictures roll across the screen.

Photos of Eric Laine and his wife Bree slowly bled from one to another. Bronze and beautiful, they waved from the prow of a yacht; holding hands, they posed for the camera at the annual Met Gala; fit and fashionable, they skied the slopes of Aspen.

Air trapped and burning in Jenna's lungs left her lips in a long, hot sigh as she studied the last photograph of Eric holding his Oscar. Elegant in a tuxedo, he smiled, his teal eyes gleaming, his face handsome, still so very handsome.

As the picture faded to black the news anchor reported it was divorce number two for the Oscar winning star. She then posed a question about the whereabouts of the first Mrs. Laine, a young sensation who mysteriously disappeared at the height of her fame. Abruptly, as if the floor beneath her chair had given way, Jenna lurched. The remote slipped from her grasp and knocked into her cup. Tea splashed onto the coffee table, and the delicate china shattered.

Chapter One

Pinehill, NY, 1999

The chartered jet made a smooth landing at a private airport in upstate New York. A cross between an SUV and a limousine was parked a few yards from the plane.

After Jenna Welles descended the metal stairs, her stylist rushed behind, helping her into the blue graduation gown and brushing her waves of platinum-streaked hair before placing the matching cap on her head. Under the blistering June sun, her make-up girl swept blusher onto her cheeks, added a quick swipe of gloss to her lips and a finishing spray to set the cosmetics.

Business and entertainment manager Alan Stark clapped his hands. "Let's get going. The ceremony starts in forty minutes. We've got to get her through the press so let's make tracks."

Jenna whipped her head toward the sound of his voice, the gold tassel dangling from her cap swishing from the movement. "Press? Please…please tell me you didn't turn my high school graduation into a circus."

"You're a big star. Your graduation is *big* news."

Shoulders slumping under the billowing satin of her gown, she sighed. "*My* graduation is a joke. I haven't attended an entire semester since I was a sophomore. I was barely here at all this year."

"Yet they've asked you to give a speech. You're the most accomplished person to ever come out of that little backwater school."

Jenna shook her head as she slid into the SUV. She had an absurd vision of standing at the podium and giving her speech with a crew of background dancers gyrating behind her.

A few minutes later, the SUV pulled into the school parking lot, and as she alighted from the car she was shelled by cameras. The squeal and pop of electronic flash units followed her to her seat. She'd missed the processional and the playing of "Pomp and Circumstance." *I am the circumstance*, she thought as cameras continued to snap.

She craned her neck to find her parents and brother in the audience stationed on the grass.

"Jen! Jen!" The familiar flutter of her best friend's voice reached her. Randi Freed stood in the aisle, waving frantically. "I can't believe you made it. I'm so happy to see you."

Jenna's first inclination was to jump up and return the greeting. Instead, she slunk lower in her chair five rows back. She knew she'd cause a near riot as bodies twisted and turned to gawk at her.

Annabelle Walker, the classmate who'd been alphabetically stationed next to Jenna since kindergarten, said, "Wow. You're such an uppity bitch now you won't even turn around to say hello to your best friend?"

"It's not that," Jenna said. "I just don't want to be the focus of all the attention. This is your day."

Annabelle snorted. "Then you shouldn't have

7

fucking come."

****

Jenna graciously gave a short speech peppered with all the usual platitudes about "trying your best" and "never giving up." She wished the graduating class of 1999 success in college, success in life, and told them she hoped everyone would be as lucky as she was and to be able to always do what they loved.

There was sufficient applause and more camera flashes, but as Jenna walked from the makeshift stage she saw resentment in too many pairs of eyes. Kids she'd never been friends with were jealous of her success, and the honor society members hadn't forgiven her for abandoning them on the final day of the Mathlete competition.

The ceremony ended with the traditional tossing of caps and mortar along with raucous cheers. Kids rushed to find their besties and parents. Jenna rushed to find her family, the people she hadn't seen in months.

"There's my girl," Sam Welles cried.

"Smellerella," her brother Kyle jeered before hugging her.

Jenna's mother tottered over, cigarette in hand, her high heels puncturing the grass.

"Mom, you can't smoke on school property," Kyle said. He took the butt from his mother, took a drag, and extinguished it.

"Oh, I'm just so excited I needed a few puffs," Lorraine Welles apologized.

Jenna's hair and makeup crew advanced to touch up her cosmetics, but she slapped them away. "That's enough."

Stepping in, Alan took charge and interrupted the

space between his client and her parents. "We want to get some photos with your friends."

Jenna angled her head to look at the flat grass. Faded lines of white chalk that, last fall, indicated yardage markings on the football field were now only slightly visible. Adults in spring dresses and suits milled about, waiting for their graduates, who were laughing, crying, hugging one another, and snapping pictures—the final ritual of high school.

"In case you haven't noticed, I don't have any friends," Jenna said. "These kids hate me and showing up with an entourage isn't helping."

"Oh, sweetie, that isn't true," Lorraine argued. "You were always very popular."

"Mom, seriously? I was never popular. I was one of the weird kids in the drama club who didn't wear the right clothes or hang out at the mall." Jenna eased into her father's embrace. "Daddy, can we please just go home?"

****

An hour later, Jenna navigated her way through cars on the Freed's lawn to get to the door and Randi's party. Cutting through back yards she'd managed to escape Alan, her staff, and photographers from every tabloid outlet. Loud voices and louder music inside the house covered the sound of the doorbell. Finally Jenna's insistent banging was answered, and Randi opened the door looking none too happy to see her friend. "Well, well, well, what the hell are you doing here?"

Jenna thrust a bottle of *Belle Epoch* and a large package wrapped in silver foil into Randi's arms. "I'm sorry. I hate when I come home to a fuss. I just wanted to hunker down in my seat and slowly die."

Pursing her lips, Randi tested the weight of the box. "If this is your swag from the Oscars, I forgive you for ignoring me."

"Oscars *and* Grammys."

"So totally forgiven."

The girls raced up the stairs and into Randi's room where she immediately tore into the box. As both a presenter and nominee, Jenna's swag bags were worth upwards of ten thousand dollars. "I donated most of the stuff but saved the things I thought you'd like."

Randi hugged a designer backpack close to her chest. The leather was butter-soft, the signature initials stamped in gold on the flap. "I like, I like. I bet I'll be the only girl on campus lugging books around in a five-thousand-dollar knapsack."

There were more overpriced items in the box—on-trend makeup and hair products, jewelry, and a gift certificate to an exclusive spa in Beverly Hills. "I-I thought we could go there during your winter break." Jenna's tone was shy and tinged with embarrassment as if she were humbly asking for a favor.

"Sounds like a plan." Randi narrowed her eyes. "Y'know for a minute there, I thought you were blowing me off to go hang out with Annabelle and the Snotty Six. Her parents are throwing her a huge party at their club."

Jenna stilled. "If I wanted to spend the day with a crew of shallow posers, I would have stayed in L.A."

"Seriously?" Randi's bow of a mouth opened wide. "I just spent my senior year being guilt-by-association-tortured by Annabelle Walker and her bitchy friends because you found fame and fortune. Am I supposed to feel sorry for you?"

Jenna offered her friend an apologetic smile. "Were they that bad?"

Randi snorted. "Not at all. After *Teen Girl* called you an 'exotic flower plucked from a bed of ordinary daisies,' they were all *so* nice to me."

"Oh, God, I never saw that one," Jenna apologized.

"Screw it. It doesn't matter." Randi shook her head and a yard of golden hair swept across her back. "The Snotty Six are history. All that high school crap is over. My best friend is a beautiful and famous movie star, and I am *so* going to use that after I get to college. Every sorority on campus will recruit me."

"You don't need me for that."

Jenna studied Randi who was petite, blonde, blue eyed, and blessed with curves. By comparison Jenna thought her own slender frame was boyish, her eyes an odd shade of light brown, and her hair, without the platinum streaks, the color of a hay bale. "I'm just today's news."

"Oh, for God's sake," Randi countered. "You've been in two hit movies, your album is number one and you're still so freaking nice. Jeeze, I miss you."

Jenna hugged Randi, then sat back and wiped her eyes.

"Are you crying?"

Nodding, Jenna sniffled. "I miss you, too. I miss all of this."

She stretched her arm pointing at the items in Randi's room. It was so much like her own, the one in the pale blue bi-level down the block. Stuffed animals and knick-knacks filled the shelves, the walls were covered in posters, and clothing littered her floor.

Randi's dorm room was destined to be a landfill. Jenna realized a sudden pinprick of sadness and wiped tears from her cheeks. "I just always thought we'd be going away to college together."

Randi draped one arm around Jenna's shoulder and squeezed, then worked the cork on the champagne. It opened with a delicate pop. "Poor baby, I'll be thinking of you when you're drinking this at a red-carpet gala and I'm playing beer pong in some filthy frat house." Handing Jenna the bottle with its froth of bubbles spilling from the neck Randi ordered, "Drink up."

Jenna smiled and took a dainty sip. "Okay, but cut me off before I get too buzzed. You know liquor and my mouth don't get along."

"Get along? Half a glass of wine and you turn into a dock worker. It's hysterical." Randi rolled her baby blues and urged Jenna to drink more. "You are such a lightweight and way too lame to be a celebrity."

The friends laughed, hugged some more, and drank the expensive bubbly.

Chapter Two

Los Angeles, CA, 1999

Alan Stark took one last glance in the hand mirror and smoothed the gray at his temples.

"I can touch that up for you, sir," his stylist offered.

"No, I like the gray."

Alan felt it conveyed stature. He waved his slender hand, dismissing the woman as he continued to gauge his appearance in the mirror. His nose, thin but arced between close set eyes, took up most of the space on his narrow face. It didn't matter. Being handsome wasn't his priority. The streets of Los Angeles were infested with the beautiful. He cared only for what his looks imparted about his lifestyle. A collection of custom-tailored suits and power ties were more important to him than having a perfect jawline.

Stepping over to his mahogany wall-unit, he eyed decanters on glass shelves. Small lights had been specifically installed to showcase his collection of crystal. He poured an expensive cognac into a snifter and swirled the liquid before bringing it to his nose to sniff its spicy perfume. He took a sip. It was his celebratory ritual, and today he had something big to celebrate. Inspired Artists, the top talent agency in the business, inked Jenna Welles, his biggest client, to another three-picture deal with Panorama Studios.

Her story read like one of those old Hollywood myths where a lovely ingenue is discovered at a stoplight and skyrockets to fame. In Jenna's case it had been a community theater production which led to a small part in a musical that had become the year's biggest box-office hit. With just a five-line solo she'd stolen the movie and became an overnight sensation. Alan had wasted no time signing her.

He also wasted no time getting her parents out of the way. They were a suburban cliché, the dad committed to a nightly beer and his armchair, the mom a perpetual coffee drinker who spent her days on the phone. They'd agreed to leave their teenaged daughter in Alan's care.

He sipped again, savoring the honeyed heat rolling across his tongue. The Millennium was the era of the blonde popstar, and he had put Jenna at the top of the pyramid. She had a four-octave range and the "it" factor that made other teen queens and their autotuned voices, pale by comparison. She was also a hell of an actress. To further define her image Alan had decided on the stage-name Angel and made her brand purity. There were no wardrobe mishaps, no tabloid scandals, and no boy-band bed-hopping. She was, to the MTV generation, what 1930s' burlesque queen Gypsy Rose Lee had been to striptease. Wherever Angel went, she metaphorically let one strap slowly slide from her shoulder to leave everyone wanting more.

****

Angel.

Jenna wasn't sure she loved her stage name. She wasn't sure about her platinum hair color either. Most of it was her own but the silvery locks that hung in luxurious ribbons to the tops of her buttocks were sewn to tight braids at the back of her scalp. The mass felt heavy. She wound it into a bun and shoved it all under a baseball cap. Twining it back into her trademark waves would be up to her hair stylist. She stepped from the bedroom of her suite.

"This photo session should only take an hour or two and then we have to prep you for your interview with *Panache*." Alan was sitting on the sofa, a perpetual presence, directing, advising, and dictating how she spent her days. She supposed, as her manager, it was his job.

"You have two premiers next week, a gala at the Griffith Observatory, and you're handing out water at a 5K for pediatric diabetes. Your P.R. rep has you right at the finish line so there will be plenty of press."

Jenna nodded as she took it all in though there was no need to remember her very tight schedule. Alan always reminded her. He didn't miss a beat or steer her wrong and her star was still on the rise. Competition in Hollywood was fierce with new talent jumping straight from the cradle and into the spotlight.

"After the interview you're coming back here to the hotel. Go to bed early and get some sleep," he ordered. "You have an early shoot tomorrow, and I want you looking fresh."

Again Jenna nodded. She was obedient. She was Angel, the good girl Alan Stark had created.

****

Later that night, Jenna sat with her feet stretched out on the coffee table in her hotel suite. The blitz and bustle of her day should have exhausted her but instead left her wired. Her life was an adrenaline rush of filming, recording, touring, and red-carpet events—an undeniably exciting lifestyle with everything she could want or need within reach. She stood and paced the room, a spacious corner apartment—a beautiful but elegant confinement.

She had everything, everything except freedom. She'd cast it aside to live in the glow of the limelight. It was the certainty and concession everyone in the industry accepted, the tradeoff rendered for living a first-class lifestyle.

Her dinner arrived and after finishing, she idly placed her plate back on the cart and slid it toward the door. Though room service would come to retrieve it, it still made her antsy to look at the dirty china, utensils, and crumpled napkin just sitting there. Setting the table and stacking the dishwasher had been a chore she'd performed from the age of nine until she'd been whisked away from home three years ago, at fifteen. She wished to just clear away the mess herself, but the everyday minutiae of everyday life was not ascribed to her schedule.

Washing clothes, grocery shopping, even throwing a bag of popcorn in the microwave was no longer a part of her routine. She glanced again at the dinner cart. *If you want something done ask a busy person to do it*. And with every second of her day usually eaten up Jenna wondered, as she so often did, *am I a busy person or just a person being kept busy?* The thought stayed with her while she waited for room service to arrive to collect the cart.

Once it was gone, she plopped into the plush cushions of a chair and took a deep breath. "Now what?" she whispered. Being liberated from the grind, even for just one night, felt oddly like forgetting to put on underwear. Something was missing.

TV held little appeal. She thumbed through a stack of fashion magazines, distracted and bored. She thought to call Randi, but the time difference was its usual inconvenience. Standing, Jenna stretched and ambled around the room again. It was a posh suite of marble, high-end but generically pale colored furniture, scaling windows, and a terrace that offered a view of a city grid ablaze with so much light the streets looked bejeweled. What would it be like to be there? To be down in those streets with no security and no Alan. To be a part of the throng instead of watching it from her ivory tower.

Jenna knew of a club opening in West Hollywood, an exclusive, invitation only event. An envelope, addressed in hand-printed calligraphy, the flap fastened with a red wax seal, had been delivered to her suite weeks ago. If not for the creative packaging she might have discarded it but the invitation had been too pretty and too clever to throw away. She slipped it from the top drawer of the secretary and turned the envelope in her hand.

Should I go? L.A. club hopping was definitely not on Alan Stark's approved list.

"C'mon Jenna, you're eighteen and earn your own money. Do you really need to ask for permission to go out?"

She picked up her cell.

****

At precisely ten-fifteen the phone in Jenna's hotel suite rang to announce that Meghan Morrissey was waiting for her in the lobby. Jenna had been ready since nine, the time they were supposed to meet. Meghan was the wild child of Hollywood icon Jack Morrissey, Jenna's most recent co-star. They had become passing acquaintances because Meghan frequently visited the set—visited still dressed in the preppy uniform of her exclusive private school. Looking at her now, Jenna had to purposefully cut short a gasp. Meghan was in a short black skirt and mesh top, her small areolas visible through the filmy fabric. Stockings with intentional runs and snags, spiked leather jewelry, and macabre black liner rimming her eyes completed the Goth-streetwalker look.

Meghan eyed Jenna in her simple, black cocktail dress. "What the fuck are you wearing?" The question held a bite of accusation.

"DeLaurent," Jenna answered as she gingerly ran her hands along the structured taffeta of the beautiful dress.

"Oh for fuck's sake. I didn't ask *who* you were wearing. You aren't on the fucking red carpet." Meghan sighed and shook her head making an army of earrings chime. "My mother wears DeLaurent."

A warm flush traveled from Jenna's throat to her face. Meghan was brash, recognizably wasted, but correct. The designer dress, with it wide belt and pleated flounces, was gorgeous, but not an outfit for the opening of a hot new club. "All my evening clothes are couture," Jenna said dipping her head as if shamed by the pricey garment.

"Couture. Pfft, that manager of yours," Meghan huffed. "*You* need to tell your stylist what *you* want to wear once in a while. I'm surprised Stark is even letting you out of your cage."

Jenna bristled. "I'm not in a cage. I do what I

want."

Meghan scratched at her raven-colored hair and raised a pierced brow to drive home her point. "That's not what the tabloids say."

"Tabloids lie," Jenna said. Still, she took a nervous glance around, half expecting Alan to be hiding behind a potted palm. "Let's just go."

"Okay, but we're making a pit stop first." Meghan pulled Jenna by the hand through the lobby door and nudged her into a limo. Picking up a half empty bottle of tequila lying on the seat, she took a long swig, then pounded on the divider. "Hey, go back to my house," she ordered, as she handed the bottle to Jenna.

"I don't drink hard liquor. "I'm only eighteen. I sneak a little wine once in a while but no booze."

"You want a hit of X?"

"No! I don't do drugs and I'm absolutely not into any wild—"

"Holy shit." Meghan took another long pull of tequila. Whatever didn't make it past her laugh, dribbled into the weave of her mesh shirt.

"*Tabloids lie*," she mimicked Jenna's words. "You need to have some fun, Goody Two Shoes."

****

The limousine followed along a curving road, into gated Bel Air and Meghan's house. It was California splendor at its best. Landscape lights illuminated an enormous white stucco structure capped with a Spanish tiled roof, the wavy ceramic a lustrous topaz. Lines of cypress and blousy palm trees created fencing along the property. The limo stopped in the circular drive in front of a set of tall doors with etched glass panels.

"Welcome to my mother's divorce settlement,"

Meghan sniggered. Her steps were wobbly as she walked through the doorway, and on the winding staircase she had to steady herself by holding on to the wrought iron banister. She stopped once to swallow more of the tequila.

In her bedroom, she foraged through racks of clothing. "You really need to lose the couture but if you have to have designer…here. This is fresh from Fashion Week in New York."

Meghan tossed a thin scrap of red to Jenna. It was a slip of a dress with narrow satin ribbons that crisscrossed the bodice. The garment was a sexy temptation the scarlet color of a winter amaryllis. It was something Alan would never approve of. Jenna's heart began to thrum a little as she tried it on.

"Wow," she said as she regarded herself in the mirror. The tight bodice pushed her breasts up to form a deep spill of cleavage. And the hem was farther away from her knees than what she was used to. She loosened the ribbons to allow more room for her breasts.

"Oh for Christ's sake," Meghan said giving the strings a yank, "leave it the fuck alone. Most of Hollywood has to pay big bucks to fill out a dress like that. There isn't a bitch in this town as skinny as you are with *real* tits that are that big." Meghan reached toward Jenna and fondled her. "Yep, all you."

Jenna slapped at the hands molesting her bosom, and stepped into a pair of mile-high, narrow heels. She declined the leather studded jewelry Meghan offered but agreed to add more makeup to her eyes.

Grabbing the bottle of tequila from the floor, Jenna took a sip, then a larger gulp that immediately had her gasping. "Okay," she said, still choking. "Let's party."

Chapter Three

Crimson, L.A.'s club of the moment, was jammed as expected, and photographers grappled for a square of sidewalk, poised to catch the invited celebrities. Autograph seekers also crammed the street trying to get a glimpse of the glitterati, or get into the club that in a year's time would be an empty cave. The A-List was fickle. Jenna and Meghan were whisked inside by security and then led to the VIP section. Even the famous were ruled by a caste system and for the moment Jenna Welles, a.k.a. Angel, was at the top.

The reality hit her the moment she stepped into the proverbial limelight. She was famous, young and famous, *rich* and famous. She could go to places like this every night of her life if she wanted to. She wasn't restricted to the affairs Alan chose for her. Moving forward, she was going to have a personal life and friends her own age, friends who could enjoy the energy and excitement of the club scene with her.

Crimson was electrifying, the dance floor a theatrical extravaganza of smoke machines and lasers. The bars were edged with neon and balloons and confetti sporadically dropped from the ceiling. The rhythmic bass of hip hop raged through speakers. Alt, R&B and techno screamed. The music was channeled straight to Jenna who danced the entire night, stopping only occasionally to drink champagne the club owners offered, an expensive vintage that slipped down her throat with too much ease. Sometime around one, Meghan vanished, taking the limo and a B-list actor with her.

Jon, one of the owners, took a tipsy Jenna by the hand. "Ah, my Angel, come sit with us."

"Yes, do sit, darling girl," agreed his partner, Caz.

Delighting in her company, the two men proceeded to pummel her with banal dialogue.

"Where has that dreadful Morrissey brat gone off to?" one asked.

"Oh I think she left with that delicious boy from the new cop show on FOX," the other said.

"Well her taste is improving. At least she isn't blowing any of our waiters in the alley."

"Such language. Shame on you. Excuse his potty mouth, Angel."

The blather went on and on making Jenna dizzy. No gay men were *that* gay but like everyone in L.A. Jon and Caz adhered to a brand. Theirs was fabulous nightclub queens and they played to their audience.

The constant thump of music began to pound in her temples. She excused herself and wove her way to the restroom to call a taxi. The ladies room was empty. She'd lost track of her purse and her cell phone and there was no pay phone in sight. Jenna dropped bonelessly onto the couch in the lounge, thinking she wouldn't want to go to a place like this every night after all. She'd had more alcohol and more fun in the last three hours than she'd had in the last three years, and this, she thought through cobwebs, was probably not such a great idea.

"I'll have more fun but less of it at one time." She

tilted her spinning head back against the arm of the sofa and raised her sore feet. An hour later she was still there, curled up on the sofa, sleeping soundly.

****

Mop in hand, the bar-back silently cursed as he looked at the clock above one of the cash registers. "Shit...three-thirty," he cursed again. His bosses had already retired to their loft upstairs and the manager was gone. What the hell was he supposed to do with the body in the ladies room? Stepping behind the bar he filled a glass with water. If drinking it didn't bring her around, he swore he'd pour it over her head. He marched across the floor and back to the bathroom.

Why did this place have to have its grand opening on a Monday? he thought soberly. *Would opening on Friday or Saturday be too ordinary for L.A.?* He had a job interview early in the morning, an interview for a real job, and had hoped to get at least three hours of sleep.

Bending down, the young man nudged the girl's shoulder gently. "Hey, babe, wake up. Time to go." He said the words with enough volume to rouse but not startle her. "Come on, sweetheart, rise and shine."

"Mmm, fuck off," the girl mumbled as she rolled one shoulder and buried her face in her arms.

He gave her a gentle shake. "No you don't. The party's over."

Again she responded with a snuffling noise and a clearer "Leave me alone and let me fucking sleep."

Typical bratty Hollywood behavior. "I'd love to let you *fucking* sleep, sweetheart, but I'd like to go *fucking* home and I can't leave you here."

Turning, she pulled at yards of hair plastered to her

face. "Please," she begged. "I'm so fucking tired."

Surprised, the young man blinked. The raspy groan of her voice as she cursed had defined his expectations and he hadn't expected such a soft and lovely face to be hidden beneath the twining mess of hair.

He stared, his eyes lingering for several moments before he realized he'd been holding his breath. He exhaled a slow draft of air and went back to the business of studying her. Her wide set eyes gleamed golden, her nose was slightly upturned, and her lips curved into a full pout. Her skin was like every soft thing ever referenced in a poem—velvet, cream, and rose petals. With a lilting grin the sleepy girl glanced back meeting his stare with her own.

It was the first of the thousand times Jenna Welles and Eric Laine would gaze into each other's eyes.

****

Eric took a deep breath, so that his heart, beating fitfully, would relax back into its normal rhythm. He assisted the girl to her feet, offering the glass of water. After taking a sip, she placed it on a nearby table and dropped back onto the couch.

"Uh-uh. Time to get up." He tightened his grasp to keep her upright.

Folding into him, she rested her cheek against his chest and hummed softly as if she'd tasted something sweet. An immediate flash of heat warmed him as the tops of her breasts swelled from the bodice of her dress. Encircling her waist, he unintentionally brought her slender body in intimate alignment with his own. His hands slid with ease along her back, the material of her dress so silky-fine he could feel the dimples in the slope just above the rounded curve of her ass. For one weak-minded moment, he thought about how easy it would be to slip the flimsy dress from her pale shoulders. She was murmuring agreeably to the hands massaging the small of her back.

"Damn," he whispered as he swept her into his arms and carried her from the club. Taking a girl in such a vulnerable state was not and never would be Eric Laine's style. He deposited her into his car and headed to the 101.

Once on the freeway, the breeze or more likely noise from the rattling engine of his beat-up convertible roused her from her stupor. From the corner of his eye he caught her hazy regard. She seemed to be reading him. "Are you the guy from the bathroom?"

"Uh huh."

"Good."

Strange. Although Eric cleaned up nicely for work, he still didn't give off a Boy Scout vibe. Imprinted on him was the surly attitude born from a derelict childhood and very few people trusted him at first glance.

Fifteen minutes later, he pulled into the narrow alley that separated his rented bungalow from his neighbor's and carried her inside. The place was one small room with what passed for a kitchen in a corner and a bathroom the size of a phone booth in another. A mattress on the floor served as his bed. He shoved the pile of clothing on it to the floor with his foot and laid her down. Before leaving the club, he'd made a quick sweep of all the tables trying to find her purse and ID so he could bring her home, but they weren't to be found. Eric prayed she was at least eighteen so he wouldn't end up spending the next year in jail.

Gently tapping her shoulder he placed his phone next to her. "Here, call your parents and let them know you're alive."

Sleepily, she pushed the old touch-tone away and mumbled something about not living with them. Dark lashes fluttered for half a heartbeat before she fell back into a drunken slumber.

Eric showered, and changed his clothes, sleep for him was no longer an option. He drank coffee dark as ink and laced with so much sugar it was like a sweet shot of adrenaline. He couldn't show up for his job interview with only one eye open. He had been on a merry-go-round of work going from one low paying job to the next. The gig at Crimson as a bar-back, the grunt who hauls the ice and supplies to the bartenders, would mean decent money until the novelty of the place wore off. He had been down that road before.

He stared at his sleeping house guest and wondered whose arm she had strolled in on. Crimson's grand opening had been an invitation-only event so she must belong to someone. Stepping out through his doorway he turned to take another look at the girl, wondering how whoever she was with could have forgotten her. He locked the door and hopped into his car.

As he drove, he said a small prayer for the interview to go well. He'd made a vow that after he turned twenty, he would get a respectable job, but it wasn't easy without a high school diploma. His references weren't exactly stellar either. He'd done some odd jobs for an attractive divorcee who lived in Laurel Canyon, but the only *references* she gave him were to a few unhappily married friends.

He parked his car and walked to the construction

trailer. Even being a day-laborer was a step up from what he'd been doing. Tom Larity, the owner of the company, and a man of about sixty, looked as though he still put in time breaking a sweat. He seemed like a regular guy and Eric liked him immediately.

Tom extended a work callused hand. "So, tell me kid, how'd you hear about the job opening?"

"I work at a nightclub. The guys who own the place said you built it. Caz Taylor and Jon Terrio?"

Tom nodded. "Good guys. You ever do any construction work before?"

Eric glanced around at the bedlam of blueprints, dented file cabinets, and broken power tools awaiting new cords, blades, and switches. "I know my way around a hammer and saw."

"Tell you what, I'm shorthanded right now so I'll give you a try. You can start tomorrow."

"Great. Thank you. You won't be disappointed."

Eric beamed as he shook his new boss's hand and then sprinted from the trailer. A smile stayed fixed and steady on his face as he drove home. When he opened his door, he discovered the girl was still there, sprawled out on his makeshift bed.

Once again, his breath caught in his throat. The top of her dress was low enough for him to see a hint of pink nipples. The bottom had ridden up to her waist and her thong didn't cover much. An immediate and arousing sensation settled low in his belly.

Eric was no stranger to women. He'd lost his virginity young, at barely fifteen. His father had thought it time for his son to "become a man" and offered him up to a twenty-three-year-old barmaid who worked at a local dive. Since then, sex had been meaningless. The opportunity to be smitten or to have an adolescent crush on a girl had been stolen from him. He dropped to his haunches and stared more at the girl, torn between the recognizable feeling of lust and something completely unfamiliar.

One of her arms was stretched over her head the other across her middle. Her long, slender legs were turned to the side, her knees bent. Had she been awake, she could have been posing for a sexy calendar. Eric watched her breasts gently rise and fall and he found himself breathing in time with her, mimicking the rhythm of slow, easy sex.

He shed his jeans and T-shirt and joined her on the mattress. Resting on one elbow, he leaned down and gave her a gentle nudge. Her eyelids, heavy with sleep, fluttered from the effort of opening. She offered an unconcerned yawn. Then, as her eyes snapped into focus, the terror of having a strange man hovering over her became unmistakably etched on her face. Her bottom lip began to tremble, a small quiver that gained momentum so that in a short while she was shivering. Something like a heavy hand pressed against Eric's chest causing pressure that left him momentarily unable to breathe.

"Shh…" he whispered. "It's okay. You passed out at the club last night and I brought you here. I'm not going to hurt you. I swear."

She shuddered, her big eyes fixed and wide, her breath thready.

"I swear," he repeated. "Please don't be afraid."

Rising from her spot on the thin mattress looked to be an insurmountable effort and she lay there pushing against her temples with the palms of her hands. "I'm dying," she more groaned than spoke.

He offered a whisper of a chuckle. "You aren't. You just need to sleep it off." The last thing the girl was apt to tolerate was his voice echoing against the walls of the barren room, so he lowered his voice to a murmur. "Just shut your eyes and go back to sleep."

Barely nodding, she eased deep into the mattress. Eric stretched alongside her, and then wrapped himself warm and protectively around her. Two strangers lay there, arms and legs entangled, as though it was the most intrinsic and natural thing to do.

****

Jenna woke up, her head muzzy and eyes bleary. She heard the steady rhythm of breathing close to her ear. *Oh, God. Where am I? What did I do?*

Her memory of the night seemed to have been swallowed up by something thick and viscid. Slowly, very slowly, it began to clear. The man, lying next to her and sleeping soundly, had brought her home.

No, not home, here, wherever here was.

Forcing down the rising panic, she eased onto her side to face him. She took a quick, cautious look. Sunlight spilling into a window cast gold highlights through his sandy colored hair. Jenna had a hazy recollection of talking to him, of his being sweet. Using her knuckles, she rubbed at the makeup blurring her vision and looked more intently.

He was young, his features strong. His nose was straight and his lips, just plump enough, nested between hollow cheeks. Tapping a fingernail against her teeth, Jenna studied the perfectly handsome symmetry of his face. She felt a sudden capricious desire to brush stray locks of hair from his forehead, to touch him. Her sight traveled down from the cords of his neck, across the wide expanse of his shoulders, going to where a light dusting of hair covered his chest and flat stomach. His lips parted, and he uttered a sleepy groan as he threw one well-muscled thigh over hers and draped an arm across her waist. Jenna's dress had scrunched up past her hips, and as he languorously shifted position, she felt his hardness pressing against her.

Air skipped into her lungs. The young man's erection was tight and flush against her, separated only by his cotton briefs and her lacy thong. He moved again and a heady shiver of arousal warmed her. It was a fiery tingle that spread from the apex of her thighs up to her breasts, and down her legs to her toes. Jenna's sexual experience had never gone beyond an awkward French kiss one time at a party.

Now in Hollywood, with Alan on constant guard she never dated. Long buried feelings of youthful passion coursing through her bloodstream prickled her skin. She lay there in a stranger's arms, reveling in the sensation.

What seemed like only moments later, he opened his eyes. They were blue, rich, and faceted like an aquamarine. Jenna almost knew before his lids parted, they would be that color.

With their mouths close enough for a kiss and his fingers twined at the small of her back he smiled. "Good afternoon," he said, then politely added, "sorry about that. I didn't mean to get so personal.

Stretching, he yawned, got up, and ambled to the bathroom not appearing overly concerned or embarrassed by the bulge distending his briefs. He returned a few moments later wearing unbuttoned jeans and wiping his mouth with a towel. He had obviously brushed his teeth.

The inside of Jenna's mouth felt like a preschool art project—paste gone awry. She had to pee, was dying of thirst, and after sitting up felt the first stabs of pain penetrate her skull.

"What's the matter, Babes…hangover?"

Jenna clutched her skull, and through slitted eyes looked at the young man smiling down at her. He offered his hand, holding hers tightly until her body acclimated to being vertical.

"This is the fourth or fifth time I've had to help you stand up. I think it's time you told me your name."

Busying herself with the ribbons on the bodice of the dress, she didn't meet his stare. "It's Jenna."

"Eric Laine," he said, dipping his head and making the ridiculous offer of a handshake.

"Where am I?"

"My house," was his simple reply.

House was an understatement. Jenna didn't need to move her throbbing head in any direction because the sweep of her eyes was enough to take in the place, wall to wall. It was a cubicle.

"Did I by any chance curse at you last night?"

"Repeatedly. You have a mouth like a truck driver."

"I apologize. I was drinking champagne."

Jenna watched his gaze move from her bare feet, up to crumpled red ribbons, and finally to a complicated mass of hair that fell like streamers over her shoulders.

"Of course you were," he said on a laugh. He placed warm hands on her shoulders and pointed her in the direction of his tiny bathroom. "Go splash some water on your face; you'll feel better."

When she returned, she had swiped at the make-up caked under her eyes, rinsed her mouth with mouthwash, and taken care of other personal duties. Eric handed her two aspirins and a cup of coffee in which he'd added a heaping spoonful of sugar. Feeling horrible and shaky, she accepted the offer, her body craving the sweet brew. By slow degrees, more of the fog cleared and then like hearing a hammer hit a bell she woke to the full gravity of her predicament. She was alone with a man she didn't know. She had absolutely no idea where she was or how she was going to get back to her hotel. She had no idea how she was going to sprint unnoticed into the lobby in the towering heels and red dress.

But Jenna's last and most alarming thought was she'd missed the morning's shoot and Alan was going to kill her.

Chapter Four

Alan Stark's voice was an edgy bristle through the telephone line. "What do you mean she didn't show up on set?"

"Just what I said," the director shot back. "She's a no show."

Slamming down the receiver, Alan punched in a new set of numbers. "Lombardo! Where the hell is Angel?"

"I don't know, Mr. Stark, I drove her home after her magazine interview. She said she wouldn't need me until the morning. I've been looking for her all day."

"Find her." Alan broke the connection and paced like a lion at feeding time. *Think. Where the hell is she?*

Grim scenarios raced through his mind, an abduction by some lunatic fan at the forefront. The idea that she would go somewhere without his permission was incomprehensible. Still, he played a mental recording of all new restaurant, gallery and nightclub openings she'd been invited to. Then he remembered the invitation to Crimson. Two of L.A.'s most successful entrepreneurs were launching a new place in WeHo, their latest in a string of upscale clubs that catered to the young and ultra-hip. Angel, he knew, was at the top of that list and had wanted to go.

Had she dared?

He held on to the edge of the marble vanity in his

dressing room, the pressure turning his knuckles white. *Had—she—dared?*

****

"Do you know what time it is?" Jenna asked in a small voice.

Eric shuffled the pile of clothing on the floor with his foot, uncovering an alarm clock. "Three fifteen."

Her eyes popped huge and undecided, the same look of stark panic that keeps a deer frozen on a highway. The girl was troubled by more than a simple hangover. She looked as if a burden bore down on her, weighty and unalterable.

"Look," he said, "you had too much to drink, and you lost your purse, so I brought you here. Nothing happened. I was a perfect gentleman." He offered a bow to emphasize his point, a hackneyed parody of a regency romance. "I'll take you home, you can cancel your credit cards, get some rest, and by tomorrow you'll be good as new."

Jenna nodded, but stood there, her chin wobbling and tears gathering in the corners of her eyes. A feeling of doom settled as Eric took in her waif like expression. *Please be eighteen, please be eighteen, please be eighteen.* "Tell me you aren't a freshman in high school," he said.

She straightened and tipped her chin up. "Of course not. I graduated last June."

A laugh fell from Eric's mouth at how proudly that particular declaration rolled off her tongue. Once again, his focus trailed from her scraggly mass of hair to the wrinkled, red dress. "Did you wear that outfit when you gave your valedictory speech?"

"Shut up," Jenna answered as teardrops spilled

down her cheeks."

"Aw come on, I'm just messing with you. Don't cry." He brushed his hands up and down her arms in a gesture of comfort. "Things can't be that bad."

"I didn't show up for work today," she admitted.

"Oh." He dipped his head in sympathy. The threat of unemployment was a burden he carried every day. "Will you lose your job?"

"No, I have a contract. But I'm in the middle of filming and I'm sure I cost the producer a ton of money."

Ah. Eric took a step back. *Producer*, he should have known. A knockout, leggy blonde, wearing half a dress, passed out in L.A.'s newest club had to be in show business. "So you're an actress?"

Jenna's mascara caked eyes narrowed. "Don't you know who I am?"

"Sweetheart, I don't have cable and I rarely look up when I clear dirty glasses from the V.I.P. lounge. But feel free to give me your autograph."

She hugged her middle as if to steady both emotional and physical tremors. "I'll sign it *to the last person who saw me alive before my manager murdered me*." The sarcasm of her words sounded like they held more than a bite of truth.

Eric pulled her back into his arms. He had little tolerance for bullies, and something inherently built inside of him wanted to protect her. Still, he was the one to eventually back away from the embrace. He stepped to his sink, tore a slice of paper towel from the roll and wet it. Returning to where she stood, he dabbed at the skin under her eyes. "Let's get you home so you can call whoever you need to call."

"I-I'm staying at The Royal Wilshire, but I can't walk into the lobby looking like this. The press will be all over me."

"Press?" Gently placing his forefinger under her chin he tipped up Jenna's face so that they were eye to eye. "Holy shit." He just realized who she was.

****

"Holy shit," he repeated. "You're not just an actress…You're a star. There's a big poster of you in the window of Excel Records. Angel, right?" Folding his arms across his chest his sight again traveled from her feet up to her head, this time in slow scrutiny. "Wow, you look a lot different in person."

Jenna felt her lips tremble and she bit her bottom one to keep from succumbing to any other involuntary shaking. She was never touching another drop of alcohol again. "Thanks."

Eric raised a brow, his expression decided. "I bet the tabloids would pay me a lot of money for your picture. Angel…hung over in East L.A." He splayed his fingers as if he were announcing a title. "Stand still while I go find my camera."

"No, no, no, no, no." Horrified, Jenna forced swollen feet into Meghan's impossible high heels and rushed toward the door.

In an instant, Eric was behind her, his hand covering hers to stop her frenzied attempt to turn the stubborn knob. "I was kidding. I don't make money by cashing in on people's fuckups. In the places I've worked I'd be a rich man if I did." He eased her around so she was facing away from escape. "Does this place look like the apartment of a rich man?"

Jenna took in, corner by corner, the small

apartment with its worn furniture. The mattress' only companion was a pitted table and pair of mismatched wooden chairs. The natty interior of the bungalow told pop and movie star Angel that the boy who'd found her asleep in the nightclub was most definitely not rich.

****

Jenna was quiet on the way back to her hotel. For two years, Alan had her on such a rigid schedule her only reprieve from living out of a suitcase were the rare occasions she could squeeze in visits with her parents or Randi. Personal mementos were back home in Pinehill. She lived as devoid of a home as the young man at the wheel, just on a grander scale.

He broke the silence. "So how does someone bring a movie star home from a late date? Do I drop you off in front of the hotel or do the gentlemanly thing and walk you to your door?"

The remark was a lot less funny than he'd intended and Jenna automatically fingered the ribbons hopelessly twisted across her breasts. "I told you I can't walk into the lobby like this. I'll have to sneak in the back way." She dropped her head on to the torn vinyl seat back. "I can't do that either, I don't have my key card."

With one hand casually draped on the steering wheel, the wind ruffling his hair, Eric tipped his head toward hers. "I've been cleaning up the messes celebrities make for almost three years now. They get trashed all the time. You're not the first. Just go to the desk and get another card."

Jenna sighed again. "You don't understand. My manager created this image and I'm…I'm…" She dropped her face into her hands. "I can't be photographed like this. He'll have a stroke."

"Correct me if I'm wrong," Eric said, "but doesn't *he* work for *you*?"

"Yes, but it's Alan Stark. He's one of the biggest entertainment managers in Hollywood and I'm really lucky to have him."

"That doesn't explain why you sound like you're afraid of him."

Jenna couldn't argue with the statement and turned her head to stare at the blurry horizon and avoid the question.

****

Eric stole a quick glance at her sitting next to him silently gnawing on her thumbnail. This girl certainly wasn't like other celebrities who bulldozed their way through clubs, announcing their arrival and their standing. Maybe that was why he hadn't recognized her—she didn't reek of self-importance. He took the next exit ramp and drove in the direction of a small shopping center with a cheap, national chain store.

"Stay put, and keep your head down, I'll be right back." He jogged to the store, returning a short time later carrying two plastic shopping bags. "Here." He handed her the packages. Inside one was an oversized sweatshirt and stretch pants. A pair of canvas sneakers and sunglasses filled the other. "Does this big-time manager of yours have any objection to exercise?"

Jenna took the sweatshirt from the bag and clutched it to her chest. "Oh. This is so nice…you didn't have to…" It seemed as if a lump in her throat made it impossible for her to finish expressing her gratitude.

Eric took her in his arms once more, something that had become a habit in the last twelve hours.

Brushing her tangled hair from her face and tracing the line of her jaw with his finger, he leaned toward her and covered her mouth with his. The kiss was gentle but thorough, his tongue sweeping the inside of her mouth possessively, while he held her tightly. She slipped quietly and easily into his embrace, her fingers firm against his shoulders. When the kiss ended, they both stared at one another thunderstruck.

Eric Laine, who never gave a backward glance at the women he was with, and Jenna Welles, who had just experienced her first real adult kiss, disengaged from one another and sat in silence for a long, lingering minute.

"I'd better get you back to your hotel." His tone was sharp enough to snip the imaginary filament that held their gaze.

"Yeah, I-I need to get back."

Eric drove his car to the rear entrance so even in disguise she wouldn't be seen emerging from his dented, old beater. She waited by the elevators until he returned with the hotel manager and a new card. After being dismissed by the concierge, he walked through the back door, waving his arm over his head to say good-bye.

He never turned around.

Chapter Five

Alan snapped at his gardener, his housekeeper, and his personal assistant all day. His behavior was a warm-up exercise for what he planned to do to Angel's driver, Nick Lombardo, when he arrived to pick him up. They had exhausted the minutes on Angel's cell phone with constant calls and filled her voice mail to capacity. Nick then spent the remainder of the afternoon loitering in the Royal Wilshire's lobby hoping to spot her.

"Tell me you've found her," Alan demanded as the car pulled up.

"She checked into her suite at about five thirty Mr. Stark."

"Five thirty. You're through. You'll be lucky to get a job driving kids to the prom."

"Mr. Stark I—"

"Save it," Alan said, as he climbed into the back of the limo.

Blood pounded in his temples. Heat rose from his neck to the top of his head. He'd been drinking steadily, hoping alcohol would temper his mood. It hadn't. Angel had gone to that club and hooked up with someone, he was certain of it. She had no girlfriends, he'd seen to that. The only explanation for her disappearance was that she had hooked up with someone. *Damn her.* Alan was seething by the time he reached the hotel and scarcely able to speak to the desk manager when he told him to ring Angel's suite.

"She's asked not to be disturbed, Mr. Stark. Would you care to leave a message?"

Alan gave no reply. The muscles in his cheeks twitched his answer.

****

Jenna pressed the message button on the furiously blinking house phone as soon as she stepped into her suite. There were clipped messages from her director's assistant, and two dozen enraged voice mails from Alan. The ire in his voice had escalated with each one. Deciding the confrontation with him could wait, she called the front desk and asked them to hold all calls. A little over an hour later, she called for a taxi to meet her at the back.

"Here we are miss, that'll be seventeen even," the cabby said as he pulled to a stop in front of Crimson. Jenna paid the driver, sprinted to the entrance, and pulled the heavy glass door open. Stepping inside the brightly lit space, she watched as the staff rushed about to prepare for the night ahead. She flinched when a squawk of feedback pierced the air.

"What am I doing here?" she whispered, walking with slow cautious steps toward the bar. *I'm just here to pay that sweet guy back for the things he bought me from Save-Mart.* She answered her own question with an acceptable reply—one that was a lie. She wanted to see him again.

A door somewhere toward the back opened, and a figure, blurred by the light, stepped through. The height, the dip of his shoulders as he walked, his stride easy even though he carried a large crate, told Jenna it was him. A feeling like light, tingly fingers brushed

41

against her skin.

He looked surprised when he saw her. "What are you doing here?"

"I-I wanted to thank you."

"Not necessary," he said, his tone pointedly blunt.

Jenna stood unmoving, her feet, anchored to the floor by the weight of embarrassment and confusion. His kiss had been a blast of hot sparks that shot through her body with such impact she could still feel them. Why was he acting so cold now?

He stood, leaning against the bar, still as a statue except for the glancing sweep of his blue eyes upon her. He was freshly shaved, his hair tamed by gel, and his red bow tie hanging, undone, from the loop of his collar. He looked tall and handsome, and so bothered by her presence. Embarrassed, Jenna looked down and stared at a stream of light raining onto the glittering floor tile.

****

Blinking, Eric forced his sight away from her, away from soft pink lips and wide golden eyes. Jenna was pretty, and not in the way most L.A. women were. She was nice too. As simple and unceremonious as that sounded, Angel, the girl who was really Jenna, was nice, a sweet girl way out of his league. He wished she would turn and walk away before he did something stupid, like kiss her again.

Gingerly, she reached into her purse. "Here, I hope this covers it."

Eric stared at the two crisp, hundred dollar bills she held in her hand. He tried to tell her he didn't want them, but a sudden shock of embarrassment tightened his throat. Her offer was like a sucker punch. He didn't see it coming and he almost snapped his head back from the force.

"I don't need your money, the clothes were a gift." He covered her hand and crushed the bills within it, grabbed an empty beer keg from the top of the bar, and walked away.

"Wait. I-I was just trying to pay you back for the favor," she shouted to his back.

Turning, he rested the keg on the floor. "I wasn't keeping score."

Ordinarily Eric would have pocketed the cash without a thought. As a kid, he had never been too particular about where money came from, so why did he feel such shame heating his face? A quick glance into Jenna's eyes told him why. Because she knew the cheap polyester sweatsuit and canvas sneakers had cost him his entire night's salary. She pitied him.

"I don't need your money," he grumbled.

An awkward silence was interrupted by a sudden click of footsteps rending the air. Eric turned at the sound. Jenna froze in place. "My manager," she whispered.

"Where the hell were you today?" The voice was an inauspicious utterance, a quiet yet menacing echo in the empty space. "Just what the *hell* were you thinking staying out all night?"

Eric silently appraised the man, Alan Stark. He was a deliberate figure of neatly trimmed dark hair, and narrow shoulders tailored under fine fabric. Eric watched as bony fingers seemed to slither from his snowy white cuff and twine around Jenna's wrist. The big shot manager yanked her close but her response to the violent pull didn't seem to come as a surprise and her face remained blank. Eric took one long stride, grabbed Stark by his silk tie and slapped him. The sound was a high-pitched clap that pierced the air followed by the thump of his body hitting the floor.

"Don't ever put your hands on her again."

Jenna's gasp was as sharp and resonant as the slap. "Oh my God, Alan."

Bartenders and various members of the staff rushed in the direction of the noise. Jon rushed to Alan with Caz fluttering close behind.

"Mr. Stark." Jon immediately offered his hand. "I cannot apologize enough." He leveled a look of wrath in Eric's direction. "You're fired."

Eric stood, rigid except for the rapid rise and fall of his chest. He regretted the slap, but immediate and intense anger was sparked by something he couldn't explain. The son of a bitch manhandled Jenna, and Eric simply lost it.

"I'm sorry," he whispered the words to her, softly, his voice a low confession. But she didn't answer, nor did she look at him. It was the response to violence he was well used to. It was the same response he'd gotten his whole life when, as a child, he'd tried so bravely to stop his father from hitting his mother.

Head hung low, Eric glanced at Jenna. The crumpled bills had fallen from her hand—the two, hundred dollar drops of disinfectant she'd meant to use to clean up her mistake.

"I'm calling the police," Jon said.

Brushing dust from his suit jacket, Alan looked remarkably composed given he'd been scattered to the floor like a broken bottle. "I'd happily have him arrested but Angel doesn't need the fallout. As for *firing* him…that's your call."

His head pivoted slowly at the circle of staff members who'd gathered around the spectacle— handsome bartenders and pretty waitresses, most of whom were waiting for their big break. Eric watched as they posed for Stark's benefit as if his scrutiny was an audition. His dark eyes, staid and serious, stopped at Eric. "I've been in the business for a long time and can tell when someone has a certain star quality." Alan casually brushed the sleeves of his jacket more and straightened his tie, his ego an apparent cloak covering a simmering fury. "The macho thing has been done. Casting agents are looking for something a little less…ordinary. If you're trying to break into the business, forget it. Keep your day job."

He turned to Jenna, whose face was pale and unreadable, and swept his arm before her to usher her from the club.

He didn't, Eric noticed, touch her again.

****

Jenna and Alan rode to the hotel in silence.

"You acted very irresponsibly."

"I made a mistake," she said, as she sat wilted against the leather seat.

Alan pounded the car window, his hand rounded. "A *mistake*? You violated your contract. They can sue you. I've seen scores of stars become yesterday's news. Is that what you want?"

Jenna shook her head. Fatigue crept silently into the limousine. She felt weighted down by it, wishing to be anywhere other than confined to a seat and forced to listen to Alan.

"You need to trust me and do what I tell you to do.

No one…and I mean *no one* takes better care of their clients than me. You're worth millions because I'm the best."

From behind the smoky glass of the limo the glow of streetlamps overtook the last pinkish burn of the early evening sky. "Money isn't everything," she said wearily.

"Really?" Alan was quick to squash the rare comeback. "Spout your clichés to some girl wrapping up greasy burgers at a fast-food place. Better yet tell that to your parents when they're trying to scrape together the tuition for your delinquent brother's fancy school."

"Kyle isn't a delinquent. He's sixteen and sneaks a beer once in a while. The prep school was your idea." Jenna's voice broke and she covered her face with her hands. Her head was still splitting.

Alan leaned close and whispered. "I'm just trying to keep your relatives in check. But maybe you'd like your middle-income parents to come out here and manage your career. Your mother, with her polyester stretch pants, would make a great stylist."

"Don't make fun of my family." Jenna's voice was small, and tears slid down her cheeks.

"C'mon now, don't cry," he said as he took her hand. It's my job to take care of everything. I will fix this."

She nodded and wiped her eyes. He *would* take care of everything.

Everything.

****

Eric stood quietly watching Jon Terrio and Caz Taylor argue about his fate.

Jon insisted he be immediately dismissed but Caz, mother to all the staff, pouted and whined until Jon relented and agreed to keep him. Grateful for not being fired, Eric worked with steadfast speed and energy, running rings around the other bar-backs to keep ice bins stacked and tables clear of dirty glasses.

After closing, he cleaned up with the same vigor and wiped dregs of alcohol, soda, and sugary lime juice from the bar's surface till it shone like glass. From the corner of his eye he saw a blur of bright orange and pink as Caz, strutting like a runway model, headed toward him. "You're doing a fantastic job here, Eric."

Nodding, Eric apologized. "Thanks. I'm really sorry about before."

"Mmm, a young man's passion." Caz swept his hand through his waves of salt and pepper hair and stared for a brief moment. "So," he crooned, "what possessed you to bitch-slap Alan Stark?"

Eric stiffened. He'd never considered himself the type of guy to "bitch-slap" another man, but Stark's delicate looking jaw didn't seem as though it could withstand a punch. "He was getting too rough with Jenna."

"Jenna, is it?" Caz sang, eyes lighting with excitement. "How do you happen to know the divine Miss Angel by her real name?"

"Shit," Eric said under his breath. "It's no big deal. I met her last night and she…um needed a ride home."

Spreading his arms wide, the flouncy sleeves of Caz's shirt fluttered as if a gentle breeze blew his way. He leaned back into the bar railing. "No big deal, indeed. I saw the way she looked at you as that dreadful man took her out of here."

Eric avoided the inquisitive expression on Caz's face and continued to drag the cloth across the railing as his employer lingered.

"Unfortunately Stark isn't someone you want for an enemy in *this* town. Rumor has it he never lets her out of his sight. I was surprised to see her here without him."

"Are they—"

"A couple?" Caz finished the thought. "Darling, that story is as old as The Hollywood Sign—beautiful starlet sleeping with an older, influential man. Anything is possible…but Angel and Stark, ugh that's just too nasty to even imagine."

Eric committed what was left of his energy to rubbing the bar's already glossy finish. The personal life of a star as big as Angel wasn't his business and he fought the swelling relief that filled him. "Well, if she comes back, I'll keep my distance. I don't want to cause you and Jon any more trouble."

"If she comes back?" Caz half sighed half sang, "from the way Miss Angel was looking at you I'd say she'll be back. The beautiful ingénue and her brooding young man are what romance novels are made of."

****

At the far end of the bar Eric's friend and co-worker Mark Chambers had been adjusting the CO_2 tanks for the soda guns. He got up and followed Eric to the men's room and stepped to the urinal to pee. As he moved to the sink to wash his hands he said, "Long night."

"Not bad for a Tuesday," Eric answered.

"You want to grab some eggs or a burger? There's a drive-in a couple of blocks from here. My treat."

Eric shook his head. "No thanks, bro. I start a new job tomorrow and I need to get some Zs."

Both men finished washing up, their reflections peering back from a long bank of mirrors. They looked a lot alike. Eric, at twenty, was just a few years younger than Mark claimed to be. They were both about the same height and had the same coloring—tawny skin and blue eyes. Mark fluffed his fingers through his light brown hair and overhead lights caught the shine of expensive highlights. People often took them for brothers.

"You sure I can't change your mind? You worked your ass off tonight for me. The least I can do is spring for a meal."

"The least? I'm the one who owes you." Eric smiled. "I'd still be sleeping on the beach, without a dime in my pocket, if you hadn't shown me around this town."

"Then if you won't let me feed you, I'll pour myself a nightcap." He gave Eric a two-fingered salute and went back to the bar.

Alone, the club's lights dimmed, Mark sipped an expensive, top-shelf scotch. Reaching into his pocket, he slipped an amber vial and tapped a small amount of powder from it onto the bar's surface. Grabbing a straw from a container, he fed his nose, and dabbed the residual powder onto his gums.

"How the hell did you hook up with Angel the virgin star?" he whispered into his glass.

Mark, an aspiring actor, sipped as a leering grin curved his lips. Mirrored tiles, set behind shelves, cast a dozen images back at him and he swept his hands through his hair as he'd done in the men's room.

"My best friend knows the brightest star in Hollywood. There's got to be an opportunity in there for me."

Chapter Six

Far from being an expert carpenter, Eric was grateful to his boss Tom for giving him the opportunity to work and learn. He pored over blueprints until they became as rudimentary as the alphabet. He worked harder than any man on the crew and received a raise sooner than he had ever expected.

Beaming, he studied the paycheck he held between his callused fingers. He calculated the tips he'd made the previous week at Crimson, and added that figure to his check. A feeling, peculiar but welcome, filled him. It was pride.

"Hey, kid," one of his coworkers called. "We're going to go grab a beer at The Trade Wind. You in?"

"Sure."

Eric liked the guys he worked with. They'd made him feel like one of them from the beginning. None of them brought eight by ten glossies to the job, ran lines, sang, or talked about their auditions like staff members at most clubs did. Yes, he thought, guys with beer guts who drove pick-up trucks home to Glendale and the Foothills were okay by him.

Tom called for the bartender. "Give my boy over here a cold one," he said, slapping Eric on the back.

It was a typical Friday with beer drinking and camaraderie continuing into early evening. Country music played on the jukebox and as the hour crept toward seven, most of the crew began filtering out. Eric glanced at the clock above the cash register. He had just enough time to shower and report to job number two. He picked up his car keys, left too many bills on the bar as a tip, and made his way to the exit. He was barely outside when someone came up behind him and grabbed him by the collar.

As Eric turned, his body went immediately into the stance of a fighter. It was automatic, a bracing of legs, a tightening of stomach muscles, and the shoulder leading tilt that puts all of a man's weight behind a punch. He easily knocked the hands away. About to shove his assailant to the ground he stopped short, stunned when he realized the man who'd grabbed him was his father.

"Shit."

Eric hadn't seen his old man in more than three years. Instantly, he backed away from the stench of alcohol and the sight of tobacco-stained teeth in a face that too closely resembled his own.

"What's the matter? Ain't you glad to see me?"

Eric took another step back. Denny Laine was only thirty-seven, but the boozing and drugs made him look closer to fifty. Other than the ever-deepening ruts in his skin from chain smoking, nothing much about him had changed. He wore a T-shirt so old and faded the motorcycle logo printed on it was a shadow. The sleeves were rolled up with his usual off-brand cigarettes tucked into the fold. A heavy chain, threaded through a belt loop, hung from the waistband of his jeans and disappeared into his pocket. Denny wore scuffed black boots, and his greasy hair was drawn back into a scraggly ponytail. For as long as Eric could remember, his father had been striving to look like a biker but had never in his life accumulated the cash to actually buy the wheels.

"What the hell are you doing here?" Eric waved a plume of smoke away. "How did you find me?"

"It was easy enough," Denny snorted. "Your mother saves her birthday cards." Laughing, he spat a wad of phlegm onto the sidewalk. "Did you really think putting a return address on them meant you'd ever get one back?"

The statement, delivered with such flippant contempt, made embarrassment heat Eric's face. He said nothing and just stared as Denny sucked more smoke into his lungs and spat again. A globule of gray added to the greasy smears of old gum and discarded wrappers on the sidewalk.

"I went by that dumpy apartment of yours and one of your wetback neighbors told me where you worked. I figured I'd find you in the nearest saloon."

Eric shot his father a look of disgust tempered with what, shamed him to admit, was hatred. Denny continued speaking, appearing unaware of Eric's eyes hot and angry upon him. "I got in a little mess back home. I figured here's as good a place as any to lay low. Afterall, you owe me."

"Owe you? Eric snorted a flat laugh. "For what?"

"For raising you. Taking care of you."

Shaking his head, Eric said, "Fuck you," turned and walked away. Denny Laine had never taken care of any of his five children and none of them *owed* him anything. If Eric hadn't filled his pockets with cans of tuna and stuffed bread down his shirt, he and his younger brothers and sisters would have gone hungry most nights.

"Hey!" Denny called, trailing after. "Don't you fuckin walk away from me you little dick-weed."

Long immune to the jab, Eric continued toward his car. In his father's limited vocabulary, dick-weed was a compliment. Little pussy, little prick, little piece of shit—it was always *little* something or other. But Eric wasn't little anymore and tuned out the insults.

"Hey!" Denny yelled again. His garbled cawing and seamy appearance had drawn attention from the people entering and leaving the bar, so Eric quickened his pace.

Denny barreled after, making threats as he raced to catch up. "I'm talking to you."

He reached out and clamped a hand on Eric's shoulder but instantly let go. The space between Eric's neck and arm was the not the same narrow junction of bone and flesh Denny had so often crushed in his grasp. "Hey, son," he said, his tone softening. "I'm in a real jam; I just need a place to hang for a day or two, till this mess blows over."

Although he wanted no part of his father's troubles, nor did he believe he owed him a smattering of loyalty, concern for the siblings Eric left behind prompted him to ask what happened.

"First of all, it wasn't my fault," Denny said. He tapped another cigarette from the pack and struck a match to the tip. He tilted his head back, inhaled, and blew an easy stream of smoke into the air. "One of those trash Jackson girls got herself knocked up and is telling everyone the kid's mine."

Eric huffed. "Got *herself* knocked up?" He thought back, trying to recall the ages of the four Jackson sisters. He knew of none even near his age, only a pack of small runny-nosed toddlers always squalling in the next yard. With slow resignation, he shook his head and laughed pitiably. "Same old Denny."

Gritting chipped teeth and tightening his wiry arms, Denny lunged only to meet a wall of resistance that sent him falling backward on to the pavement. Eric watched a jolt of shock claim his father. Then Denny's eyes, which had widened as he hit the concrete, narrowed, and his brows lowered. He slowly pushed away from the ground and stood. Eric gulped a short breath as the memory of a small boy's fear touched him. It lifted quickly, and Eric, so intent on staring down the wrath in his father's bloodshot eyes, wasn't prepared to avoid the rock Denny used to smash into his face.

****

Tom Larity reached Eric just as he was about to be hit for a third time. The rock was a goose-egg size, solid chunk of stone with a spiny surface that had sliced at Eric's skin. Tom grabbed Denny around the throat and sent him hurtling toward one of the crew who, with one punch, rendered him unconscious. Blood oozed between Eric's fingers as Tom helped him to his feet.

"What the hell is going on here kid? Who is that son of a bitch?"

"My father," Eric whispered. The admission was more painful than the searing bruise quickly growing and palpating beneath his bloody cheek.

Tom was silent, as he looked back and forth between Eric and the motionless body on the ground. "He's your father? Your own father hit with you with a goddamned rock?" Tom stepped close to the sprawled figure and shook his head in disgust. He drew his foot back and gave Denny a hard kick to the ribs. "C'mon, kid, let's put some ice on that eye."

Angling his head toward his shoulder, Eric raised his arm to let the sleeve of his T-shirt absorb the blood. "Nah, I'm okay."

Through a blur, he looked out at the gathered crowd, humiliated not potent enough a word to describe his feelings. Tom shooed everyone back to the bar and tried in vain to get Eric to go to the emergency room. He didn't push the issue.

He also didn't interfere when Eric picked his father up from the ground and dropped him into his car. *A man didn't get involved in another man's personal business.* Eric knew Tom Larity was *man* enough to know this. They shook hands, and again Tom offered help if Eric needed any. Driving away with semi-lucid threats from Denny echoing in his ear, Eric knew he should have left him to rot in the gutter where he belonged.

****

Alan and his date accompanied Jenna to the wrap party for her latest movie *Stalked* as if she were thirteen and needed chaperones. It was absurd; skinny, morbid looking Alan and a zaftig woman on the downside of her lingerie modeling days, hovering over her as though they were her parents. Jenna wore her smile like a mask for the benefit of the press as Alan clung to her side, ignoring his date. Scanning the room, she desperately searched for someone to rescue her. There was no one.

Stalked, a crime thriller, sported a cast of weathered character actors playing cops. The only other young women in the film beside herself were day players about to be murdered, or already dead.

Throughout filming, she had no opportunity to forge any friendships.

"I'm going home."

Alan waited for several beats before answering as if debating whether or not to grant his permission. "Have Lombardo park the car and make sure you get to your room."

"No," Jenna said. "Not the hotel. I'm going home…to visit my family. They were supposed to be here, but my dad has the flu."

Alan shook his head dismissively. "I'm afraid not. You have to re-record the title song for the soundtrack. You'll be in the studio day after tomorrow."

"Oh, God, I forgot."

"You need to let me hire an assistant for you."

Babysitter. Alan would hire a keeper who would report her every move to him. "The job is my friend Randi's as soon as she graduates. Good night."

She said her good-byes to the crew, and then rushed from the party. Through the usual hail of camera flashes Nick Lombardo shuttled her to the limo.

"Back off," he ordered as he pushed through the crowd and secured Jenna inside. "Let's get you to your hotel," he said as he slid into the driver's seat. When not being a rugged bodyguard, he was a most genial chauffeur.

"I want you to drop me off at Crimson. It's that place where you and Alan found me a few weeks ago."

As the car pulled away from the curb Jenna studied the reflection of Nick's eyes in the rear-view mirror to gauge his expression. She wondered how soon after she stepped from the car he'd be on the phone to tell Alan where she was. She started to raise the glass divider then stopped. "Nick?"

"Yes."

"Um…you don't need to tell Alan where I'm going, do you?"

"Miss Welles, I work for you." The Brooklyn born Lombardo laughed. He was a big man, big even by bodyguard standards, and the sound was the hearty bellow befitting a man his size. "I work for you," he repeated, this time his tone all business.

"Thanks," Jenna said.

The car's inky paint reflected the brilliance of highway lights on the 405. Once on Wilshire, the limo inched forward among sedans of immeasurable value, their passengers loftily hidden behind tinted windows. At the club Nick eased to a stop and opened the door for her. "I'll be right out here. They have tight security inside but call me if anyone gets too uncomfortably friendly."

As the club's security swept Jenna through the crowd she turned once more toward Nick. "Could you do me one more favor?"

"Anything."

"Call me Jenna."

****

A burly member of Crimson's personnel released the hasp on the velvet rope in the same quick motion as striking a match. A hundred more L.A. names would breeze through the doors and Jenna glanced sympathetically at the crowd of people still waiting in line, patient and hopeful. Using her celebrity to her advantage left her feeling as if she'd taken something that didn't belong to her, pocketing an item unattended to at a merchandise counter. Alan did her table stealing and line cutting, and Jenna had never really tasted the sour flavor of guilt.

Once inside, she was all alone and not sure where to go. Caz and Jon, the two owners, saw to her comfort once they spotted her. "VIP table," Caz snapped to one of the waitresses.

"No," she argued. "I'd really rather stay down here."

She was probably the first and only celebrity to ever decline entrance to the noble shelter of a VIP lounge. She politely declined a glass of champagne and ordered a soda, stirring and looking around to see if Eric was here and hadn't been fired after all. Her heart began to patter as she spotted him, wide shouldered, all rangy muscles, a bus tray balanced on one shoulder. From a distance, she watched him disappear behind the kitchen doors.

Her heart raced more as the doors swung wide and he walked out again, this time with a crate perched on the same shoulder. He was swallowed up by the crowd and Jenna lost sight of him until he appeared on the other side of the bar. He bent to place his burden down, his face in profile. He turned and Jenna drew a quick breath in anticipation of seeing him. But, in place of the perfect features burned into her memory, she saw one beautiful aquamarine eye set deep above his cheekbone, mirrored on the other side by a slit swollen shut surrounded by raw and bloated skin.

A breath of shock had barely passed her lips when she saw a familiar soap actress, a slender woman with breasts exceeding the limits of nature, nudge her way through the crowd. She leaned toward Eric and gently laid a hand against his bruised cheek. A soft yet suggestive kiss followed. She mouthed something close to his ear, and again traced his bruises with her fingers, the soft brush an intimate caress.

Jenna watched, then rose from her seat. "Excuse me," she whispered, laboring to get through the crowd before Eric turned to see her staring like the last puppy in the box. It was foolish, she knew, to be so devastated over a guy she had kissed only once.

Nevertheless, she felt as though her heart had been stepped on.

****

Eric waded through a tight collection of bodies to pick up discarded glasses. He placed them on a tray and brought them to the kitchen to be washed. His cheek throbbed with every step and the vibration of the music compounded the pain. His eye had gotten worse. It was practically swollen shut and it made the already difficult task of maneuvering through the mob almost impossible.

The VIP section was teeming with celebrities. Eric circled the area to collect empty champagne bottles and more dirty glasses. Sitting on one of the leather couches, a soap actress he'd been seeing, was tittering at some comment made by a tough-guy, action-hero. Leaning against him, she smiled, appearing absorbed by his company. But, as Eric bent to wipe their table, she inconspicuously stroked the inside of his thigh. She was starting to become a little too obvious for his taste. Sleeping with her had lost its appeal, and her earlier offer to "nurse him back to health" left him cold. From behind his tray, he removed the fingers sliding higher between his legs.

Clearly unaware that his companion was groping

the bar-back, the action-hero gave her a kiss before standing to visit the restroom. His head barely cleared Eric's jaw as he brushed by him. Eric progressed to the next table where a swimsuit model was snorting cocaine with her rock star boyfriend. The rock star, a former teen heartthrob, was gaunt, his complexion waxy and his trademark hair thinning at the crown. His companion, the super-model, looked like a bag of bones with too many teeth. The magic of photography could create any illusion. None of the "beautiful people" were as beautiful as the camera portrayed them, Eric thought, until, stepping down the stairs and walking around the dance floor, he came face to face with an Angel.

****

Jenna was inching her way to the dance floor, weaving through the gridlock of bodies. She managed to avoid liquid spilling from a clumsily held martini glass and then veered to the right to sidestep the elbow of a man solid as a bank vault. Hands up and palms facing outward, she turned and found her fingers against the crisp pleats of a tuxedo shirt.

Her eyes made a slow journey, button by button, up to the red satin bow tie. It jerked a little between the white tips of the collar. She cautiously looked up further, to see the face, Eric's. His lips were parted, open only wide enough for a shallow breath to pass through. Other than the slight tremble of his mouth as he breathed, his face was still. One eye stared back at her. The other was swollen shut.

He made no effort to move, nor did she. Her hands still rested against his chest as a crush of people continued to push them closer together. He bent his head closing the gap even more. "Don't go anywhere," was all he said, before pressing through the crowd.

****

In the kitchen, Eric dumped the empties into the sink quickly, and quicker still glanced at his image in the stainless-steel door of the industrial refrigerator.

"Fuck," he mumbled. If his eye looked that bad in the hazy reflection of the door, how grotesque did it look in person?

His anxious heart bumping against his ribs made his eye pulsate with more intensity. She was here. For over a month he had been on guard, making unnecessary trips to the front door and wondering if he would ever see her again. But she hadn't come back. Against his better judgement he'd bought a magazine with her picture on the cover and worn the ink from the pages reading and rereading the article about her. Just when he had given up any hope of seeing her again, she was there, thrust into his arms.

Returning to where she stood, he took her hand, and led her through the crowd and out the back door. He steered her around the dumpsters to the far side of the building away from the blast of music. With his back against painted brick, he pulled her close and rested his aching head on top of hers. Her hair smelled of vanilla and citrus, a scent so clean it could have accompanied his last breath and he wouldn't have minded. He stayed like that, unmoving, saying nothing, finally giving in to the pain that had been bombarding him all evening. Eventually he lowered his arms so that they were around her, at first holding her gently then hugging fiercely.

She looked up into his face. "What happened?"

His reply was a weary sigh, a sad breath that

exhausted any optimism he'd ever allowed himself. This was his life. He was a fool to think he could walk away and start over. Being in a dirty alley was symbolic of what he was, what he would always be.

"I have no business being with you." He straightened and eased her away. "C'mon, I'll take you back inside. I shouldn't have brought you out here. The last thing you need is to get involved with someone like me."

"Wait." Jenna raised her head and their eyes met. "What I *need* isn't your call. That's for me to decide, and I don't seem to do enough of it."

A staggered breath left Eric's lips. He threaded his fingers with hers and pulled her back into his arms. He bent his head, burying his face against her throat, her skin smooth and warm against his skin. The alley and the distant streetlights seemed to blur.

He brought his lips down to touch hers in a whisper of a kiss. Soft and gentle brushes gave way to a deeper kiss, one with an intensity that had them both gasping. She was limp in his arms as if dizzy from the onslaught. The passion that passed through their bodies was like an electric current fusing them together, not allowing them to part. They kissed more, kisses so frantic they had to slow the pace. Then kisses so potent, so arousing, they had to end.

"We have to stop." Eric's words rushed out with his breath. "I have to get back inside and you…this…this is no place for you."

"I-I…" Jenna seemed incapable of forming words and nodded.

Eric brought her back inside, holding the hand of the girl he had just fallen hopelessly in love with.

****

As Eric and Jenna stepped through the narrow passageway, a pair of eyes followed them. A photographer, his squat body fitting perfectly between the dumpster and a stack of empty liquor cartons, snapped away. Hiding in the back alleys of clubs and restaurants was a profitable occupation. Something interesting always rolled out of the service doors.

An aspiring actor taking a few snorts of coke in a doorway might get his big break, and a no-name ingénue, getting plowed against a wall, could land a part in a hit movie. All the unknowns taking a little hit of something, or getting a little action in an alleyway, might make it big and eventually provide a paycheck for a patient photographer. Balding, chain-smoking Larry Belka was just such a man.

As the back door of the club creaked shut and the yellow sliver of light blinked to black, he packed away his camera equipment. The night's hours of crouching on pavement strewn with garbage was going to pay off. Tabloids would go to war to bid for the first ever shots of America's teen sweetheart making out with a busboy.

****

Long after last call, Eric was still busy cleaning and stocking liquor cabinets for the next day. He thought about asking Jenna to leave so she wouldn't witness him mopping the floors or see how twisted his eye looked in the bright light. But want prevailed, a burning he'd never before experienced, and he asked her to stay and wait.

While he finished cleaning up, Caz and Jon held her captive at a table to fuss over her. Once the bar was wiped down and the coolers restocked, he was officially off duty. He hoped Jenna wasn't bothered by the curious looks from the bartenders and cocktail waitresses. Though celebrities patronizing clubs in L.A. were as predictable as an eighty-degree day, stars of Angel's stature didn't usually dismiss their bodyguards and hang around waiting for one of the grunts.

His friend Mark sidled over and flashed a too-white and too-wide smile. "Aren't you going to introduce me to your girl, Eric?"

Always on, Eric thought—a trait of the aspiring actor. He made an abrupt introduction before Mark started running lines. Taking her hand, Mark lowered his head and then raised his eyes. They were a portrait of seduction, the lids hooded and one brow a millimeter higher. "Hello," he said in a deep and fluid voice. "I'm a huge fan."

Eric stepped between to shield her from *the look.* "We were just leaving." Reclaiming her hand, he bid his friend goodnight and walked outside to the parking lot. "I hope my buddy didn't bother you."

"Not really." Laughter fell from Jenna's lips. "What's with the face?" she asked.

"You mean this?" Eric dipped his head and tried to impersonate Mark with his good eye. "He wants to be an actor and it's his *look.* He practices it in the men's room mirror."

Jenna laughed harder. "You're kidding."

"Shh," Eric hushed her. Mark was ambling to his car, his arm around one of the waitresses, a pretty brunette, newly hired.

"Night, buddy," Eric shouted. But before the taillights of Mark's restored coupe blended into the mix of traffic, Eric and Jenna were giggling again like children.

"Okay," Eric said, as he regained his composure. "I have to stop. I shouldn't make fun of him. He's my friend and other than *the look*, he's harmless."

****

Mark Chambers slapped the ass of the young woman lying on her stomach. It was a playful gesture but still left stinging red handprints. She turned and raked her fingernails down his hairless chest and tweaked a nipple, the pinch firm. He rolled on top of her and with a swift and forceful movement entered her. He twined locks of her hair in his fingers, tugging hard enough to stretch her skin taut over her cheekbones and make her eyes water.

A lazy smile of pleasure was no longer on her lips. Her eyes were wide, and she breathed in short gasps. Mark pumped with intensity, the girl's hair still roped around his hands.

Chapter Seven

Stretching languidly, Jenna remembered the best night of her life. She and Eric had driven to the beach and talked till sunrise. They watched a reflection of gold and copper sparkling along the waves of the outgoing tide in each other's arms. His explanation of what happened to his face had caused an awkward silence, and she swallowed her shock and sadness when he admitted his father had beaten him. He didn't embellish and out of kindness she hadn't pushed.

The sun eventually rose higher, turning the sand a bright orange that faded to pale pink and then dusky amber. Eric and Jenna kissed with innocent passion, his lips brushing hers then glancing along her neck and shoulder. He never tried to fondle her breasts or reach between her legs. As much as her young body craved his touch, the fact that he hadn't made their time all the more romantic.

Eric was the one to end the kissing, telling her he didn't want to get too carried away. "My dirty car isn't the place for this."

After he drove her to the hotel, he promised to call the next day. Jenna stretched more and stared at her new cell, willing it to ring.

****

Eric was slumped in a chair, asleep when the raspy sound of his father's voice woke him.

"Where the hell am I?" Denny scratched his oily scalp and looked around the room. When he spotted his son, he grunted. "Eh, what a shit-hole."

Eric shifted in his seat. "If you don't like it, get the fuck out."

Opening his mouth to speak, Denny was seized with a coughing fit. He rummaged through the tangle of blankets at his feet, sputtering like a derelict car on a wintry morning. "Where the hell are my goddamned cigarettes?"

Tired and achy, Eric shook his head and stepped around the mattress to get to the bathroom. He closed the door to tune out his father's confused burbling and turned the sink's faucet handles. Splashing water on his face made him wince. His flesh was so sensitive to pain even the cool drops stung.

He stared into a rust-dotted mirror. *Crap, I look bad.* The skin around his eye was bloated to at least four times the size making it impossible to open. A dark purple welt spread across his cheek to his ear. The side of his nose was swollen, and his upper lip so puffed out he looked as if he were sneering. The bastard did him good this time.

"What the hell am I going to do with you, Denny?" Eric mumbled into the sink. He gently patted droplets of water from his face, but like the water, even soft terrycloth burned. When he stepped from the bathroom his old man was sitting up and sucking on a cigarette.

"Try not to set my *shit-hole* on fire," Eric said.

Looking full of bravado and smiling, Denny rose, bones creaking audibly as he labored to stand. He puffed out his chest. "Watch your mouth you little piss-ant. Or do I have to give you another beating to show you who's boss?"

"Beating?" Eric curled his hands into fists, clenching and unclenching them to stop the eager spasms building in his arms. "You hit me with a rock, you fucking coward."

Denny took another slow pull from his cigarette, the tip glowing as an inch of dead ash fell to the floor. He squinted and grinned, showing a row of yellowed teeth. "It's a father's right to keep his kids in line."

Slowly, Eric stepped over, close enough for his chest to almost brush against his father's soiled T-shirt. "Try and keep me in line now, Denny. Go ahead, try."

****

Sitting at the table on his stone patio, Alan pushed his cup away. He paid little attention to the greenery surrounding the expanse of California limestone—the vibrant hibiscus, fuchsia, and varieties of palms that edged the pearly stones. He took no notice of the sunshine glinting on the crystal water of his pool or how the ocean, set behind it, reached to infinity. Alan's attention was fixed upon only one thing, the picture of Angel on the cover of *The Exclusive*. She was in a back alley in a clinch with the hood from Crimson. The caption read "*The Angel and the Busboy.*"

Alan read the attached copy then neatly folded the paper in half, repeatedly running his thumb along the edge creating a razor-sharp crease. He summoned his housekeeper, ordering her to bring him a drink that he swallowed in one angry gulp. When he set the empty glass down, he did so with more force than he intended and cracked the expensive tumbler.

"Son of a bitch."

Alan Stark hated when anything he owned was

ruined. He picked up his phone and scrolled through his contacts until he found the number of the Steven Powers Investigation Agency.

****

Jenna and Eric took their romance slowly, getting to know each other in cautious measures. They spent whatever free nights they could, comfortably assigned to the sofa in her hotel suite. The media fury about the young star's affair was too explosive to allow a proper date in public.

She was a bit more open about her childhood and explained she'd been a nerdy girl who'd never aspired to prom court but secretly wished to fit in. Without much detail, she told Eric about her family and how life had been happy in an unremarkable and garden variety way before fame. She admitted how it stole most of the normal benchmarks of growing up. She admitted to being lonely.

"So how come your folks haven't moved out here?"

Shifting under the shelter of his arm she exhaled a tired breath and Eric responded with a comforting squeeze.

"My dad is too close to collecting his pension to leave his job. And all of this is—" she waved her arm around the room "—a lot for my mom to take in. She enjoys the bragging rights and loves the new house I bought her, but she's only comfortable in Pinehill with her friends and her routine."

Eric nodded, thinking about his mother who'd be here, racking up room service charges if the situation was reversed.

Jenna rested her head on his shoulder; they sat

quietly for a time. "I miss my family. I would go home more often but I always seem to have some commitment that keeps me on the road or here in L.A. I'm glad I have a break and can at least fly home for Christmas."

As he kissed the top of her head the airiness of a lemon rind mixed with a note of sugar filled him. "I'll miss you but I'm happy you're here now."

She leaned closer. "Mmm. Me too."

Sinking into the luxury of the silky cushions, Eric relaxed with Jenna in his arms, content and happy he'd skirted any questions about his own home life when she asked, "What is your family like?"

"Ah." He took a deep breath while scrambling for an answer. "You've seen the evidence of my reunion with my old man." He tapped his finger against a cheek that was still stained bilious green and lavender. Smiling to cover his embarrassment, he grabbed the television remote from the coffee table. "Let's watch TV, okay?"

He clicked on an action movie, violently noisy and intrusive, pretending to focus on an eruption of flames and bullets slicing the air. But as he watched, eyes unblinking, his thoughts were of how to tell Jenna where and what it was he came from.

His parents, one of whom he'd finally put on a bus bound for Oregon and hopefully a jail cell, and his siblings crowded his mind. Chaos, tears, but mostly fear and neglect pounded inside his head. Both of Eric's parents had been sixteen when he was born, then carelessly added four more children they couldn't afford to care for. Never able to hold down a job, both of the Laines traded food stamps for cash to support drinking and drug binges. His small town on the outskirts of Portland was little better than a slum, yet his family had earned the distinction of being the neighborhood trash. *How*, Eric thought wearily could he rise above the shame and ever admit it?

Jenna the nice girl from suburbia was miles out of his league, Angel the superstar…lightyears.

Chapter Eight

Pinehill, NY, Christmastime

In her new room, in her new house, Jenna and Randi sat amid a jumble of wrapping paper, ribbons, and bows. With Nick and an entourage of security the girls had set out on a last-minute holiday shopping spree at a local mall.

"Wow, Jen, did you ever think you'd be able to buy out the stores the way you did today?"

"Ah," Jenna answered, "it's good to be rich." She gulped from a bottle of vintage *Meursault.* "It's also good to have a driver who'll buy the *good* wine for his underage passenger."

Having skipped lunch both girls became instantly tipsy. "Here's to good wine and good drivers."

"Cheers."

More than half the items, pricey jeans, sweaters, and shoes neatly packed into bags were for Randi. Jenna lay back, crinkling the paper and giggling. "So if I'm so fucking rich, why the hell didn't I have all this shit gift wrapped?"

"Jenna Welles! Nice mouth. Hollywood is a bad influence on you."

"Nah, you know it's the wine."

One of Randi's pale brows lifted, the rest of her face assigned to skepticism. "Oh, come off it. The wine cursing is just an excuse to let loose. No one should have to be as good as you are."

Jenna's eyes expanded to purposeful circles, wide and animated. "But I am. I'm the sweetest, purest little starlet out there." She rolled to her stomach, rested her chin on twined fingers, and batted thick lashes. Her grin was gamine, artless. "I think I'm going to win "Favorite Virgin" at the People's Choice Awards this year."

Giggling, Randi raised the bottle. "To your virginity, may you lose it soon."

Jenna grabbed the wine, brought it to her lips and swallowed. "Amen to that."

Leaning across the bed, and almost falling in the process, Randi reached for a tabloid lying on the floor. She slapped at the cover. On it was a picture of Jenna and Eric, his arm halfway up to cover their faces. "I can't believe you're dating such a hottie and you haven't done it yet. *What* are you waiting for?"

Jenna snatched the magazine away, and stared longingly at the cover, remembering the day the picture was taken, remembering how quick Eric was to throw himself in front of her, as if protecting her was built into his genetic code.

She laid the magazine down and sighed. "He hasn't tried."

"What! Why the hell not?" Randi shot to attention then slowly folded back down, her shoulder brushing Jenna's. "He doesn't have any…y'know, problems in that department, does he?"

"No!" Jenna shoved her friend, almost toppling her from the bed. "We fool around. We just haven't gone…all the way. He said he wants to take me somewhere special, drive up the coast to Big Sur or

Carmel. He's just waiting for the right time."

Randi hugged a pillow, a soft square of goose down covered in creamy damask. "You know what they say. No time like the present."

After draining the remaining drops of the vintage white, Jenna giggled. "Well, unless *you* plan on fucking me, my virginity is safe for today."

Randi laughed so hard she finally fell off the bed. "Jenna Welles, Hollywood *is* a bad influence on you."

****

The girl in Alan's bed stretched tanned arms and slowly wiggled her index finger. Her nails were long and painted glossy coral. It was an invitation for him to come back to bed, but Alan just looked away, his mood flat and uninspired.

The young actress had served her purpose, but he had already showered and grown bored with her presence. She was pretty with wide dark eyes and long red hair. She had invested in a great pair of tits but spent too much time in the sun. In ten years' time she'd look like a piece of beef jerky. He cocked his head toward the door in dismissal and knowing the drill she gathered her clothes from the floor and dressed.

As she left, he glanced over his shoulder. "Call my office after the new year. I'll set up a meeting for you with a casting agent I know." Alan never said good-bye, and the girl, whose name he had already forgotten, didn't seem to care.

Once dressed, he went downstairs and strolled to the bar in his office. He plunked three ice cubes into a glass and poured a healthy shot of single malt from a crystal decanter. He sat at his desk sipping the liquor slowly, savoring the flavor, and debating whether or not to light a Cuban. He decided to wait until after he opened his "gift."

Reaching into the top drawer of his desk, he carefully slipped the package out. It was a manila envelope delivered by courier a day ago, from his private detective. Alan had intentionally refrained from opening it. The thickness of the package gave him reason to hope it would be worth the wait. He ran his fingers over the envelope, caressing it as if he could coax the contents to give him what he desired. He removed the papers and thumbed through, hoping something would catch his eye before he began to read in earnest.

Alan broke into a smile, a rare, upturned slice of lips, and lit his cigar.

****

Eric sat in Alan Stark's office wondering if he had purposely scheduled their meeting at exactly the same time Jenna's plane was scheduled to land. *Of course, he had.* How stupid could Eric be to think otherwise? He should have been at the airport greeting his love with a big bouquet of flowers, instead, he was fighting the sour congealing of his stomach's contents. His head was on the chopping block. Whatever Stark wanted couldn't be anything good, or anything Eric would want to hear.

Stark had called him at the club the day before and insisted they meet. "I advise you to show up, Laine. Especially if you want what's best for Angel." Eric hated the way Stark said the word Angel, crooning and mellow, as if saying it gave him pleasure. He hated how he looked at Jenna, spoke to her, hated the possessive net he cast whenever he was near her.

As he waited, his skin became a damp shroud over muscles tight with both worry and anger. Stark stepped into his office and regarded Eric with a slow and disparaging stare, a gawp almost edged with humor as if to ridicule him. "I'm glad to see you dress for business appointments." Stark's tone was an extension of the mirth inked in his dark eyes.

Eric raised his head, deliberately slowly, "I have no business with you."

"That may be, but I have business with you."

Stark settled into the chair behind his desk, a large leather piece resembling a throne at a dais and picked up a sheaf of papers. He tapped as if to straighten them, toying with Eric, smiling the keen glow of someone about to utter checkmate.

"You have quite the resumé." Alan sifted through the papers one by one slapping them flat on the desk as he read the litany of crimes noted on each page. "Burglary…assault…"

Slap, slap. "Breaking and Entering." Slap. "The list goes on and on." Slap…slap…slap.

"Grand Theft Auto is my particular favorite." He let that page gently flutter to land on the others.

Eric froze in his seat. "You son of a bitch."

A man, tall and imposing, moved from his spot in the corner like a deadly apparition. "Do you need me to stay, Mr. Stark?" he asked in a deep, dangerously calm voice.

Smiling, Alan waved him away never taking his eyes off Eric. "Please wait outside, my business isn't quite finished with this ah…person." Alan returned his attention to the papers still in hand, flipping casually through them. "Besides a very impressive criminal record, there are also some really interesting accounts of your love life in here—a fling with a bit player on a television series, an ingénue from a low budget horror movie, and a more recent liaison with a soap star."

Eric stood, his eyes riveted upon Stark gingerly holding the papers. His hands were soft, pale and narrow, and if not for the dusting of black hair they'd be a woman's. The sight of those hands delicately holding his life was an assault to Eric's system and he felt as if he could easily vomit.

The triumph on Stark's face was restrained yet confidently set. "You're not good enough for her, Laine. But of course you already know that."

Eric's jaw clenched into a steely tightness that kept it locked. When he was finally able to speak his words were staggered spurts of humiliation. "You're…a…a scumbag."

"Of course I am. You don't get to the top in this business if you aren't." Stark settled back into the comfort of the chair and added. "*My* client has endorsement deals in the works and they hinge on her clean-cut image. You'll tarnish it. You…and your family."

Eric watched as Stark's grin bloomed wider as he gave the knife one last turn, the fatal twist that completely severs a heart from its arteries. "You did know your mother was arrested for prostitution. According to the date you must have been about, eight…nine years old. Correct?"

Desperate, Eric reached across the desk and in a quick swipe snatched the papers, sending Stark's chair almost toppling backward. Stark managed to grab the edge of his desk, pulling himself and the chair forward.

The resounding thud prompted the linebacker to rush back in. Stark stood hands splayed on his desk. "I have a dozen copies of that. Take it, burn it, do what you want with it, one way or the other Angel will know what's in it."

Eric leaned close, the heat in his eyes blistering but the lump in his throat preventing further speech. When cornered, Eric Laine automatically lashed out. He raged and punched and vented his anger like a dog, starved and beaten. He wanted to do it now, to curl his hands into fists and release the thunder like artillery from a cannon. Instead, he turned and with great effort, held his head high and walked away.

****

Jenna performed a remote broadcast for the New Year's Eve Time's Square celebration from a studio in Los Angeles. She rang in 2001 on television at nine o'clock. When midnight came to California, three hours later, she was back in her hotel suite alone. Eric was working.

It wasn't until the next day that they were able to share their New Year's kiss. Exhausted from a night of carting and stacking, and being doggedly ordered about by bartenders and waitresses, he fell asleep during the third quarter of a football game with Jenna curled next to him. She regarded his face while he slept as if trying to commit it to memory. Mesmerized by the handsome planes of his face she brushed back the locks of hair that obstructed her view.

Awards season was approaching, and Alan had her committed to spots performing, presenting, or both which meant constant rehearsals. This would be their last day together for a while. She slowly let her head fall onto his shoulder and released a melancholy sigh.

He woke. Eyes, open only wide enough to reveal hints of turquoise, glittered a smile. His voice was a groggy murmur. "Hey," he whispered, and kissed her temple.

He stood and stretched, and the slow reaching motions made Jenna think of a cougar, all lean, graceful muscle. Transfixed, she watched as his shoulders dipped, first the right and then the left, his biceps lengthening and then tightening as he moved. A pale blue T-shirt stretched across his chest and stomach, and more purls of muscle covered his ribs.

He looked down, and his lazy smile made Jenna blush. Hooking two fingers into the waistband of her jeans, he coaxed her from the couch slowly, languorously pulling her close. Her breasts, tender and tingling, grazed his chest, and her pliant thighs met with his harder ones. On a fragile whisper she begged, "Make love to me."

Eric threw his head back making a feral sound from deep within his throat, a painful sounding groan. "I can't...I'm sorry, I can't." His fingers slid against her bare skin as he withdrew them from her jeans. She lowered her eyes toward the floor, a burning humiliation flaring through her pores and staining her cheeks.

Her attempt at seduction was clumsy.

"Jen...Jen, look at me." The air his voice rode on skimmed her ear but sounded a mile away. "Please, look at me," he pleaded. "I want you. More than you can imagine but there are things that complicate everything..."

He fumbled over the words, plowing his hands

through his hair and scrubbing at his scalp as if to force a simple construct of thought. "It would be different if you weren't who you are and I wasn't who…Crap," he whispered. "I'll be right back."

Jenna sank down onto the couch as he sprinted from her hotel room. His words echoed. "*It would be different if you weren't who you are.*" He'd bought in to the virtuous Angel propaganda. Her elbows rested on her thighs and her feet were turned inward like a disappointed child's. She dropped her chin into her hands and sighed. Jenna Welles, a.k.a. Angel, was going to die a virgin because her PR rep was doing such a fantastic job.

****

Eric returned to Jenna's suite holding the crumpled stack of papers he'd stuffed into his glove compartment. He'd read it the night he snatched it from Stark. Typed in bold, black ink Eric's list of offenses was irrefutable proof of how base a human being he was. Stark was right. Eric, with nothing but a catalogue of shameful behavior to claim, wasn't good enough for her. He had known it from the start, but was too selfish, too hopelessly in love to let her go.

After placing the papers on the coffee table, he took her hands and looked deep into her eyes. "Jen, your first time is supposed to be special, something you never forget. I don't want you to regret choosing me."

"Why would I? What's going on? What are those papers?" Jenna's brows knit tightly together, two furrows of skin worrying the space between her soft, golden eyes.

"All the things I haven't told you about myself." His voice was quiet, somber, shame filled.

"I know enough," she argued.

"No. You don't," he said on a tired breath. "You don't know how selfish I am. If I wasn't, I'd do the right thing and walk out of this room and never come back."

"Don't say that, please." She rubbed her stomach as if to dull a sudden pain, and her skin erupted in cold bumps. At Eric's urging she picked up the papers and looked at them, her complexion washed of color. He shrugged impassively and inclined his head toward the couch. "Read it…please."

The first page was a cover letter addressed to Alan from a detective agency. Gasping she dropped the papers as if they scalded her. Eric bent to pick them up, and one by one, handed them back to her. "Please," he repeated. "Read it. I should have told you all of this sooner. I should have thought about your image, but I was only thinking about myself."

"My image?" Jenna whispered. She rounded her fingers and tapped the sides of her fists against the table in a slow rhythm. "I…am…not…an…image. I'm a person."

"A famous person," he interrupted. He gently laid his hands over hers to stop the steady bang against the glass. "And like it or not you *do* have an image, a certain reputation and ruining it isn't my call."

She sighed, her eyes wide and lost. "And making me read this isn't your call either. I'd rather throw it in the fireplace."

"No." He put his arms around her as she stood and gripped the papers to her chest. "If you don't read this, you'll always wonder. I'll always be some secret you couldn't face."

"You won't," Jenna argued.

"I will," he insisted. "The only chance we have is for you to know me…really know me, the good and the bad."

She stepped back from his embrace and nodded. "Okay." Slowly, her eyelids lowered, and she stood breathing steady and softly. "Okay," she repeated. "I'll look, but only because you asked, because *you* need me to. No other reason."

He nodded and took a seat on a small club chair. And with his fingers locked together watched solemnly as the love of his young life pored over his tarnished biography.

****

Jenna read page after page, her teeth nibbling her bottom lip. "This was all before I met you, I don't care about any of it."

"Still…you can't just blow it off."

The humility in his voice stung. Jenna watched as he turned, his face angling right and then left as if taking slow appraisal of the elegant suite and the uncorrupted cleanliness of her environment. It was everywhere until he dipped his head and she saw his eyes settle on his dirty sneakers.

"You can't just stuff it all back in an envelope and forget it any more than you can forget who you are."

"Oh I'm not forgetting this." Jenna stood, the burn on her cheeks now scalding and rising up into her scalp. "I won't forget what Alan did." Emotions, tightly swaddled, broke free and she yelled, the sound high pitched and untamed. Tearing at the pages, she sent them exploding like confetti from a cannon. "Who the hell does he think he is?"

Her rare burst of fury continued to skim the air. Oxygen was thick in her chest and she breathed and swallowed gulps of it until she calmed, and the red haze of rage softened. She focused on the one thing that brought all back into focus. Eric.

"How did you get those?" She indicated the scraps at their feet. "I don't understand."

Clasping his hands behind his head, he released a tired groan. "It doesn't matter."

She kicked at the papers. "Of course it matters. Alan had no right to pry into your life. I'm going to fire him."

"Don't. At first, I wanted to kill him, but then I realized he wouldn't be doing his job if he *didn't* have me checked out. He's just trying to protect you."

"Protect me? From you? From being happy?"

Eric grabbed Jenna by the shoulders. "Look at me," he prompted, giving her a gentle shake. "Being angry with Stark doesn't change the fact that I did all those things. If he could get information from sealed juvenile records so could any number of reporters. We need to talk about it."

"Why? What's the point? You were a kid. I already know things were tough for you growing up. I love who you are now and whatever happened before doesn't change that. Alan had no right to invade your privacy. It's unforgivable."

"Unforgivable or not if you won't let me explain then I'll always be the guy, the guy on those pages."

Jenna gazed at Eric with the light of a thousand stars in her eyes. She pressed close and kissed him. "Never. You could never be a man reduced to something so simple. I know all I need to know about you." She kissed him again, his face warm in her hands.

"Still," he said tipping his head and kissing her palm.

She repeated a version of her earlier statement. "Okay, I'll listen, but only because *you* need me to know."

****

Eric Laine told Jenna Welles, the girl he loved, his story. He had been taught by his parents how to steal, how to devise a persuasive lie, and how to make tears spill from his child's eyes for money. He had been taught by the cheerless streets of his childhood how to fight, and how to survive. He had stood before a judge for the first time at the age of twelve.

Jenna, her eyes wide, beautiful, and accepting, never wavered from his. They never showed disapproval or worse, disgust. Still, as he spoke, he felt mildly nauseous like he'd been steadily inhaling noxious fumes.

"I stole food because I needed it. I stole candy because I wanted it." He took another pause, another slow breath. "I cut school and got into fights…a lot. It was how I blew off steam, but honestly the fights didn't always come to me. Most of the time I went looking for them." Eric lowered his head and continued his confession, not to gain absolution, but to peel away whatever romantic notions Jenna had of who and what he was. They sat for a long while. He spoke in flat tones with his love quietly listening.

When he finished, she shrugged a casual and indifferent lift of her shoulders. "It was a long time ago and you were a child. You should be proud of yourself for turning your life around. A lesser person would have become a hard-core criminal."

Eric angled his face at the scraps of paper still scattered at their feet. "Jen, grand theft auto is a felony. I *am* a hard-core criminal."

"Oh."

Solemnly he began his explanation of what led him to a two-year sentence in a juvenile detention facility. He had been thirteen and the inheritor of his father's frustration—a thump to the chest with an elbow, a cuff to the ear, another cuff to the mouth.

"My school sent a social worker to my house to find out why I was always so beat up. The day she came I had a real nice bruise across the jaw, and my lip was split wide open." He paused and rubbed his eyes in the manner of someone who had been reading small print for too long. Unbolting the memories and admitting to them were no more and no less shameful than he'd imagined. They just were. They were a part of him. He spoke to his own twined fingers and continued.

"Denny never hit my brothers or my sisters. If he tried, he had to get through me first. That seemed to suit him just fine. He told the social worker I was violent, and he couldn't control me. I was removed from my house for the safety of the other kids." Eric grunted a sad laugh. "Removed...like a stain."

He glanced at Jenna who was sitting composed and with her own fingers locked together. If he looked too hard or too deeply into her eyes, he was sure he'd see her love withering up till nothing was left but the compassionate pity one feels for a stray animal. He shrugged and gave her a weak smile he didn't feel.

"I was placed in a halfway house for delinquent boys. There were ten kids in the place, all smart-asses like me."

Eric closed his eyes remembering the bleak and filthy house, the heavy draperies that never parted to allow a slice of light into the squalor, the rank smells of cabbage and cigarette smoke that lingered. He remembered a woman with ruddy skin and her boy whose leering smile and beady eyes followed Eric. Always.

"The matron who ran the place had a son. He was about twenty, a big dough-ball, and he...he liked me."

For the first time since Eric began speaking, he heard Jenna react, a small, pitiable groan she cut short. The sound died in her throat, but shock altered her eyes like a darkening lens.

"He...um...used to come to my room, and uh...touch me." Eric shuddered from the memory and pinched the bridge of his nose hard. "He was a lot bigger than me. I pushed him away...but...but...he was a lot bigger than me."

Eric stood and wiped sweaty palms onto the thighs of his jeans. When he resumed speaking, it was in the dull monotone of someone under hypnosis.

"It went on for a while. He'd lock my door and corner me. He'd go a little further each time. I knew eventually he was going to do more than just touch me with his hands."

"Stop. You don't need to finish this," Jenna cried. She rushed from the couch, but Eric held her an arm's length away, his eyes blank but still connected to hers. "I stabbed him with a fork. He came into my room one night and I jabbed a fork into one of his fat thighs. He squealed like the pig he was and then I hit him. I hit him, and hit him, and hit him."

Eric dropped his hands from Jenna's shoulders to slap dead against his legs. He spat part laugh part growl, caught now in memories fatal as a spider web. "A couple of other boys pulled me off him and dragged me away. I begged them to let me go so I could kill him. I'd never wanted anything so bad in my life than to kill him."

Jenna never reacted, her face a steady collection of features that might have been a model for an anatomy catalogue, an unblinking perfect display. But in her eyes Eric saw what looked to be no less than murderous rage.

"I stole his car to get away, away from the group home, away from my parents, away from everything. I didn't get very far."

In three cautious steps Jenna was close enough to press her face into his chest. "None of it matters now," she whispered. "Nothing you've said changes the way I feel about you. Everything you've been through is in the past. We're together now and I love you. I'll never hurt you and I'll never leave you, not ever."

He crushed her in his arms. "I love you too, Jenna, but you deserve so much more. You deserve a man who's decent and smart, and worthy of you. I don't know that I'll ever be that man."

Rising up on tiptoe she cupped his face in her hands and squeezed as if holding something broken together. Her eyes reached deep into his, looking beyond the fathomless blue of his irises. She looked into his very soul. "You already are."

****

Jenna and Eric drove along the I-15 to Las Vegas. At 1:00 a.m., they entered The Jacks are Wild Chapel and were married by the Reverend Lucky Marshall. They were married in jeans and T-shirts. No one, not even the minister guessed who the bride was.

Tears sparkled on Jenna's lashes as she declared her love for the young man who had known such little comfort and kindness in his life. Eric stood tall, too composed, proudly holding her hand. Their eyes held as they promised to love and cherish one another but saying the words couldn't make the sentiment any stronger.

They already loved. They already cherished.

After the short ceremony, Mr. and Mrs. Eric Laine checked into a motel off the main Vegas strip. He paid cash for the room using money he withdrew with his bank card, his pride surely destined to outlast his finances.

Their honeymoon "suite" was an inexpensive room appointed with a double bed, armoire, and television. An autumnal palette of faded greens and golds complimented dated wallpaper. "Not exactly what you're used to," Eric said as they stepped into the small space.

Jenna never gave an even cursory glance around. She thrust herself into her young and handsome husband's arms almost toppling him onto the tight weave of the industrial carpet. Her head smacked hard into his chin and they both let out a simultaneous "ouch!"

"I'm such a klutz," she said. "I don't know how to do this. I'm not going to be very good at it."

Rubbing the spot where she'd hit, he smiled, his eyes hooded and gleaming. "Luckily for both of us, I do, and I am."

Tilting her head, Jenna's expression was a raised brow, pursed lipped inquiry caught somewhere between a simper and a smile.

"Fuck," Eric whispered. "I didn't mean to sound like such a dick…I didn't mean…"

"Shh," she laid a finger against his lips. "Let's start over."

He swept her into his arms and carried her to the bed. He drew alongside her for a kiss much as he had on the night they met. This time there was no anxious breath of surprise as he bent forward to press his mouth to hers. She welcomed the touch, following his lead like a dance.

"This is new for me too," he admitted. "I've never been with anyone I loved." Eric pulled her T-shirt from the waistband of her jeans, removing it so slowly his fingers teased each rib. Free of the soft cotton, Jenna lay motionless except for the rise and fall of her chest. He studied her, examining every inch of skin—her throat with its pulse gently fluttering, the hollow space between her collar bones, slightly damp with longing, and then her breasts covered in filmy white lace. "Jesus," he whispered. "I can't believe you're mine."

A sigh fell from Jenna's lips and Eric had to command himself to take his time. His desire was an intensity he'd never before felt, the urgency to be joined with her so great his heart's pounding resounded loud and fierce in his ears.

Her eyes fluttered shut as he cupped her breasts. The feel of his hands heating her skin through the lace more tantalizing than if she were naked. He kneaded her flesh then brought his mouth down and sucked through the web of flowery silk.

She groaned and gripped the bedsheets, her back bowed into an arc so her breasts tipped higher to meet his mouth. He trailed lower savoring skin in unhurried inches. His control spent, he undid her jeans and pulled them away, casting aside panties covering the center, the very heart of what he craved. Jenna gasped as his breath blew softly against her, then moaned pleasurably as his mouth covered the lips of her sex. He stroked and laved until he felt her shudder of pleasure against his tongue.

Almost faint with excitement, Eric strained large and hard against the fly of his worn jeans. Jenna opened her eyes to the sound of popping as he tore at the buttons of his 501s. Still reeling, drunk with desire, she reached up and slid her hands under his T-shirt, desperately needing to feel his skin, bare and smooth against her palms. Her fingers glanced across his chest and she timidly followed the line of fine hair down the center of his stomach, stopping at his navel.

He covered her hand with his own and guided her further down. "Touch me, Jen. It's okay to touch me."

She molded her hand around the warm shaft cupped within the white briefs. He breathed short pulls of air through his teeth as she explored his length. As he stood to strip out of his clothing, Jenna followed his every movement. Her eyes remained on him as he returned to the bed, his body sun-kissed and glistening like a slow pour of whiskey. His weight settled on the bed and she inhaled the scents of soap and shampoo mingling with a faint musk of perspiration. His essence.

"Are you nervous?" he asked. His voice was sensually deep, and his chest rose and fell in a steady rhythm.

"No." Jenna swallowed hard, her eyes roving his wide shoulders and muscled arms, the hard ripples dividing his abdomen, and his strong thighs dusted with hair. She could feel more easy heat seeping into her face when her eyes once again went to the long thickness jutting straight and strong from his body. They kissed again passionately, more ardently because it was a lover's kiss, a kiss between a man and woman on the threshold of intimacy.

"I love you," Eric whispered. His hands roamed one last time against the rose petal softness of her skin before he slipped his fingers between her thighs, each glance making her body burn with anticipation. "I don't want to hurt you. I'll be gentle...I promise." Then he began to slowly caress the vee between her thighs before slipping his finger inside her.

"Jesus, Jen, you're so tight."

His words were buried under her moans as he dipped and stroked, glazing her with a finger slick from her own need. The pressure, so sweet and sublime, made Jenna's body tingle as though something weightless as smoke floated against her skin. Eric eased on top of her and kissed her as he pressed to enter, rocking slowly, breaching higher and deeper until he filled her. Fighting the urge to withdraw and plunge again into the tight haven, he stopped to let her adjust. His breath was a thready rasp against her neck. "Are you okay?"

Jenna responded with a nod, the sting of his tearing through her virginity an insignificant flash of nothing compared to the hard heat now pulsing so exquisitely inside of her.

He rocked gently and she instinctively matched the

slow, rolling rhythm. He took her face in his hands. "Look at me," he whispered on a ragged breath. "Open your eyes, I want to look into your eyes while I love you."

Jenna nodded, her dark lashes fluttering as her lids parted. Her golden irises were luminous, Eric's as blue and infinite as a summer sky. They rocked slowly, their bodies twined, their eyes locked as they reached higher and higher, connected in every way possible.

****

Morning arrived too soon.

"We have to check out by eleven unless you want to stay another day," Eric said.

"I wish I could." Jenna answered, rising on tiptoe to kiss his stubbled cheek.

He placed a finger under her chin, tilting it upward to examine the raw marks his day-old beard had made on her neck and kissed them gently. "Sorry about those." He pulled her into his arms and swayed. "So I guess we have to get back."

"Afraid so. I have to be in the studio this afternoon to run through dance steps for my new video."

Their short honeymoon was over.

****

Myriad thoughts rushed through Eric's mind as they sped along the highway back to Los Angeles. He sat quietly in the driver's seat, holding Jenna's hand, and staring ahead as the road cut through the desert. He was happy, happier than he had ever been in his life. But just at the edge, uncertainty pushed against a fragile wall of contentment. He clasped her hand more tightly.

"Everything, okay?" she asked.

"Perfect," he said, smiling. "I was just,

y'know…thinking."

"About what?"

"You, I was thinking about you."

Jenna rested her head on his shoulder. "Good…Now tell me the truth. Why so quiet? Did I wear you out last night?"

A laugh followed an ersatz yawn. "Three times last night and twice this morning. Maybe you teenagers have that kind of energy, but I'm an old man."

"Okay, my twenty-year-*old* man." Though Jenna giggled, her cheeks bloomed pink. "I guess it's a good thing you're not the one who has to dance for three hours later today."

Sobering, he let her hand slip from his as she turned wide eyes toward him.

"Are you upset because I have to work today?"

He instantly laced his fingers back through hers and squeezed. "No, no of course not. I know you have commitments, obligations, and things. It just makes me realize me how reckless eloping was."

"Do you regret getting married?" Panic was crawling into her voice and Eric brought her fingers, still intertwined with his, to his lips and kissed her knuckles.

"Never. You're stuck with me forever, Mrs. Laine."

"Then what's wrong?"

He sighed. "Three years ago, I made a promise to myself that I would stop acting on impulse and use my head. I swore I wasn't going to end up like my old man."

He downshifted as the sienna-colored brush along Nevada's flat roadway became an incline of rocky terrain and they entered the Mountain Pass. The sky above the Mojave was a constant and cloudless blue.

"Last night, I ran off with you without giving a thought to where we were going to live or how we're supposed to adjust to the differences in our incomes. I don't expect you to sleep on a mattress in a bungalow in East L.A., but, Babes, you know I can't afford Beverly Hills."

We'll work all that out." Jenna's eyes softened with love and trust. "I have faith in us. I have faith in you."

The newlyweds silently held hands for the rest of the ride. When they reached L.A. Eric pulled his dust grimed and exhausted vehicle onto a side street where the I-10 and Highway 5 met. They had called Nick and he was already there and waiting to take Jenna to the studio.

"Welcome home, Mr. and Mrs. Laine."

"Thanks," Eric said. "We're keeping this to ourselves for now."

"Wait, how did you know?" Jenna interrupted.

Grabbing her small satchel from the car Lombardo gave his big bear shoulders one shrug. "Oh, let's see, a spur of the moment trip to Vegas…neither one of you is old enough to gamble. I figure you must have gone to elope. Don't worry, my lips are sealed."

Chapter Nine

Jenna's legs were jelly and her timing completely off. She missed cues and stumbled around the studio like a drunken wedding guest doing the Electric Slide. She was tempted to tell her exasperated choreographer she couldn't dance because she'd barely gotten any sleep, couldn't dance because she'd spent the entire night making love with her husband.

"Okay, sweetie, let's try that again. From the top— five, six, seven, eight."

Jenna tapped her foot twice, pivoted on her toes, and fell into one of the male dancers in the chorus.

"Okay, kids, take five."

The choreographer took a long pull from a bottle of designer water. An assembly of attractive, firm-bodied, young men and women dressed in the typical dance garb of tights and thin soled, leather slippers, dispensed to corners of the room. "Angel, is everything all right? You seem distracted."

Jenna sighed languidly. "I'm just off today. Everything's fine."

Everything was better than fine. Everything was perfect. It suddenly made sense to her why The Roman Empire fell, why duels were fought, and why the alpha lion mauled the other males in the pride. Sex. There was no force more powerful or more motivating than sex. She took another lazy breath, released it slowly, and reassessed her thoughts. It wasn't sex. It was love. *Sex with someone you love, that was powerful, earth shattering.*

The choreographer snapped her fingers. "Sweetie, are you still with me?"

"I'm sorry. I was up late last night."

"Let's call it a day. I just want to go over one thing with you before you leave." She dismissed the dancers and walked to a table littered with paper. Her stride was a ballerina's—head held high, back arched and toe-to-heel steps. Jenna followed, her muscles refusing to move in any way resembling the graceful patter. The thought had her mind drifting to Eric and she blushed again.

The choreographer picked up a clipboard. "I wanted to know if you had any of the kids from this video in mind for the tour."

"Tour?" At first, the word didn't register, then hit Jenna like a face full of ice water. "Tour?" she repeated.

"The U.S., Europe, and Australia...your world tour. Your manager asked me to give him a list of dancers."

"World tour," Jenna said again, this time on a whisper. "Excuse me." She hurried to the dressing room to change.

"Angel, what should I tell Alan?"

"Don't worry about that. I'm my way to see him right now."

****

Jenna tapped her fingers restlessly against her thighs as she rode to Alan's office. Nick had barely pulled the limo to a stop before she bolted through the doors.

97

"Wait," he shouted as she was swallowed by a mass that came from nowhere. Abandoning the car, he rushed through and pulled her into the haven of the building. "You can't just run off like that!" Nick nodded toward the security personnel sitting at the dais. "Bring her up to Stark's suite," he said and then rushed back out to move the car.

In the elevator, Jenna stood, her breathing labored, her eyes fixed on the door. As it opened, she sprinted through and bypassed the receptionist. Inside she found Alan relaxed, arms folded and one bony hip leaning against his desk.

"Angel," he said, and nodded.

"Don't call me that. It isn't my name." Her voice quavered but she stood firm.

"Very well, *Jenna*. I was just on my way out to a dinner appointment, but someone called from downstairs and said you seemed…distressed. Naturally, I canceled my plans for you."

Alan's dark suit was free of wrinkles as always, and every hair combed neatly into place. The severe military grooming was unnerving. His eyes, heavy lids that draped over obsidian irises, caused her stomach to knot.

"When were you going to tell me about the tour?"

"It's in the planning stages. No need to bother you with it."

"No need? You can't plan something as involved as a tour without telling me. What if I-I…had something to—"

"Something to what?" he interrupted. "Something more important than your career?" He tapped his fingertips together and cocked his head. Still, not a hair moved, the cuffs of his white shirt an even and balanced distance from his jacket's sleeves. "You've told me a million times how you love the stage and performing live. This is a tour of your own. You'll be the headliner, not an opening act. Isn't this what you want?"

"I meant live theater, where I started. I want to do a musical."

Alan snorted, the sound edged with disdain. "Jesus Christ. You were never in the *theater*. That community production you were discovered in was the equivalent of a high school musical." His tone was tempered with amusement, as if Jenna were a precocious toddler wheedling for candy—cute yet bothersome. "You're eighteen. Let Lupone and Peters have Broadway for a little while longer. You asked to be on stage and I'm putting you there, this is a win, win for everyone."

Jenna's mind scrambled to find an argument. There was none. A tour would take her to places most girls could only imagine. What she couldn't imagine was leaving Eric. *He'll come with me. Of course, he'll come with me. We'll see the world together.*

Then she remembered the report, the vile and disgusting report Alan thought would ruin them. How would her husband react to her invitation to go anywhere with Alan's insinuation at every turn? How could she expect him to tolerate a year, maybe two of Alan relentlessly jabbing him with needles of hostility. Jenna's mouth felt suddenly dry and arguing with him seemed unimportant.

"You don't make any plans without my say so from now on," she managed to say.

Alan nodded, but Jenna saw victory in his half-smile. She turned and stepped from the office, the inside of her mouth still dry as chalk.

****

Eric refused Jenna's offer. He'd said no as simply as if she'd asked him if he'd like another cup of coffee. "No thank you."

Days later, the argument, far from exhausted, slipped unavoidable into every conversation.

"I wish you didn't have to work tonight," Jenna said as she tightened the belt on her robe. She was going to bed and Eric was going to Crimson. He threw his arms around her and kissed the top of her head. "I'm sorry. I know our schedules suck right now."

"Not as much as they will once I'm on tour."

He sighed and pulled her closer. "We'll work through it. I don't like it, but we knew there'd be times we'd be apart."

"You don't understand." She fought a strong desire to stamp her foot. "This isn't like being on location for a couple of months. I could be on the road for two years. Rehearsals alone will tie me up for months."

Eric's arms went taut, his grasp crushing her ribs. She clung, gripping the back of his shirt. "It's too soon. We shouldn't be apart so soon."

Though he gently stroked her hair, Jenna still felt the hurried pounding of his heart.

"It's not like you're leaving tomorrow," he said, but the optimistic words fell flat as his breath blew across her temple. "We'll work through it."

"Why won't you come with me," she begged. "Who turns down a free trip around the world?"

"His arms fell away as if he'd been carrying something heavy. "What would I do with all my *free* time on this *free* trip?"

"See the sights, go to museums, absorb the culture."

"Right." His expression was stony, and Jenna saw his eyes measure one item of elegance in her suite, and then another, and another. "Because I'm the opposite of cultured."

"That wasn't what I meant," she said on a sigh. Then she brightened, snapping her fingers and smiling. "Tour crews employ dozens of people you could...there's always something that needs to be..."

Slumping his shoulders, Eric hung his head as if defeated. "Jen, I'd take a bullet to the heart for you, but please don't ask me to be one of your gofers."

She smiled as the perfect idea blossomed. "Not a gofer, part of the stage crew. It would be a way for us to be together."

But his resistance was immediate. "They're union guys and won't like having the star's husband force his way in." He took her back into his arms. "Besides, Babes, I like the job I have. I'm learning all about construction and the money is pretty good. Even if I quit to follow you, where will that leave me once your tour is over?"

Shaking her head she admitted she didn't know. She rose on tiptoe so their embrace was cheek-to-cheek, heart-to-heart. "I could set you up in business once we're home."

The kind offer, floating so softly from Jenna's mouth was nevertheless a slap, one that stung and burned and would chafe for days.

****

Jenna chose not to tell her parents about her sudden

marriage to a man they had never met. News that big was something to be delivered in person. For the time being, she and camera-shy Eric opted to keep their marriage a secret.

She made quiet inquiries about buying property so they would have a place of their own. Alan, not receptive to the idea of her buying a house, was less amenable to her looking in trendy Santa Monica instead of the more affluent Malibu or Brentwood.

"It's what I want," she told him, "something small, near the water."

Jenna galled Alan more by buying a co-op, a one bedroom fixer upper. When she admitted her "boyfriend" Eric would be sharing the place, Alan's reaction was so explosive it was like another "shot heard round the world."

Chapter Ten

By January's end, Jenna finished recording the cuts for her new album and afterward spent her days in rehearsal for the videos. On rare occasions when their schedules didn't conflict, she and her secret husband plastered, and painted, and made love deep into the night. It was as close as they could get to a normal life.

Jenna playfully pushed Eric away. "Stop!"

They'd been making out in the back of her car enroute to a furniture boutique. Nick pulled to the curb and parked, then followed the newlyweds inside. A few people on the sidewalk rushed to be near the young star but once sheltered in the shop she was free from attention. A saleswoman hurried over.

"We're looking for a couch," Jenna said. She was acting very grown up even though her smile was the wide-eyed gleam of a kid peering into an ice cream freezer.

The saleswoman, dressed in the same sedate, creamy hues of the store's walls and posh inventory, crooked a finger for Jenna and Eric to follow. Walking with an airy stride, she brought them to a showroom. She extended her hand toward the furniture, each piece yards from the next and bathed in the glow of architectural pendants that appeared to float from the high ceiling.

"Wow," Eric said. "This looks like the stuff in your

hotel suite."

"Hotel? Hardly." The saleswoman pursed her lips into a peevish moue. "All of our pieces are custom, hardwood construction, imported fabric…" Her voice trailed off as she stepped over to a low boxy sofa with a tufted back and legs in a pale wood. "This is young, modern, and the designer is a favorite of just about anyone who's anyone."

"I love it," Jenna gushed.

Eric was less impressed. "Is that real suede?"

The saleswoman gave the fabric a loving caress. "We can order it in any color you like but this blush is gorgeous."

Staring longingly at the sofa, Jenna didn't flinch when the saleswoman heralded a price of twelve-thousand-dollars.

"Jesus," Eric whispered. "I have to work three months at two jobs to make that much money."

Tugging on his arm Jenna whispered back. "I wasn't thinking. Let's go somewhere more reasonable."

Reasonable, the word bit into his skin. "Excuse us for a sec."

The saleswoman nodded while he and Jenna stepped away. "Buy the couch if you really like it, Jen. You shouldn't have to settle for reasonable just to spare my feelings."

"Are you sure?"

Eric gnashed his pride between his teeth and swallowed. But as he and Jenna walked back to the smiling saleswoman to buy her expensive sofa, Eric knew she had already settled.

She was married to *him*.

****

Alan realized it had been a mistake trying to keep Angel away from the "Busboy." She was a willful child, daring to do what was forbidden. Her insurrection had also weakened her dependence on Alan and shifted it to another man—another man clearly unworthy of her. Losing Angel wasn't an option. Getting her back under control was going to be a battle and he was going to need an aide-de-camp. Luckily, he'd recently hired just such a person.

He buzzed for Bree Davis, his new associate, and waited. Unlike the other lackeys in his employ, she didn't spring to attention. From his doorway Alan watched as she stepped across the hall. He admired the way she carried herself. *All business*. Her high heels made a light clacking sound on the marble. Not an annoying sound, but one that would tell a blind man she was slender and graceful. Bree was put together as always in a suit of cream-colored silk with a hint of something lacy underneath. Her dark hair and long nails were impeccable. She was pretty-ish but maximized her assets to the fullest, a sweep of shadow to set her eyes in an attractive angle, and red lip liner to draw her mouth into a sexy pout. Alan was an expert at recognizing the tricks of well-applied cosmetics.

"Please sit," he said, gesturing to a chair facing his desk. "I'll get straight to the point. I want you to be more of a senior associate and actively involved with handling Angel."

Bree's eyes expressed no emotion. They neither glittered excitement at the prospect of advancement, nor did they glow with gratitude. Relaxed, Alan settled into his chair. *Perfect*, he thought. His new employee was both ambitious *and* unflappable. *Perfect*.

He pressed his fingertips together. "Angel is getting off track. I need someone to steer her in the right direction, someone who will do whatever it takes."

Bree smiled, her scarlet lips stretching over perfect white teeth. "Are you asking me to advise her professionally or—"

"Be her friend," Alan interrupted. "She's a big star but not very experienced, especially when it comes to men. Her current entanglement isn't the best thing for her…*career*."

"Entanglement?" Bree Davis raised a dark brow. "Isn't she living with her boyfriend?"

"For now." Alan slid a titanium credit card across his desk. "I also think it's time for you to have an expense account. Hit some clubs, see what's trending."

She stood and slipped the card into a gold clutch with a signature F stamped into the leather. "Any particular club?"

Once again Alan leaned back into the comfort of his chair. "There's a place on Wilshire you can start with. See if anything interesting is going on."

****

Eric had restocking the beer coolers down to a science. Smiling, he slid the last bottle atop the pile and closed the lid. Tomorrow, it would be some other grunt hosing off mats and stocking shelves. Caz and Jon had promoted him to bartender, working alongside Mark.

Twenty minutes later, he stepped through the front door of his apartment with every intention of waking Jenna to share his news. Naked, he climbed into bed, and curled up to her spoon fashion. He nibbled at her earlobe. She arched in response as his hands roved over her stomach ending their journey at her breasts. A soft groan fell from her lips when Eric's practiced fingers made their way lower skimming over the front of her panties. His hands glided over the satin vee between her legs easily, she arched again, instantly rousing to her husband's touch.

"I'm madly in love with you, you know," he murmured.

"Mmm…I'd hate to be this easy for someone who wasn't." She rolled lazily onto her back. Her dark lashes fluttered against the silken skin of her cheeks, and her eyes, the lids heavy, opened. She offered him a dreamy smile. They kissed, slowly, heat and arousal building each time their tongues met, each time their hands glanced over skin, each time words of love drifted on a breath. They stopped only long enough for Eric to sheathe himself in a condom. He slid fine satin from her hips and down her legs. She opened to him, and he easily found his way inside. There was no need for his hand to guide the way. They were a perfect fit.

Jenna was wrapped around Eric as he rocked into the warm pocket between her thighs. She drew him deeper and deeper, enveloping him with her body, her heart, her love. His pleasure was like nothing he had ever known. No woman had ever made him feel this way, nor could any other woman ever again. Of this, he was certain.

Chapter Eleven

Eric threw a pair of khakis into his wife's suitcase. They were new. Three button-down oxford shirts, new underwear and socks, and his decent jeans shared space with Jenna's clothing packed into the large pullman. Adding to his limited wardrobe was his attempt to impress his in-laws. He and Jenna were going to New York to tell them they had gotten married.

The trip home was actually a pit stop between talk show appearances to plug *Stalked*. She'd persevered in keeping a fence between Eric and Alan by insisting her agent skip the journey.

A day later, Jenna and Eric landed at a private airstrip on Long Island, checked into a suite at The Waldorf, and were rushed to a West Side television studio for her appearance on *Live in New York*. He waited in the green room and watched a film-clip of her movie playing on the television. When the clip ended, the camera closed in on her, and she smiled as the audience applauded. She glowed.

Sipping from a water bottle Eric studied her image. Under the studio lights her eyes gleamed like honey spilled from a jar and her hair was the pale yellow of buttermilk. His own eyes, he was sure, were playing tricks on him because the more he stared the more he swore she emanated a pearlescent glow. *Maybe not*, he amended the thought. The girl filtered through a camera lens shone as Angel, a beautiful and talented star. But that girl wasn't his wife. Jenna was his wife, and she was so much more than what the world saw. She was a girl with layers and weight, smart, introspective, and with a quick sense of humor that never failed to make him laugh.

He recalled a day they'd been drinking wine while working on their small apartment. Tipsy, Jenna had smashed her thumb and cursed with the vigor of a dock worker. Scoring through any childish amusement Eric had listened, his laughter contained, to her scream about horses, monkeys, chickens and their genitals, before getting her ice. As she continued to swear her face flushed red. "What is it with me, wine, and the *F* bomb? It's got to be some kind of disorder."

"I work with carpenters all day. We bash our fingers…we curse."

Jenna held the cubes to her thumb until the cold had deadened the pain and the pulse had stopped beating under her nailbed. She grinned and then dropped the ice, melting and slippery, down the back of his shirt. Eric loved her playful side, loved her serious side, and loved how a smile or pensive frown could so easily turn into a passionate smolder.

The door to the green room opened and she walked in almost spilling into his arms.

"Ready to go?" he asked.

Twisting around, Jenna shifted her attention, her eyes roaming the room as if needing to be assured it was empty. It was a worrying habit of hers Eric noticed when they'd started dating. It was a tic like touching the jamb before walking through a doorway. She rarely spoke in confidence without checking for "bugs."

"Ready to tell my parents that I've been lying to them for two months?" she finally whispered.

Giving her shoulder a gentle squeeze Eric pulled a set of keys from his pocket and dangled them under her nose. "I sent the limo packing and rented a car so we could drive up to the country alone. It's already here in the studio garage so we won't be followed." He knew his wife would be relieved to be released from the precincts of a too large vehicle and too ostentatious arrival.

The tense slash of her mouth thawed into a smile. "That sounds great. Perfect in fact."

****

In little more than an hour, Jenna and Eric exited the highway and climbed and descended a road with a gradient of rises and dips. Paddock fencing edged the road in spots, most of it listing crookedly and in need of paint. Eric hadn't expected New York to be like this, never realizing so close to the gray legion of buildings and trumpet of traffic, he would find red barns and fields dotted with livestock. As a kid, he had taken solace in the quiet simplicity of nature. His childhood town was a hilly grid of streets that hoarded litter, broken glass, and crumbling mortar, but miserly refused to share a patch of green. It was only when looking out into the far distance he could realize the beauty of a tree or clear, blue sky.

As they entered Pinehill, Jenna pointed out landmarks from the Revolutionary War. "George Washington slept here…and there, and there. He apparently got around."

Eric chuckled. No one would ever guess his sweet wife's sense of humor listed to the side of sarcasm. He took quick glances out the side window with interest.

"Turn in here," she said. "I want to show you the block where I grew up."

He steered into a street with clusters of houses all lined up neatly, and exactly the same distance from the curb. He guessed about twenty years ago a farm had been paved over, the land divided, and identical split-levels sprouted up on identical square plots of land. There was a certain comfort about the neat structure of the clean little development. He imagined Jenna, as a child, riding a bike on the smooth sidewalk, pink streamers riffling from the handlebars.

They traveled on, up more bending roads till they reached a stately colonial stationed high up like a citadel behind a fortress gate. Once past decorative fencing and up the cobbled driveway, the front door of the house flew open and Sam and Lorraine Welles sprinted across the lawn, waving their arms in greeting.

"There's my pumpkin," her father exclaimed, hugging Jenna so hard his glasses slipped from his nose and bounced on the unyielding, winter grass.

"My baby, my baby," Lorraine cried, pulling her away from Sam. "Let me have a good look at you." She held Jenna at arms-length and squinted as her eyes took in every inch of her. "You look thin. Have they been giving you enough to eat?"

"Mom, I'm not away at camp. There is no 'they.' I eat whenever I want to."

Lorraine lit a cigarette and puffed. "I wish you'd take better care of yourself."

"And I wish you'd quit smoking."

She puffed again discharging a long stream of gray at the already somber sky. "Cigarettes calm me down."

Lorraine Welles was a nervous collection of narrow bones covered in black stretch pants and gem encrusted sweatshirt.

Jenna shook her head. "If you didn't drink two pots of coffee every day, you'd *be* calm."

She introduced Eric, and Sam shook his hand, pumping rapidly. "Looks like a nice young man here, hon. That talk I planned to have with him might not be necessary."

"Daddy!"

They were a nice looking couple, Eric noted, Jenna having obviously inherited their best features. With the right clothes and buffed to sophistication, they'd fit in anywhere in L.A. It was too bad they never visited.

"Let's get inside before we freeze to death," Lorraine said, shooing everyone into the house. "Sam, get their bags."

He trotted over to the luggage, but Eric grabbed the suitcase and small carryon before Sam had the chance. A tall rangy kid of about sixteen with features and coloring identical to Jenna's was standing in the open doorway. He backed into the house to allow Eric to enter. "Dude, where's *your* bag?" he asked smirking.

So, this is Jenna's family. Eric thought. Nice, ordinary, her mom on the jittery side, her dad a bit corny, and her brother a wiseass. Maybe finding his niche among these people was not going to be as hard as he feared.

They sat down to lunch and Jenna's mother fluttered around the kitchen like a baby bird, hopping from place to place, doling out food and drink. If a glass was an inch low, she refilled it. Sam engaged Eric in the appropriate "guy" dialogue about sports and construction. "I've got a nice collection of tools in my shed. I can't see hiring someone to fix every little thing that breaks." From Lorraine's eye roll, it was apparent he fixed little.

Kyle interjected sarcasm into the luncheon conversation that Eric caught but went unnoticed by his parents. Jenna ate her food in silence.

After lunch, Kyle slapped Eric on the back. "You're bunking with me. C'mon I'll show you my room."

"I thought you went to boarding school?"

"I do, compliments of my big sister. I came home to see her and to meet you."

They climbed the stairs, Kyle opened his bedroom door and cocked his head. "You can have the bed, I'll be okay on the floor with a sleeping bag. You might want to grab your shit out of my sister's suitcase before my mom finds it in there."

Eric thrust his hands into his pockets. "Listen, Kyle…about your sister and me. It's not just some casual—"

"It's cool. I'm not stupid like my parents. I know you're banging her."

Eric stilled, his body tense, his jaw tight. "Watch what you say."

"Why?" Kyle folded his arms akimbo, his smooth, young jaw sketched around a mouth bent in a dark glower. "It's true. Isn't it? The newspapers say you're living with her."

Eric looked beyond the boy, at trophies and bookshelves, staring as if something interesting caught his eye. "You don't understand."

"The fuck I don't. I've read all about you. You're a

busboy and my sister's rich and famous. It doesn't take a genius to see why you latched on to her."

Eric swallowed the accusation. It made logical yet brutal sense. He felt his value hollow, his self-esteem now puddled at his feet. "I'm not using her. I love her." The blanket statement was his best and only offer.

Scoffing, Kyle's response and expression showed Eric he'd as soon spit on him as believe him. "Love her? Yeah, you and half the guys in my dormitory. There's ten assholes on my floor alone that have her poster on their ceiling. Believe me you're not the only one getting off on her."

Eric fought not to wince, none too happy with that bit of information. "I'm not going to tell you again. Watch your mouth."

"Why?" Kyle's aspect ebbed into a relaxed glow, his eyes fixed in a grin. "What the fuck are you gonna do, beat me up with my parents right downstairs? C'mon, Busboy, bring it. I'm almost as tall as you, and I work out. Give me your best shot. It won't be the first time I got into a fight because of her."

He said nothing, watching scorn lift from his brother-in-law's complexion and leave in its place damp eyes and the gentle humility of a boy, one hurt or embarrassed. The kid was so earnest in his invitation he felt an instant pull of admiration for him.

"We don't have anything to fight about. I told you I love her."

Kyle wiped his nose with the back of his hand. "You better. I'm not kidding. I work out."

****

When Jenna and Eric returned from their trip into town, her father was relaxing in his lounger, laughing uproariously at something on television. Her mother was in the kitchen humming as she prepared dinner. Kyle was across the hall in the den, earbuds jammed into his ears, tuning them out.

Sam brought his chair to an upright position with a thump and stood. "Did my little girl show you all the sights?"

"Yes, sir. We went to the old cemetery behind the church and stopped for coffee at the restaurant that used to be the blacksmith's."

Sam gave Eric a light rap on the arm. "Did you get over to the shopping center? They just opened a Seafood Factory. Ever eat there? Food's great."

"I'll bet it is," Eric answered.

All of Eric's replies to Sam were polite without being condescending, Jenna noticed. Her parents were nice people but rated low on the interesting meter. An action movie playing at the multiplex and her mother's panic attacks were the only things that ever got their heart rates accelerated.

Hang on, Mom and Dad. They're about to soar.

"Daddy, can you come into the kitchen. Eric and I want to tell you and Mom something."

Brow wrinkling, Sam coughed into his fist. "Sure, Pumpkin. Nothing wrong I hope?"

"No, Daddy."

"I'll get Kyle," Eric offered.

In the kitchen, Lorraine had each dish simmering with egg timers set. She was the only woman Jenna knew with a drawer designated specifically for those gadgets. The ticking seemed ironically appropriate. In seven minutes, the carrots would be done, and her mother was going to have a heart attack.

Having the family enter before being called to the table caused Lorraine to drop a lid onto a pot with a clank. As if she sensed an impending disaster, she turned the flames down on all of the bubbling pots and pans to a simmer. "Is everything all right?"

"Our little girl has some news for us," Sam said, inching closer to his wife.

Both Kyle and Jenna assumed stations near to their mother. Eric took the cue and stepped within reach of Lorraine. Whichever way she chose to sway there would be someone in position to catch her.

"News?" she repeated in a thready voice.

Jenna gave her mother no time to construct a catastrophe. "Eric and I got married in Las Vegas over the new year."

Kyle took hold of Lorraine's arm. Sam walked quickly to the sink, opened a cabinet, and retrieved a glass and pill bottle. He filled the glass with water, opened the bottle, and returned to his wife. He placed a small yellow tablet onto her tongue and handed her the glass. Lorraine obediently swallowed the pill, then fell into her husband's arms and cried.

****

Three emotionally charged days later, Jenna and Eric boarded their return flight to L.A. The trip was by far less turbulent than meals marked by fretful questions, more bouts of crying, and dire predictions about what could go wrong in a marriage so hastily entered into and not blessed by God. When they arrived at their apartment, at eight o'clock that night, Jenna and Eric, jet-lagged and guilt ridden collapsed into bed.

Chapter Twelve

Bree Davis hadn't watered the Devil's Ivy on her desk and now it was half dead. She dropped the clay pot, straggly leaves drooping over the side, into her wastebasket. Greenery was epidemic in L.A. and there was no need for that particular aesthetic to invade the indoors. She was part of an ambitious breed of professional women with no time to devote to plants. Like children and pets, they were overrated.

She retrieved two thin tubes from her top drawer, Mua's Russian Red lipstick, and cinnamon breath spray. She gave a quick spritz to cover the lingering essence of vodka and spices from her two-Bloody-Mary lunch, and then carefully painted her lips. Grabbing the eighteen-hundred-dollar designer bag she'd saved six months for, she strode out the door, the wide straps of her work satchel slung over the opposite shoulder. At Alan's insistence, she was going to Jenna Welles' house to present her with a potential project, engage in some girl talk, and become "friends." What Alan expected Bree to discover was a no brainer. His starlet was living with a busboy, and that should tell him all he needed to know.

Bree cruised along the Santa Monica freeway and found a spot in front of the building. She lit a cigarette, took three long drags, and tossed it. After another spritz of breath-freshener and a reapplication of Russian Red, she stepped to the curb. Nick Lombardo, the faithful guard dog, pushed away from a gray sedan and escorted her into the lobby.

"Where's the limousine?" she asked.

"Too showy, draws too much attention."

She nodded a quick thank you to the short-on-words bodyguard as the elevator door slid shut. Jenna was waiting by her open doorway. "Hi. C'mon in."

Bree returned the smile. "Your apartment is lovely," she said, but her tone lacked sincerity. Her head pivoted about a cubicle of high-end furniture arranged against flat planes of gypsum-board and on squares of worn parquet flooring.

"Thank you," Jenna replied. "Alan said you had a script to show me."

Bree nodded. "After the misunderstanding about the tour, he wanted to make sure you were apprised of everything." Ruby lips froze into a smile where a purse of displeasure actually wanted to be.

Jenna gestured toward the couch. "Make yourself comfortable. I'll make some tea."

A few moments later, she returned with a cup in each hand, and handed one to Bree. Jenna's signature platinum waves were twined into a loose braid that glowed pearly against a table lamp, her scrubbed-clean skin a creamy perfection. Bree glanced sidelong at Stark Management's number one client, but no matter how much glitter Alan sprinkled on the young star, Bree failed to be dazzled by her. Then again, she viewed all of L.A.'s entitled through the "green eyes" of envy.

She removed a sheaf of papers from her satchel to discuss the script. She began at a pace, clipped and with no inflection in her tone—all business.

"This is the best thing I've read in a long time. Last year the studios were at war trying to gain the film rights to it, but luckily for us, Panorama won. It has Oscar written all over it."

She sped through the pitch like quicksilver to the touch and ended with another toothy smile. It was good material, but more importantly, going be filmed opening scene to end on the craggy hillsides of Yorkshire, England. Alan was determined to keep the distance between his starlet and her boyfriend by scheduling a film during a break in her tour. Bree's mission was to sell her on the idea.

As she continued to regale the merits of the script, the tumblers in the lock clicked and the front door opened. She turned in the direction of the sound as the Busboy stepped inside. Her hands shook as she placed her cup onto the table and she gazed, spellbound like a teenager spotting her crush. It was only when Jenna, bounded off the couch, that Bree broke her stare. Jenna rose on tiptoe and kissed him. "Honey, this is Bree Davis. She brought something for me from Alan's office. Bree…Eric."

Bree took a small sip of tea and nodded. "Hello." The word scraped, breathy and low from her throat. Eric smiled and his ivory teeth gleamed a contrast to his bronze skin. Mud and grease were spattered on his jeans and T-shirt—a supple, white cotton snug over tight muscles. A dusty baseball cap was tilted back on his head.

He lifted wide shoulders in apology for his appearance. "I'd shake your hand but…"

Bree had to grip an imaginary railing before

toppling, head over feet, and falling into the amazing sea-blue of his eyes. "That's quite all right," she answered, barely spitting the words.

"I had to dig around on the job," he explained. "And then I got a flat on the way home. I'm not usually this filthy." He shrugged, looking adorably embarrassed, then kicked off mud caked work boots. "I'll get out of your way. Nice to meet you, Ms. Davis."

Bree sipped more tea, glancing in his direction as he strode down the hallway stripping out of his shirt. A small china cup pressed to Russian Red was the only thing preventing her tongue from falling out of her mouth.

****

Stalked debuted in the tradition of old Hollywood. It was a glamorous, *to-be-seen-at* event. Television cameras and the papers covered the gala. Eric, who avoided the spotlight whenever possible, knew he was about to be blinded by its glare. For Jenna's sake he was required to dutifully pose for pictures, most of which he knew would have captions labeling him as "The Busboy."

Jenna's hand rested in his as their stretch limousine rolled into white hot shafts of light. Across from them, perched at the edge of the leather seat, Alan, with Bree Davis at his side, gave instructions. He claimed Jenna's hand and spoke, ignoring Eric as if he were a tree she was relaxing against.

"Bree and I will step from the car first, I'll make a small statement about how hard you worked on the film and so on...that will give the photographers enough time to gather around the car for you. Nick will be holding the door...and Laine, as you come out, help

Angel from the car, hold her hand, nothing more. I don't want shots of her being mauled in every paper."

Eric fixed Stark with a glare. "Is that okay with you *Jenna*?" he asked, carefully pronouncing her name.

"Look, Laine." Alan's tone was glacial, rime frosting every word. "Like it or not, tonight she's Angel."

As he alighted from the car, Eric did as he'd been instructed. He stood at her side, still as a rod, as the whine of electronic flashes stabbed his ears and explosions of blue and white blinded him. He and Jenna walked the red carpet, Jenna waving at fans and smiling her greetings to the other celebrities. She stopped several times to sign autographs.

She was poised, as always, and elegant, a vision in silvery blue. Light and wispy, fabric swirled around her legs and beads sparkled under the lights. Her pale blonde hair was set in waves and flowed down her back. *Fairy Princess*, Eric thought, as he held her hand and looked down at her; beautiful, ethereal, a fantasy— his fantasy come to life.

****

The film was received with all the appropriate reactions—gasps, screams, laughs, and finally a roar of applause at the end. After the movie, Jenna posed with her costars and the film's director. Eric faded into the background as photographers snapped away.

An after-party was held in what was once the estate of a silent film star and Alan quickly shuttled Jenna away to give interviews. As she disappeared through the crowd, she turned to Eric and mouthed the words, "I love you."

Alone, he ventured about with no particular

destination in mind. Bree stepped toward him, her hips an easy sway as she walked. "Are you enjoying yourself?"

He angled his head in the direction of the waiter serving champagne. "I'd be having a better time if I had a beer instead one of these." The champagne coupe looked too refined for his callused hand. "This is okay but not really my style."

She lifted lashes heavy with mascara. "Come with me, I can make sure you have what you want." She led him out of the ballroom to the bar on the terrace, her body gilded in fabric fine as gold-leaf. The gown was a shimmering and mere shadow of silk that plunged deep in back, stopping just above the curve of her buttocks. As she leaned toward the bar, she arched her body so that, Eric, devoted husband or not, couldn't help but notice the view.

"What type of beer would you like?" she asked over her shoulder.

He pulled his gaze away. "Whatever they have on tap is fine."

Bree turned, handed him a frosted mug with a froth of foam and tapped her glass to it. "This picture is going to be a big hit. You must be very proud of Angel."

"I'm always proud of *Jenna*."

"Ah," Bree arched one dark eyebrow, tipping an angular face sketched with an almost nonexistent grin. "Jenna, is it? I should have known from the way you reacted in the car you're not very fond of her stage name."

Scanning the crowd, Eric watched Hollywood's beau monde mingle. There was an artifice to the gathering—too many beaming smiles and too much laughter riding every word. He took a lazy swallow from his mug. "Angel is a concept Stark invented. Jenna is who she is."

Bree dropped her lashes into another slow flutter. "You seem sweet, very protective of her. She's a lucky girl…You clean up nicely too if you don't mind my saying so." Her compliments wafted on a throaty breath, her voice predictably husky. "It's so warm up here. Would you mind taking a walk with me? I could use some air."

Eric pointed out the obvious. "We're outside."

"Yes, but it's so crowded."

Breaking from the crush, he followed her to where a serpentine length of marble steps led down to a formal garden. Gas lanterns guided the way to fuchsia, canna, and bird of paradise growing amid spumes of palm fronds and tall cacti. A mammoth fountain with cherubs chiseled onto the top tier stood center. The landscape was old-world Hollywood at its finest.

Bree listed slightly, leaning into him for support. Her breasts grazed his biceps. "These shoes," she complained, "are impossible to walk in." Plucking at the side-slit of her dress she raised her foot to show him the thin heel of her shoe. "High fashion is definitely not designed for comfort…or mobility."

Sliding his hands into his pockets, Eric stepped away and half-leaned, half-sat against a low stone partition, his feet casually crossed at the ankles. The platinum orb of the moon was low on the horizon, illuminating the sky and almost washing away the yellow of the lanterns. He felt Bree's eyes upon him as she offered a too deep and too lingering appraisal.

Her tone became more of a breathy murmur as she spoke, her words a veiled invitation. "I'm sorry, I don't mean to stare. It's just…well. Have you ever considered a career in the business?"

An easy laugh tumbled from his lips. "No, Ms. Davis. I'll leave the acting to my…to Jenna."

"It's a shame." Her eyes were hooded and lazy, seductively disappointed. "As a professional *and* as a woman I have to say you should be doing something to capitalize on your looks."

"My looks?" he said, laughing again.

"Yes, your looks. Don't you have a mirror?"

Eric shrugged. He never looked too closely at himself, never probed too deeply into eyes that held his memories. "I think we should get back up to the party."

"Wait." Bree's hand, her fingers long and pale, the nails polished the same gold as her dress, came to rest on his forearm. "I think you should consider what I was saying. You're an extremely attractive man. You have a great speaking voice and a certain quality. I'd love to do something for you."

Eric knew women well enough to recognize flirting. He and Bree Davis locked eyes for just a moment. The spill of water from the fountain was a gentle ripple of sound, and the garden's flowers heady scented. She oozed femininity, and in a different circumstance he would have considered her invitation.

He shook his head. "I'm sorry, I'm really not interested."

****

"You were marvelous, darling. You are going to be huge."

The star of a long-running network drama, whose

once striking good looks were forgotten under layers of flesh and time, toddled off after paying Jenna the compliment.

Alan, still glued to her side, whispered, "She should know all about being huge."

Jenna glowered at him. "I'm a big fan, and I like her. She was just honored for her work with P.E.T.A."

Alan yawned. Careers on the waning side of fame bored him. "She does it for the press. The fatter she gets, the more charities she signs on for." He angled his head toward the crowd and sucked air through his teeth. "I'm going to have a long talk with your PR rep tomorrow. I see too many B-listers out there."

Frustration had stripped away any of the night's joy or pleasure, then the sound of a voice, familiar and booming, brought her smile back. "There's my Angel." Actor Jack Morrissey gathered Jenna in a hug. "You were terrific, kiddo, star quality."

"Thanks, Jack. I had a great co-star."

"Y'know, I'm famous for being a no-show at these things, even when I'm in the movie. But I came for you." Jack scrunched up one side of his face attempting to wink, but both glassy eyes were fixed in a narrow squint. He reeked of alcohol.

His daughter Meghan stumbled by, giving Jenna a sloppy wave. "We need to hit up some clubs again, girl."

Alan shook the actor's hand but quickly piloted Jenna away. "Big star, bigger booze hound."

"He's a nice man. He taught me a lot."

"Well the movie's out and you don't need him anymore. He's a lush. And stay away from that kid of his. She's a train wreck."

"Unbelievable." Jenna mouthed the word so Alan wouldn't hear.

She stepped away but he caught up and steered her about the room. At his insistence they lingered with the up-and-coming, breezed past the down-and-out, and hit the breaks for the high-and-mighty. Jenna spoke to hot young directors, rich old producers, and a dozen stars with Oscars on their mantels. She never failed to be awed when in such company. Being considered one of them was still a foreign concept and she wondered if it would ever sink in. It was amazing. It was exhilarating. It was daunting.

Eventually she found Eric. He and Bree were at the bar standing close. *Too close*. Bree Davis's reaction to Eric hadn't gone unnoticed by Jenna the day in her apartment. She broke away from Alan and rushed over. Sliding her arms around her husband's neck she said, "I'm ready to call it a night."

"Gets my vote," he said, his smile beaming down on her.

"This isn't a democracy, Laine, you don't get a vote." Stark, pithy, eyes ever riveted upon Jenna, glared disapproval as Eric enveloped her in his arms. "Must you maul her in public?"

Eric's lips parted, as if he might say something. Instead he closed his mouth into a tight slash. Jenna hugged him again, showing her silent appreciation for his gracious tolerance of Alan and his constant indignities

Eric kissed her temple. "Babes, do you want to go home?"

Alan was quick to interrupt. "This is a Hollywood premier, not a dive bar on the strip. She isn't a 'babe,' she's Angel and a big star. She makes a grand entrance *and* a grand exit. If you've had enough, feel free to leave."

Looking as though his patience was exhausted Eric repeated, "Jen, do you want to go home?"

"I'm her manager," Stark shot back. "She leaves when I say she leaves."

Eric eased Jenna away, his hands on her shoulders. He dipped his head as if to ask a question, one she answered back with a nod. He turned and steeled his eyes at Stark. "You may be her manager but I'm her husband and I'm taking my wife home."

****

The shocking announcement of the nineteen-year-old virgin star's marriage heightened both Angel's popularity and her media value. For weeks, stories with every imaginable spin about the young actress and her handsome blue-collar husband appeared in both tabloids and the legitimate press. *The Exclusive*, the worst of the rags, ran weekly photos of Jenna, the shimmering mantle of her alter-ego Angel, cropped next to gritty pictures of Eric in jeans and hard hat. Reporters camped outside the building where Jenna and Eric lived. Fans, spurred by the media fever, descended like the faithful to a religious shrine.

When an overzealous fan successfully scaled the stucco facade of their building and almost made it through the living room window, it became sadly obvious to the newlyweds that they would have to give up their small home and move to a more secure location. Jenna bought a house in exclusive Malibu.

Chapter Thirteen

With *Stalked* sweeping the box office and Jenna's album sales topping the Billboard charts, it was no great surprise when seats for her concert tour quickly sold out. The initial run was for six months, but new dates and venues opened as fans clamored for tickets. Her rigorous rehearsal schedule abruptly and indefinitely curtailed any stolen romantic moments she shared with her husband.

In mid-May, two weeks before the Memorial Day weekend, Jenna and her entourage of backup singers, dancers, musicians, stagehands, sound techs, makeup artists, hairdressers, wardrobe people, security team and, *of course* Alan Stark, embarked on the tour. Eric joined her in New York for her opening night concert, and then flew home to Los Angeles to supervise the moving of their things to their new home in lofty Malibu. As Jenna sat on her state-of-the art tour bus, absently watching the skyscrapers of the city smudge then blur away, the vehicle sped to the next destination. She thought about how terribly she already missed him.

****

Eric unlaced his boots, then took them off before opening the back door. Even the mud room wasn't meant for the amount dirt compressed into the deep treads of his soles. Once inside, he brushed dust and debris from his jeans, but as he stepped into the kitchen, clay caked his socks, and fell onto the marble.

"Shit," he whispered, looking down at the rust-colored clods that had shattered against the floor. He tossed his socks into the mud room and wadded up a mass of wet paper towels to clean up the dirt.

Wearily, he grabbed a container of orange juice from its lonely spot on a refrigerator shelf and took a long swallow. He thought about taking a seat at the shining center-island but didn't want to get any dirt on the expensive white fabric covering the stools.

Sitting in the great room was also not an option. The airy space, an expansive cube of windows that stretched from the floor to the upstairs loft, was also white—bright, glaringly white. Having had no time to shop for real estate, Jenna bought the house sight-unseen and already furnished. Every table, chair, and scrap of fabric in the house was white. During the walk through the realtor, the clack of her heels an unwavering echo, had proudly boasted the names of all the different fabrics—washed almond, pure pearl, and the nonsensical, almost alabaster. *It either was or it wasn't*. He sighed as he looked at a blizzard of identical shades of nothing.

The only place any color was to be found were in enormous, canvases that hung on the walls—modern, ugly work that looked like artists spat paint at them.

Eric climbed the winding staircase, his steps slow and tired. After showering, he ordered a pizza and popped open a beer. He wanted to watch a ball game while he ate, but tomato sauce and Egyptian Pima-cotton was not a good combination. After his dinner arrived, he ate at the quartz counter, hoping the red oil dripping from his slice didn't somehow seep into the polished stone.

He ate three slices, flipped the cardboard lid over the rest of the pie, and slid the box into the empty refrigerator. He grabbed another beer and went back into the great room to decide which one of the white chairs or sofas he should sit on. The couch facing the entertainment armoire was the logical place to rest, but it was covered in suede and Eric had fallen asleep on it the night before and drooled all over the thick rolled arm.

He shook his head, stretched aching muscles and again inhaled a tired pull of air. There was nowhere in the house Eric found comfort. *Igloos had more atmosphere*, he often thought. He wondered what Jenna would think of the place when she came home from the tour. Would she like the clean brightness of the house? Would she like the plush white furniture and thick white carpets?

Maybe it wasn't what was in the house Eric found so oppressive, but what wasn't in it. Jenna. Without her, there was no warmth or comfort. It was gone away with her, in which city now he wasn't even sure. It had been almost a month since he'd seen her. A month since he saw her performing and earning the money that gave him license to wander aimlessly through the pristine, glass box in search of a place to sit.

****

Jenna gulped long draughts of water as dressers peeled one outfit off and replaced it with another. Seven changes in all, done with the precision and speed of a pit crew at the Daytona 500—sexy costumes that reflected her status as a *former* teen virgin. Her makeup artist pounded her with a towel to capture the rivers of sweat running down her face and neck, and then dabbed at her eyes and lips with makeup. Stylists tugged at her, their hands sure and swift. After her headset was readjusted, Jenna was dispatched back into a chaos of light so brilliant it was what she imagined an alien abduction to be like.

Each night thousands of people screamed and cheered their adoration. It was both electrifying and frightening, the same thrill of terror as a roller coaster rattling downward from the highest crest. It was a stomach-flip like nothing imaginable.

After her shows, Jenna usually grabbed a quick dinner and was back on the tour bus to shower, sleep, and zoom to the next destination. But in big cities there were multiple concert dates, and she stayed in luxury hotels, ate lavish dinners with her backup dancers, and partied at exclusive clubs. Most nights, long after the frenzy ended, she still found herself too wired to sleep. Music still resounded in her head and adrenaline coursed through her system. It was then, in the hours just before dawn, that she thought of Eric and wished he was there to share it all with her.

****

Eric was in his usual station not acting much like a lonely husband as he prepared drinks for a clientele of mostly women. They lined the bar, watching him with the same hungry anticipation of a child eyeing a lollipop. With one hand he tossed ice cubes into the air and caught them with the metal shaker he held in his other. He flipped a liquor bottle upside down with dexterity and poured. The women continued to follow his every movement—his arms bunching beneath crisp white cotton, and his eyes, lit by the bar's low lighting, sparkling pools of blue. Bree Davis slipped through the crowd, her long limbed stride easy and her hair falling in luxuriant waves over her shoulders.

Eric smiled and offered a wink. "You're becoming a regular, Miss Davis."

She set a pricy clutch on the bar and grinned. "All part of my job. With my boss out of town, it's up to me to see what's hot, what's not, and who's making the rounds."

Eric tilted his head to indicate a space no longer crammed with bodies. "I think the A-List has found a new spot."

"You still look to be drawing customers."

Eric wasn't exactly unaware that his station was a congestion of customers while Mark idled lonely at the other end of the bar. Ignoring Bree's observation, Eric placed a coaster before her. "So what can I get you?"

"Whatever's your specialty," she answered. Her tone was a throaty purr.

"I make a pretty good martini, but I don't recommend more than one."

Bracing the heels of her hands on the railing she leaned close, displaying a swell of cleavage. "Then as my bartender you'll have to see that I make it home all right if I get too drunk."

Eric cocked an eyebrow as he grabbed a bottle of gin from the shelf. "Tell you what, as your bartender I'll make sure you drink responsibly."

Bree's answer was a timid smile, but her eyes sparked intensity. He could almost feel the scrutiny of her stare as he finished mixing the drink.

"Can you join me and have one?" she asked.

"It's too early." He leaned forward and closed the

gap between them. "Besides, I won't be twenty-one for another month. I shouldn't even be in here." He winked again. "Don't let it get around though, Mark and I go to an after-hours place when we're through, and they think I'm legal."

"If after-hours clubs aren't legal," she said, "why do you need to be?"

"Good point."

Bree gave her head a slow toss, her hair a glossy spill under an anthology of pendants and neon. "It sounds like fun. Would you like some extra company tonight?"

"Sure, why not."

Eric coughed, regretting his reply and wishing he could dive, glove tipped outward to basket-catch the words before they hit the ground. Bree's lips were pursed, the corners slightly upturned into a slaked, scarlet pout. Eric rushed away to the other end of the bar to grab a bin of ice from the bar-back.

What was I thinking…inviting Stark's assistant of all people, out?

But Eric didn't really need to examine his motives too thoroughly. He knew exactly what he had been thinking. He was thinking about the picture of his wife in the morning paper, her hair a wild cascade around her face, and her dress so low-cut and short, it allowed more leg and cleavage than he was comfortable with. He was thinking of news footage of her prancing on stage, breasts bouncing, being passed from one buff and bare-chested dancer to another. He was thinking like a macho jealous guy, resentful and wounded, and soothing his ego by letting another woman stroke it.

His mood soured, the smile vanishing. He went

back to the business of serving drinks, shoveling ice into glasses, and grabbing money like a machine. He had worked during the day in the same fashion, pounding nails with an angry vigor. It was his way of blowing off enough steam to get in a human state so he could deal with his customers at night. But it wasn't working. He missed Jenna, engaged in stupid flirtation with Bree Davis and everything sucked.

A sudden commotion began on the dance floor. Two men, on the verge of fighting, seemed oblivious of the people they bumped as they shouldered one another. With senses still finely tuned to trouble, Eric became aware of the situation long before the bouncers. He watched the scuffle on the dance floor intensify, the men drunk and untidy, wheeling threats and clumsily batting at the air. Eric glanced toward the lounge, wondering at what point the security team would notice the coming storm.

Waving his arms, he signaled for them, but the bouncers simply stood, two behemoths in black suits and headsets, small microphones pinned to their lapels. They posed, presenting an image of a bad spy movie. *Actually*, Eric remembered, one of them had recently *been* in a bad spy movie.

He called to Mark, "Grab the glasses off the bar. I'll be right back."

Using one hand for leverage, Eric easily hurtled the bar and reached the drunks before the first fist connected. He grabbed one of the men and shoved him up against a column at the edge of the dance floor. The man struggled free and turned his ire on Eric, but by the time the security team arrived, he had flattened the guy.

"Nice work." One of the bouncers threw a mock

punch to his triceps. "I'll bet that beautiful wife of yours doesn't need bodyguards with you around."

"Yeah, well I haven't been around her much lately."

He went back to the bar in a worse mood than ever. Flexing scraped knuckles he plunged his hand into a bucket of melting ice. His sleeve was blood-spattered. Splitting the guy's lip had just cost him the price of a new shirt.

Mark ambled over shaking his head. "I don't think anybody really wants you serving drinks with blood dripping off your cuff, my friend. Chill out on the other side of the bar and I'll make you a drink."

Grabbing a pitcher he added a blend of clear liquors, grenadine, and a splash of orange juice. He poured the concoction into shot glasses and Mark, Eric, and Bree drank the contents one after another.

"Party time," Mark announced sometime later after he and Eric were finished cleaning up and tipping out.

"After hours?" Bree perked up, straightening in her stool, again displaying cleavage. "Why don't you ride with me; I have a driver. We can arrive in style."

Eric declined the offer. "The place is a dive, *Miss Davis.* We don't need a limo or any style."

"Speak for yourself," Mark argued, turning to flash a smile and *the look.*

Glancing down at his shirt, Eric muttered. "Maybe I should pass and go home."

"But I've been waiting all night." Bree's liquid, big-eyed stare voiced disappointment. "I'm just not ready for my four lonely walls."

"Just roll up your sleeves," Mark said as he patted Eric on the back. "It's not like we have somewhere better to be."

What the hell, Eric thought, reconsidering. He had a nice buzz going from the shots. Why go home to an empty house?

Chapter Fourteen

Blanketed on all sides by security, Jenna was rushed through a crowd of fans. Nick was at the forefront and Alan, as always, hovered close by. At her sides, bodyguards held their arms up to shield her from the bombardment of paparazzi as she was shuttled to the super-stretch limousine waiting curbside in front of Chicago's hottest nightclub. White hot sparks like summer lightening continued to explode as the limo pulled away.

Inside the car, Alan sat, skinny legs crossed and a sour expression on his face. He gave a quick turn of his wrist and glanced at his watch. "Two thirty."

Jenna unscrewed the cap on a bottle of water and took a sip. "Alan, if you were tired you could have gone back to the hotel. I would have been fine."

"I'm not tired, but you need to save your energy for your performances."

Jenna stretched. "I have plenty of energy, and I'll get a good night's sleep on the bus after tomorrow's show."

Alan huffed a nasal grunt that she ignored.

Ten minutes later, still shrouded by bodyguards, she entered the hotel elevator and rode it to the top. Her suite at the Crown Western was lavish as were all her accommodations—large living area, spacious bath, and a bedroom with a king-sized bed covered in expensive linens. In the shower she rinsed away smoke, and sweat, and makeup thick as a mask. She shrugged into a large cotton T-shirt with the words *Larity Construction* printed on the front, one of her husband's. Slipping into the bed, she rested her head on a mountain of goose-down pillows and picked up her phone to call Eric. Seven rings later, she hit cancel. It was three thirty, one hirty in California. He was probably still at work.

Jenna thought to read for a while and try again, but before she picked up the magazine lying on the bedside table, she changed her mind and flicked off the light. He hadn't been home last Saturday, or the one before, or the one before that. He was out somewhere, and she was in no position to be upset about it.

****

Mark gulped his shot, turned the glass upside down, and slammed it on the bar. Bree took a small sip of her own, but Eric waved his glass away and shook his head. "I'm through," he said through lips that looked rubbery and uncooperative.

Bree sagged against him. "You're not wimping out on us, are you?"

"I believe I am." Eric listed against the bar as if his bones collectively parted beneath his skin.

Undeterred, Mark ordered another round and positioned himself close to Bree. He raised an eyebrow that was too dark to be partnered with his platinum streaks and spoke to her in a hoarse buzz. "You're still with me, aren't you?" He raised another shot glass and handed it to her.

"I'm with Eric," she said, her voice lazy from alcohol, but still insistent.

Moving away, she left a gap between herself and

Mark. Bree Davis was a woman who had no problem handling the advances of aggressive men in pursuit of careers in the business, but she continually backed away from even the slightest contact with Mark Chambers. There was something veiled beneath the smiles and wide virtue of his eyes. Mark had the aspect of an adorable child who turns out to be the bad seed in a *B* movie.

He offered her a vial of white powder, which, like most of the drinks he handed her, she refused. Not appearing offended, he strode to the bathroom, returning to the bar revived and ready to drink more. He tapped a steady beat on the bar rail with his fingertips. "You two are lightweights."

His eyes were wide, the pupils huge circles that all but obscured the pale blue of his irises. He spoke in rambling spurts that made white dots of spittle collect in the corners of his mouth. Despite the late hour and vast amount of alcohol in his bloodstream, he was annoyingly alert.

****

The early morning sun was squeezing through sticky contact paper covering the windows. Eric cringed as slices of Los Angeles daylight fell across his face. He raised a hand to cover his burning eyes.

Bree turned her head around and drew her lips into displeasure as if just realizing the seamy room was dirty and dank. "Let's get the hell out of here."

Downing another shot, Mark sprang to attention. Eric's body, however, seemed to be weighted to one side; still he managed to navigate through the exit without falling down the two steps. After they climbed into the limo, Bree lowered the divider to give directions to the driver.

"I'm crashing at Eric's," Mark interrupted. "Malibu, my good man."

Twenty minutes later Bree and Mark stood by as Eric fumbled with his keys and miraculously managed to punch in the correct security code on the alarm. He stumbled up the stairs, fell into his huge white bed, and passed out.

****

Eric had absolutely no recollection of the ride home and remembered little of the time spent at the after-hours. With cautious steps he made his way down the stairs, not surprised to find Mark sprawled on the white sofa, a collection of beer bottles at his feet, and a half smoked joint sitting in an ashtray. It was the sudden movement on the patio that gave Eric a jolt. He hadn't expected to see a pair of tawny legs stretched out on one of the lounge chairs by the pool. Squinting to keep the sharp talons of sunshine from scratching his retinas, he crept slowly through the French doors.

"Bree?"

"Good afternoon," she said. Her voice was a smoky invitation as she relaxed on a chaise, all lean limbed, her body covered in little more than a diaphanous bra and panties.

"What are you doing here?"

"I came in with you last night to use your bathroom, and I guess I fell asleep in your guest room. My head is splitting, and I couldn't resist taking a dip. I hope you don't mind."

Eric dropped onto a chair holding his own throbbing head in his hands. "No, it's okay."

The odors of alcohol and cigarette smoke clinging

to his shirt attacked his sinuses. He stripped out of it, crumpled the shirt into a ball, and threw it at the base of one of the potted palm trees that flanked the oval pool. He felt Bree's eye on him as she slipped her sunglasses down her nose and looked at him over the rims. A rumpled looking, also bare-chested Mark appeared with a beer already in hand and Bree snapped her glasses back up to her eyes.

"A little hair of the dog," Mark proclaimed as he sipped.

"You're out of your mind." Eric's lips were set in a grimace of pain.

Stretching, Mark lowered himself to the end of Bree's chaise. "You don't look any worse for wear."

Bree flapped the ends of the towel she was laying on to cover herself, and Eric suggested Mark take a seat on one of a dozen other chairs that surrounded the pool. "Did either of you notice what time it was when we got in this morning?" he asked.

Lighting a cigarette Mark answered around a cough and veil of smoke. "Seven I think."

"Crap. I missed Jenna's call again. She's already on her way to Wisconsin."

Bree stood and dove into the pool. She invited Eric to join her. "The water feels great," she called up to him. She offered no such invitation to Mark.

****

Hours later the intercom at the gate sounded a constant buzz as pizza deliveries and more people arrived. Music blasted on the stereo. Eric, lying on a chaise at the other end of the pool, slept through the noise.

What had started as a simple Sunday card game

had turned to full-on parties. Now Mark, most of the staff from Crimson, and friends, of friends, of friends, were in regular attendance.

****

Nick and hulking bodyguards shuttled Jenna inside the night's venue, hovering closely as she signed autographs on the way in. In her dressing room, she reached into her bag for her phone but held it for long moments before flipping it open. She eventually dialed, first Eric's cell, which went to voice mail, then the house phone. A voice, familiar, but not her husband's, boomed in her ear. "Party Central."

"Excuse me?"

"Angel, sweetheart, sorry about that. How's life on the road?"

Jenna blew a frustrated sigh into the receiver. "Put Eric on."

It wasn't the first time Mark Chambers had been brazen enough to answer the phone and it settled Jenna's question about why Eric hadn't been home the night before. He had been out somewhere with his buddy. Female giggling provided background accompaniment for the rock and roll blasting on the stereo. It sounded like a hell of a party.

"Hang on a sec, I'll have somebody go find him."

Jenna held the phone away to mute the animated chirp of Mark's voice, but his shout traveled into her receiver. "Hey, sweetheart, go find Eric. *That's* right, the hot guy in the board shorts."

After a short wait, a clicking sound told Jenna another phone had been picked up. "Hey, Babes."

She didn't answer.

"Babes, are you there?"

"Oh, I wasn't sure if you were talking to me or to one of the other 'babes' at the house."

There was long breach of silence before Eric answered. "There are a few guys from the club here, and a couple of friends of Mark's stopped by. They're just hanging out by the pool. I'm actually trying to get rid of them so I can get some sleep. I'm beat."

"You could try going *home* after work?"

Another vacuum-like void of silence preempted the chaos in the background.

"Like you do?" Eric's words spilled through the line, and Jenna could hear a crinkling of paper as he spoke. "Film and pop star Angel parties with dancers from her sell-out concert. She was spotted in Chicago's newest hot-spot Club O." His discourse ended with the sound of the newspaper slapping against something hard. "Great picture of you, too. Tell you what, *Angel*. I'll try going home after work when you try wearing clothes that cover your ass."

Jenna pressed her phone tightly against her chest. She thought about responding but instead snapped it shut with a click.

****

The hum of the dial tone could have been a stiletto. It pierced Eric's eardrums that painfully. "Fuck! Fuck! Fuck!" He shoved the newspaper off the glass table and sent the pages fluttering into the pool. Being tired and hung-over was no excuse for his surly little speech. And calling Jenna Angel, he could have cut is tongue out.

He stormed into the house and up the stairs, tossing debris as he went. Beer cans littered the treads and cigarettes floated in the dregs of liquid in plastic cups. Eric strode through his bedroom to the bath for a

143

shower but stopped short when he noticed a lump in his bed moving.

A girl who may have been thirteen or thirty sat up, revealing tiny breasts. She ran her fingers through stringy hair and squinted, but her eyes still had an unfocused glaze to them. Eric huffed as he regarded the blue tinged circles under the girl's eyes, the red, runny condition of her nose, and her dry cracked lips. She looked like an ad for allergy medicine. *Meth head,* Eric knew.

"Who the hell are you?"

Lifting her thin arms to scratch at her hair made the sheet fall further down her emaciated torso. "Got a light?"

He shook his head in disgust as the girl picked up a half-smoked cigarette from his night table. She angled her face toward him fully expecting him to light it. He yanked her to her feet causing a glass and its contents to topple to the floor. In one motion he shoved her toward the door throwing a bundle he assumed were her clothes after her. "Get the hell out and tell everyone the party's over."

An hour later, he stood in the dirty living room, his argument with Jenna still swimming laps in his head. The temptation to add to the mess by throwing what wasn't already overturned around the room was strong. Instead, he bent down and picked up the throw pillows, returning them to their place on the couch. He dropped onto cushions that had been a pristine white a few weeks ago and covered his eyes with his forearm, silently cursing himself for behaving like a teenager and trashing the house while his parents were out of town.

The sound of the vacuum motor roused him.

Cracking open one eye, he saw Mark scurrying about, picking up glasses and emptying garbage into a plastic bag while alternately dragging the machine. "These people have no respect for someone's home," he said.

He continued apologizing while begging forgiveness and cleaning. Eric joined him in the task, knowing it would take more than furniture polish and the cleaning lady's skill to restore everything.

"Man, I'm really sorry about all of this, all these fucking bimbos lying around the place spilling drinks."

"I'm the one who lives here," Eric cut in. "I didn't have to let them in the door. It got out of control. No more parties. I can't have some cokehead having a heart attack in Jenna's house."

Mark nodded his agreement. "I hear you man. Listen, I've gotta take a leak, I'll be right back."

He sprinted off to the powder room and stayed locked inside far too long to simply clear his bladder. *Cokehead,* Eric's words wandered back to him. He knew his friend was scooping white powder from a vial or folded piece of foil—travelling down a dangerous road. Shaking his head, Eric bent down to gather more debris from the floor. Mark certainly wasn't the only person in L.A. on a supplemental diet of cocaine. Eric pressed the button on the handle of the vacuum and took over the chore of cleaning the carpet.

Chapter Fifteen

Alan ran his finger down the column with the week's expenditures, comparing it to intake from sales of "Angel" merchandise. As entertainment manager he wore many hats—numbers cruncher, image consultant, and mother. The numbers were good. His client, however, was starting to burn out. He had represented enough celebrities to know that their emotions ran hot and cold. The adoration of cheering fans was a rush most people could never imagine, the downside, how fierce and penetrating misery could be when it struck. Star egos were abidingly fragile.

He entered Angel's dressing room to find her swiping at red-rimmed, puffy eyes. "What's wrong?" he asked. His tone dripped with concern and his mouth hung open in a curious oval.

"Nothing, I'm fine."

"No you're not. You've been crying. Tell me what the hell happened."

"It's nothing," she insisted.

He reached for her, holding tight to her wrist. "You're going to be on stage in less than two hours. You can't perform if you're upset. Tell me what's wrong."

"I'm just tired and a little homesick."

"I suppose a meltdown now and again is in order." Go splash some water on your face. Hair and makeup are on their way."

Alan watched her walk off to the bathroom, her spine steel-rod stiff. He grinned, knowing full well what had caused the waterworks. Bree had called earlier, and he already knew about the party at the Malibu mansion. She'd stayed long enough to witness a parade of guests settling in and drinking, girls stripped down to scraps of material that barely qualified as swimwear. She had also stayed long enough to overhear Laine, irritable and short-tempered, arguing with his wife on the phone.

Alan made a mental note to give Bree a bonus when he returned to L.A. He also stored the name Mark Chambers, a hack, aspiring actor friend of Laine's, on his roster of people who might be of use for something. With Angel's star rising higher and higher, Alan was more determined than ever to free the teenaged superstar from the confines of her blue-collar marriage.

****

For two more weeks, Jenna's bus zigzagged through the Midwest. A week later, it was on a southern route speeding through Oklahoma, Texas, New Mexico, and Arizona. By the tenth week, she was headed to the Pacific Northwest.

Each night brought new fans, who brought new excitement and electricity to the shows. But for Jenna the color had faded. Everywhere she went she was surrounded by bodyguards; still, frenzied fingers grabbed for her, pulling at her hair, her clothing, and whatever else they could touch. The name Angel was an incessant scream at her ears. After-parties now wore her out and she craved sleep like the starving craved food. She would be home for a much needed hiatus in a few short weeks she reminded herself, home with Eric.

They would clear things up and get back on track. It was the only thought that gave her the revitalization and energy she needed.

****

Eric Laine's twenty-first birthday passed with very little fanfare. Mark treated him to dinner at a new tapas place on Sunset, and they went for drinks at an old haunt on Cloverdale afterward—Eric's first with legitimate ID. It was also the first weekend he had off in months. Crimson, once bustling inside and surrounded outside by a line of customers, had closed its doors while Caz and Jon made plans to rebrand.

"Let me get these," Eric said.

"It's okay," Mark insisted. "I told you tonight was on me."

"But you don't have a—"

"Job? Don't worry about me, my friend. I've got something lined up." He plucked the cherry from his drink and slipped it into his mouth. "In fact, I can get you in this new place. Guy who's opening it is a buddy of mine. You know how the money rolls in when a club first hits."

Eric shrugged. "I don't know? I'd like to spend some time with my wife when she gets home. Maybe get some sleep once in a while."

"I hear you. The night life can wear a person out." Mark played a rat-a-tat on the brass railing and ordered another round. "I think about getting a day job every now and then, but I've gotta keep my time free for auditions."

Their conversation stalled as Eric gave his attention over to the bar's pitted top and the hazy circles of light spilling from dated, amber pendants. A broken staccato of music spat from an old jukebox as he sipped his drink. He knew Mark failed at open calls and was never cast. The bartender eventually loped over with their refills.

"You should really think about this new place. It'll be like old times—me and you together, back behind the stick," Mark said.

While Eric didn't embrace an immediate leap back into the L.A. club scene, he couldn't help *but* think about it. Couldn't help but think how his income had just split down the center with one piece falling into a hole. He thought about the astronomical mortgage his wife paid, and he *thought* about being able to contribute a little something to their high-end lifestyle.

"I'm not promising anything, but I'll go take a look at the place with you."

Mark smiled and tapped his glass to Eric's. "Just like old times."

****

San Francisco was a palette of vivid colors, buildings with window boxes overflowing with flowers, and tall Victorians that seemed to grow right out of its vertical hills. Jenna's talent was out enjoying the city while she sat, legs curled under staring out at the bay from her suite at the Fairfax. She had no desire to traverse the winding corkscrew of Lombard Street or sample the chocolate at the famous Ghirardelli square. Jenna's only thought was that she was three hundred and fifty short miles from home and two short weeks away from being back in her husband's arms. Her only desire was to make things right between them.

Two hours later, she was in a makeup chair at the night's venue, the steady hands of her hairdresser coiling her hair around the narrow barrel of the hot iron. Alan, ever on hand, rattled names from a list of attendees for the backstage party.

With her locks stretched away from her scalp and her eyes now being worked on, all Jenna could offer was a quick, "Okay."

"This is quite a lineup," Alan boasted. "PR has given out over a hundred passes." His lips were stretched into a wide crescent and he stood beaming down at her.

"Is there something else?" Jenna asked. His simpering grin was a bad omen. Alan Stark rarely smiled.

"Actually, there is." He brushed at his jacket sleeves. Fussing with his clothing was his version of stretching before exercising. Jenna knew he was warming up for something. "Prince Luca of Santorino has invited you to a late supper after the show."

"Luca?" Jenna whipped her head around catching long strands of hair in the spiral channels of the iron." Isn't he the one the papers call the playboy prince?"

"Tabloid nonsense," Alan said as picked imaginary lint from his sleeve.

"A late supper is a date. I'm married in case you forgot."

With a wave of his hand, he dismissed the stylists and makeup artist. Bracing his hands on the arms of Jenna's chair, he leaned close. "Prince Luca is the crown prince of the most exclusive country in the Mediterranean and his father is an international financier. You should be flattered someone in his position is a fan."

Jenna's back was tight against the makeup chair;

curls spilled over one shoulder while the rest of her platinum locks were still pinned to her scalp. She shuttered her eyes to veil the dark dots of Alan's boring into her. "I appreciate all my fans no matter who they are."

"Spare me. A hundred young singers are breathing down your neck, but you're the only one who has a crown-prince hot for her. This is something we capitalize on. After the backstage party you're getting in a limo with the prince and having dinner at Top of the Point."

Jenna trembled with so much frustration her teeth almost chattered. "I'll meet him, smile for the camera, curtsey or whatever. I am *not* having dinner with him."

"You most certainly are. It's already arranged."

****

Eric threw his bag into the trunk of Jenna's convertible, a glossy and expensive car she rarely drove. The trip was spur-of-the-moment, and had he planned it he would have left early enough to catch her show. With the long drive ahead, he'd have to surprise her at her hotel. He whistled as he slammed the trunk, hopped into the car and headed toward the I-5.

Six long hours later, he gave the car to the valet and entered the lavish Fairfax. The doors were heavy glass with inserts cut like the facets of a diamond. Orbs of light filtered through and glinted on towering columns, and tall palm trees set throughout the lobby. Eric looked around at an expanse of white marble and gilded molding, then at his worn canvas knapsack. He wished Jenna had left behind one of her designer suitcases. Compared to the other patrons occupying the lobby he looked like someone on the last leg of a cross-country hitchhiking trek. Dressed in faded jeans and a denim jacket, his most comfortable for the drive, he waited patiently as the desk clerks all but ignored him. Eventually one approached and asked if he had a reservation.

"No, but my wife is staying here," he explained.

"Her name?"

"Jenna Laine, but um…she's Angel. She's probably registered as Angel."

The clerk moved to the end of the registration desk and into a huddle with the other clerks. They engaged in a whispered conference, giving Eric speculative glances as they spoke. One of them returned to where he waited. "Sir, it's against our policy to allow anyone into a room unless they're registered for it. We haven't been informed that Angel is expecting her husband."

"I wanted to surprise her," Eric said on a sigh. "I guess I'll just get another room and wait."

"Sorry but we're booked solid."

Eric hadn't gotten his wallet more than an inch out of his back pocket when he noticed two men standing sentinel by the elevators. They were tall and square-faced, their bodies robust beneath dark blazers. *Hotel security.* He took a tired breath. It was late, a weekend night and maybe the hotel was booked. Not wanting to waste his time arguing, he grabbed his bag from the floor and left.

Outside he waited for the valet to deliver Jenna's car back to him, wondering if it would have made a difference if the desk clerk had seen the expensive automobile. He gave the valet a five, tossed the knapsack back into the car, and called her cell phone. She was either still on stage or in the thick of an after-party, so he tried to leave a message. As usual, her mailbox was full.

He drove to the venue and circled the near empty parking lot until he found the area where massive tour busses rested. He pounded the steering wheel as he realized he hadn't brought the backstage pass Jenna had given him. He stared dispiritedly at the mob of fans waiting behind ropes, near the busses. The only way he was going to get near his wife was to wait with them and hope to catch her attention when she left.

He inched his way through a mass of mostly teenage fans to get closer to the front. Kids, young and still in a state of post-concert exhilaration babbled on about the show, how Angel looked, what she sang, and how great she was. Eric smiled until two pimply freshmen declared her boobs to be the roundest, bounciest set of tits they had ever seen. He inched away before the boys made any more observations about his wife's body.

Eric found himself standing next to an odd little man of about fifty wearing Jenna's album cover *Heavenly* silk-screened onto a tee-shirt. "I've seen *Stalked* sixty times," he boasted. "I'm her biggest fan."

Get in line, pal.

Several times a man, his baseball capped head a barrel over an equally thick neck, came out to the fenced area to tell everyone Angel had already gone. Each time he made his statement a cluster of people left and by midnight less than twenty people remained. Eric was finally able to get the attention of the man dismissing everyone.

"Hey, buddy, can you get a message to her?"

The security guard answered with a sardonic laugh.

"You're kidding, right?"

Scanning the near empty lot, Eric exhaled a tired breath. "Look, I know you're not going to believe me, but my name is Eric Laine, and I'm her husband."

Inching close to the rope the guard tipped his face and laughed louder. "Sure you are. And I'm the second coming. Do yourself a favor and go home."

"Oh my God he is." A teenage girl, who like Eric, had refused to leave, gaped at him, her feet playing an excited drumroll on the asphalt.

Another girl, reed-thin and wearing thick glasses, rushed over. "It's him! It's him, it's the Busboy!"

The remainder of the crowd turned in unison to gawk at Eric, but it only made the guard more annoyed. "You all have to get your cars out of the lot, or they'll be towed."

Eric made one last attempt. "Look I'm leaving, but could you do me one favor? Ask Jen...um Angel, to turn on her cell phone. Tell her Eric is outside, and I'll call her in about five minutes." He walked away without waiting for an answer, the two squealing girls pattering and spinning at his heels.

At his car Eric eyed the expanse of asphalt, and the blue-white circles of light raining down on the empty parking spaces. "Don't you kids have a car? This isn't the best part of town."

The girls blurted something that required an expert in teen speed language to translate and all he caught were the words, friends, sneak, party, and left us. The corners of his mouth lifted toward his cheeks. This was a situation so comically wrong he could do little more than stand there with a cockeyed grin on his face. He was in a dark parking lot with two girls no more than fourteen and he was having no more success getting in to see his wife than they were.

Still giggling, and bounding like puppies, they gibbered on about their efforts to sneak backstage. Eric stepped away to escape the shrieking, but the girls followed and hovered over him as he placed his call. Once again, a voice announced the mailbox was full.

A sudden and blazing shock of yellow blinded him. A black sedan came to a screeching stop. Both girls immediately threw themselves behind Eric, clinging to his jacket. He brought a hand to his eyes to avoid the glare, when four men surrounded him. He heard a familiar laugh before he could focus on the huge silhouette.

"Yep, looks like a pervert stalker," Nick Lombardo shouted. Still laughing, he grabbed Eric's hand and shook it. "Hotel called the arena and said a man claiming to be Angel's husband tried to get into her room. Security just said you were creeping around the gates, so I came out here to kick your ass."

"Kick it after I say hello to her, okay?"

Nick motioned the guards to let Eric go through the barricades. "Deal."

Eric slid into the car and almost started through the gates when he remembered the two girls. Pushing the gearshift back into park, he stepped from the vehicle and placed his arms around the teary-eyed young teens. "C'mon, we're going to a party."

****

The backstage affair was a crush of activity with guests lined up by a makeshift bar, and others, with plates in hand, being served by the wait staff at a pricey buffet. Jenna coasted through the crowd, in her head checking off people like items on a list so she wouldn't miss anyone. She posed for pictures and kissed cheek, after cheek, after cheek.

Alan shuttled her into her dressing room. "The prince is on his way in. Fix your face."

Jenna glanced at the clock. "Fashionably late?"

Alan's expression soured. "He's a crown prince. He could hardly come to the party until his bodyguards made sure the room was secure."

Giving her hair a quick drag with a brush, Jenna said, "You've got to be kidding. There's enough security here for the Pope."

"Lose the attitude."

She rolled her shoulders, but knots of muscle held tight. "All right, I'm ready. One or two pictures with the prince and I move on."

"You'll be sweet and cling to his every word."

Alan cleared a path and preceded her through the crowd to where the royal and an older male companion stood. The prince was average height, handsome and poised with European elegance. He gave Alan a perfunctory greeting and turned to Jenna to present her with a single red rose.

He stepped intimately close, dark eyes narrowed, the lids seductively heavy as his gaze made an uncomfortable pause at her breasts. Cameras clicked documenting the suggestive image they presented.

"Belle," he said on a breath. "The name Angel is perfect. You have the face and body of something beautiful God has made." His hand slipped from Jenna's waist to rest comfortably close to her buttocks. "Such loveliness is hard for a man of my passion to resist."

Jenna pulled away from the presumptuous fingers sliding lower and as she turned, she pressed against something warm, firm, and familiar.

"Keep your passion in your pants and your hands off my wife's ass."

While Alan waved frantically for security guards, Nick Lombardo, who had arrived with Eric, stood like a sentry. "Ease up, fellas. He's her husband." The announcement sent the guards away.

Jenna turned, sighing her elation and throwing her arms around Eric's neck. He lifted her, spinning her around and kissing her. Photographers once again sprang to keen attention, and camera shutters blinked with dispatch.

****

Two teenage girls, one in braces and the other in oversized, purple glasses, worked the room, accumulating autographs, chowing down on lobster and pastries, and sneaking glasses of champagne. When the party ended, they were driven home to Sausalito in style with Nick at the wheel of a super-stretch limousine.

****

Jenna and Eric sprinted through the hotel lobby, the desk clerk scurrying behind and offering apologies. Eric never acknowledged the man. His eyes were on his wife.

He wasted no time by touring her opulent suite. Sweeping her into his arms, he strode directly to the bedroom. He kicked off his beat-up boots, and still holding her, bounced on to the bed. Jenna and Eric kissed and touched with wild, frenetic intensity, tearing at each other's clothing clumsily, and rolling around on the mattress like they were tumbling down a hill.

Jenna's hair was a wild cascade, spilling around them as they made love, panting and groaning their pleasure. Eric's heart pounded hard against Jenna's breasts as he gave a final thrust that brought them both shuddering and bursting with release.

Calmer, but not yet sated, Eric kissed Jenna and peeled away the lacy bra dangling from her shoulders. She obliged and shrugged, letting the satin slip from her arms. She pushed his shirt from him and then let her fingertips glance over the light patch of hair in the center of his stomach in feathery strokes. Her hand traveled lower to his erection, still hard and large, and glistening with drops of semen at the tip. Jenna rubbed her finger over the wetness and Eric shuddered again.

They touched, now slow and languid. Eric kissed Jenna's breasts, his mouth savoring, warm, and wet on her skin. Jenna thighs pressed against Eric's hips as he dipped and retreated in a sweet unhurried rhythm. "I missed you so much," he whispered.

Jenna hummed her response, fluttering her lashes against his cheek and tightening her grip on his neck. "I don't ever want to fight again."

They each climaxed once more, uttering sighs and words of love, then fell asleep twined in each other's arms.

****

Fog drifted low, skimming the water of the San Francisco bay and lifting as noon approached. "Good morning," Eric said, his voice a tired murmur.

"Hi." Jenna's voice floated soft against his throat.

He stroked her cheek with his knuckles. They stared, gazing at each other for long, lingering moments.

"I still can't believe you're here," she said.

"I missed you too much to wait another two weeks."

"I'm glad." Jenna snuggled close and Eric kissed her hair. "You're my hero you know. You showed up just in time to save me from that slimy prince?"

Eric shot upright in bed. "That guy is a prince? Crap, Jen, I didn't just start a war or anything, did I?"

She giggled. "I don't think you have anything to worry about."

"Unless he challenges me to a duel."

She turned, climbing on top of him and straddling his hips. Leaning over, platinum hair a torturous spill against his chest, she mocked the prince's words. "A woman of my great passion finds you hard to resist."

Jenna rode him, easy and quiet, until the cadence of her pace quickened, and the sounds of love's culmination spilled from her throat. He grasped her hips reaching his own release and sighing his pleasure. He brushed his fingers through Jenna's hair as she rested comfortably spent against his chest. They lay quiet, breathing evenly for the first time in hours.

He gave a gentle kiss to the top of her head. "So do you want to say it or should I?"

"You mean oopsie?" she asked.

"It was more like five oopsies."

Wide eyed, she simply shrugged.

"Not funny, Babes. You still have a tour, a movie, and then back to finishing the tour."

Jenna made lazy circles on his stomach with her forefinger. "It's too late to worry about it now. If I'm pregnant, I'll deal with it."

Gripping her shoulders, he bolted upright bringing

her with him. His fingers dug into her skin harder than he intended. "What do you mean by *deal with it*?"

She wriggled her arms trying to escape the steely grip. "Looser costumes, close ups, big bouquets of flowers…What did you think I meant?"

His hand went limp, and he took a shaky breath. "I-I thought…"

"What? You thought I would abort your baby?" Jenna rolled to the other side of the bed, taking the blankets with her and yanking them to her chin. Her eyes, wide ovals, filled with tears.

"Babes, I'm sorry. I'm just not thinking straight these days." He scrambled over to her and pulled her back into his arms. "It's so hard being apart, sharing you with the whole damned world. I sometimes get crazy and think the worst."

"You honestly think I would get rid of your baby, *our* baby?"

Eric buried his face into her hair and exhaled a long sigh. "It would kill me if you did."

****

Alan stood by the stage entrance like a hunter waiting for his prey. Glowering, he glanced at his wristwatch when Angel arrived, the Busboy's arm slung over her shoulder. She kissed him and rushed off to her dressing room.

Sniffing angrily, Alan watched Eric Laine stride to the soda machine. Alan hated how Laine swaggered in his snug jeans and T-shirts, hated his ridiculous shoulders and belligerent frown. Alan hated how a punk with no education and no class had insinuated himself into Angel's privileged world. He marched to where Eric stood swigging down a cola. "I hope you're proud of that little scene you made last night."

"It wasn't exactly a scene."

"Threatening royalty? Your crude behavior has no limits, does it?"

After swallowing the rest of the soda, Eric wiped his mouth with the back of his hand. "That crude enough for you?"

"Nothing you do shocks me."

"I don't *do* anything for your benefit, Stark."

"Or my client's either."

Alan stepped away and passed a row of vending machines on the way to the dressing rooms. Further down the hall, framed posters of musicians, sports stars, and other luminaries hung on painted cinderblock walls. Before turning into another corridor he strode back to where Eric Laine idled.

"Mark my words, I'm going to get rid of you before you ruin her with that rowdy arrogance. It follows you around like a shadow." Sniffing as if something foul tainted the air, Alan took measure of worn jeans, cheap sneakers and hair that fell in disarray around a face set in a scowl. "You're nothing but attitude. Hang on to it. It's the only thing you're ever going to own."

Chapter Sixteen

Labor Day weekend brought Jenna's sold-out show to the L.A. Coliseum and Jenna home to Eric. It was also the opening night of Hollywood Boulevard's newest nightspot, Circuit. Eric had caved and taken a job there and he and Mark were stationed in the VIP section.

The room, styled in modern washes of pale blues and bleached woods, was a contrast to the main area where industrial metal tables were set against walls splashed with neon paint.

By eleven, the club had filled but the VIP lounge still echoed emptiness. Only "names" were allowed entry. Eric watched as Jason Altman, the owner, marched to the corner of the bar where Mark was serving the star of an old teen sitcom whose trashy behavior kept her in the limelight at thirty-five.

Curious, Eric studied the scene, his new boss fuming, and pointing to the clock above the register as Mark stood appearing uneasy. After Altman rushed away to greet a B-lister on a police drama, Eric stepped over. "What was that all about?"

Mark slipped his fingers between his throat and collar as if the starchy fabric and bow tie were suddenly too tight. "He's getting antsy because there aren't enough celebs in his fancy lounge."

"Why complain to you about it? Did you promise

to deliver some big names?"

Ignoring the question, Mark shoveled ice into glasses and set them on the drain mats.

"Mark?"

No answer.

Shaking his head, Eric returned to his station. He realized why he'd gotten the job so easily. He'd been played. Hired as bait.

****

At a little after midnight, Jenna, her entourage, and celebrities who had been at her backstage party finally entered. Altman's goal of limousines at the curb and the A-List in the back had been met. Although annoyed by his friend's deception Eric still worked feverishly to serve them.

He forced a smile as he refilled his wife's soda. "It's getting pretty late. Why don't you head home?"

"Do you *not* want me here?" she asked, frowning.

"I'm pretty sure my boss was counting on it. I just don't want you being exploited."

Jenna shrugged. "My job is all about exploitation. I'm used to it." Grabbing her purse from the bar she slipped from the stool to head to the rest room. As she walked away, Bree Davis sauntered over and took her place.

Eric laid a coaster on the bar top. "Hello *Miss* Davis."

"How are you, Eric?"

He ignored the intimacy in her tone. "No complaints. What brings you here?"

She sucked her bottom lip between pearly teeth and smiled. "Clients, I never miss an opening, or one of your martinis."

Jenna rushed back over clearly upset."

"What's wrong?" Eric prayed it wasn't the way Bree was comfortably perched on the edge of her bar stool.

Worrying her fingers together Jenna said, "it's Meghan Morrissey. She's in the rest room and looks out of it."

"When is she ever *in* it?" Mark, standing close by, sniggered.

Jenna's eyes made an immediate and flinty pass at him. "I'm going to go back and check on her."

Grabbing his arm, Eric trawled Mark to an empty spot at the end of the bar. "You give her anything?"

Mark shook his head, but Eric's grip prevailed. More celebrities had filtered in, the booths filled with millions of dollars' worth of designer clothing, jewelry, and plastic surgery. Waitresses hurried about delivering drinks and popping corks as Jason introduced himself with handshakes and fawning grins.

"Don't bullshit me," Eric insisted, his hand still tight around Mark's biceps. "I've seen you party with Meghan at Crimson. What's she on?"

Shrugging away, Mark bent toward the ice sink to fill more tumblers. "I swear I don't know. I stopped hanging out with that burn-out weeks ago."

Jason Altman's toadying smile disappeared as he approached his bartenders. "Is there a reason you two are having a private conversation instead of serving my customers? These people aren't used to waiting."

Eric told Altman about Meghan, but his response was an unconcerned cluck of the tongue. "Throw her in a taxi." He brushed his hands together as if he'd finished a menial task and declared, "problem solved."

"Don't you think we should make sure she's okay before we dump her in a cab?" Eric suggested.

Before Jason could answer, Jenna ran up, looking frantic. "She's passed out. I can't get her to wake up."

Hurdling the bar on one arm, Eric rushed to the ladies room. Jenna, Jason, Bree, and the bouncers trailed behind. Meghan lay crumpled on the tile like a discarded marionette, limbs lying at odd angles.

Eric gripped her shoulders and shook. "Meghan, wake up sweetheart." When there was no response, he placed two fingers on the soft tissue of her neck just below her jawbone. She had no pulse. "Call an ambulance!"

Her skin was cool and damp, her body a weightless and wilted stem. Eric stretched her flat on her back then, tilting her chin up and her head back, he blew a long draught of air into her lungs. He checked for a pulse again. Nothing. "Don't do this, Meghan."

He knelt at her side cupping his palms over her breastbone and counting, "One, two, three." After fifteen compressions, he blew another breath and again checked for a pulse. Nothing. Another breath, more compressions, and again a dire *nothing*.

Sweat leeched from his pores and soaked his shirt. Beads formed on his brow as he continued his delivering compressions. "Where the hell is the ambulance?"

The group around Eric stood frozen, faces skewed in masks of both horror and fascination. He felt time passing in slow, separate fragments. His arms, pumping up and down, almost appeared to leave a trail as he moved. "C'mon, c'mon," he begged, over and over, his hands and mouth an almost violent press against her.

Meghan gasped. The harsh pull of air and the shock of her return to life made time, light, and sound return with her. Though her breath was ragged, she was breathing on her own.

"Stay with her, I'll be right back," Eric said to Jenna. Heart pounding and chest heaving, he sprinted from the ladies room and back to the bar. "Where's the fucking ambulance?"

He was immediately swallowed up by customers. "Is she okay? What happened to her? Did she come to?" The questions blended together to become a reedy din.

"She's okay," Jason announced as he edged close to Eric and pulled him out of earshot of the crowd. "Listen, the ambulance isn't here yet, but I've got a taxi waiting right outside. I'll have one of my men help her into it. There's no need to embarrass her by making a big deal out of this."

Struck dumb, Eric stared. Then, as if pinched to wakefulness, he railed at Altman, "Are you out of your fucking mind? Her heart stopped beating. That's a pretty big fucking deal."

Jason's expression remained wide-eyed and fixed. "I've got every penny I own sunk into this place. I can't have my opening ruined because some celebrity's brat got a little too high." He cocked his head toward the bouncers. "Take her out through the back and get her in the cab."

With the intensity of a flare sparking white hot fire Eric rounded on Jason. He grabbed the lapels of his pretentious designer jacket and slammed him into the wall. "What kind of scumbag are you?"

Jason batted at Eric's arms, the pitch of his voice

rising. "Let me go!"

Eric only shoved harder and then braced his forearm across his boss's throat. "You listen to me, asshole. If your boys try to take her out of here before the ambulance gets here, I'll crush your fucking windpipe and I won't be reviving *you* with CPR."

Jenna's bodyguards presented a standoff with the club's bouncers. Nick stood, legs braced, burly arms folded across his chest. After five minutes, an ambulance arrived. Paramedics rushed through the club with a curious swarm of customers at their heels. Celebrities who had no desire to be linked with the drama in the next day's paper, quickly left.

"I'll ride in the ambulance with her," Jenna said, following the gurney.

"No." Eric stopped her. "I'll go. It'll be chaos at the hospital, and you'll be right in the middle of it. I think Nick should take you home."

Reluctantly she agreed. Her presence would only lash more wind to an already heady storm.

"I'll see you at home." Eric kissed his wife's cheek and sprinted away.

****

Inside the ambulance, Eric held Meghan's hand and she seemed to recognize him as consciousness surfaced and burrowed back into darkness. Her hand was cold, and withered, and felt nothing like the skin of such a young woman. The ambulance, with its steady glow of red and flickers of electric blue, pulled into the emergency room bay. It was met with a horde of reporters and then as if the pandemonium could expand to no greater circumference, legendary actor Jack Morrissey stormed the gates.

"What happened to my baby?" he demanded. With shaking hands he grabbed his cigarettes and they spilled from the pack onto the ground. "Son of a bitch," he cursed. The sanguine shade of a ripe berry grew up from his throat and spread into his receding hairline. He appeared confused in the manner of someone not knowing whether to beg or to rage. He raged. "Get me someone who's in charge!"

As Meghan was being wheeled inside, Eric stopped him. "Mr. Morrissey, don't. Let them do their job."

Jack rounded on him. "Who the hell are you?" He gathered the fabric of Eric's shirt in his hands and shoved him. "Were you with my baby? Were you the one who got her all doped up?"

Eric made no attempt to remove the knotted fists pressing into his chest and allowed the older man to release his anguish.

****

Days later, an exhausted and repentant Jack Morrissey appeared at the door of Jenna's Malibu mansion with an arrangement of pale pink and white roses. Jenna smiled but struggled to carry them. The gorgeous blooms were in a crystal vase the size of a lobster pot.

Eric rushed over. "Hey, I got it."

Hands in pockets, Jack stood in the marble foyer, waiting to be invited in. "I'm sorry I went off on you at the hospital."

After laying down his burden, Eric sprinted back over to Jack and shook his hand. "I'm no stranger when it comes to losing my temper."

"C'mon inside," Jenna offered.

Two celebrities and a carpenter sat in the white

living room sipping coffee.

"She's going to be okay," Jack said, speaking of his daughter. "She's got a bit of a road ahead of her, but she's going to be okay."

Eric nodded and Jenna sighed with relief.

Hefting his shoulders Jack let them slump, rounded, toward his lap. He brought gristly hands to his face and amid a flow of groans spoke. "I really dropped the ball. I was always away filming, missing birthdays and holidays. Hell, I never made it to a single damned school function." The once strapping leading man took a heavy breath hunched in his seat, the aura of timeless strength and beauty faded.

Jenna took his hands between her own and squeezed. She drifted off into a maudlin fantasy of her future, and what kind of life she would someday be offering her own children. Would she be somewhere on location, away from a daughter who was getting dressed for her first date or on tour when her son played in his first little league game?

Jack seemed to read her thoughts. "Well, aren't we something. I came here to thank you both and I just pissed all over it." He stood to leave. "I need to know one thing, kid," he said to Eric. "How did you know what to do?"

Eric offered a modest smile. "I've had a lot of random jobs since I came to L.A. One was as a lifeguard at a public pool. You need to be certified in CPR."

Jack's voice cracked and his eyes blurred, red rimmed and misty. "The E.R. docs said my baby wouldn't have made it without you." He rubbed his hands across his face and swallowed hard, coughing to clear his throat and compose himself. "I will never forget what you did. You've made a friend for life."

He kissed Jenna's cheek and shook Eric's hand. "I'm the last guy on the planet who should be giving anyone advice, but I'll give you some anyway. Don't ever let what's really important slip away."

Chapter Seventeen

Jenna sat next to Eric on the sofa, scanning a script. She had signed to do a nineteenth century romance filmed in England after her U.K. concerts wrapped and before the rest of the European leg began. Once again, her schedule was an unforgiving gallop from rehearsals to fittings to promotional appearances as she prepared to leave. Tension squeezed the passion and joy in her marriage like a tight band. She and Eric found arguments at every junction. After Mark Chambers appeared at the door for the third night in a row, Jenna grabbed the script and stalked off to the patio.

An hour and three beers later, Eric politely cut Mark's visit short and joined Jenna outside. Relieved she'd gotten her period after their carelessness in San Francisco, she was nevertheless edgy. "Since we aren't having a baby, I guess you've decided to adopt Mark."

Eric didn't miss a beat as sarcasm flowed like rainwater from a downspout. "Yep. Then Alan will have a little brother."

Instantly, Jenna's defenses rose. "Alan has a reason to be here so often. He works for me."

"Does he? Seems like the other way around."

Rather than respond, she rubbed at the narrow slits that had become her eyes. The minutes of her days were gobbled up, every morsel of time fed into a demanding and greedy mouth. Angry, exhausted, and miserable, she crushed the script in her hands and went back inside. "I'm going to take a shower."

Later, in bed, Eric reached for her. "I'm sorry, Babes. I don't want to spend our last couple of weeks together fighting."

Jenna's arms pressed tightly against her breasts; her head sunk into a mountain of pillows. "Neither do I, but I don't see why this has to be our last couple of weeks. Why can't you just come with me? I need you."

With a quick swipe, Eric pushed his hair out of his eyes. "Need me? I wish that were true, but you have an entourage of people that take care of everything you *need*."

They lay there, chasms apart, Jenna curled on her side, neither of them having the will or desire to engage in the usual and tired debate.

"I'll visit you in London," he promised.

"Visit." She said the word like a melancholy note.

"It's the best I can do. I have a job, too, and can't just take off whenever I want."

Jenna buried her face flat against her pillow hugging it tightly. *You swing a hammer. You make a lousy twenty bucks an hour after taxes. How the hell is that more important than being with me?*

She longed to voice the thoughts aloud, to shout them while kicking at the blankets like a hysterical child throwing a good and proper tantrum. She longed to finally embrace the entitled celebrity standard. Instead she swallowed it all back and made one last appeal. "You could take the time off if you owned your own company."

Another topic they'd exhausted: Jenna offering to set him up in a business of his own and his ego refusing the *charity*. He reached for her and pulled her close. "You have to put in twice the hours when you start a business, I already told you that. And there's still the chance it would fail. I couldn't take that kind of risk with your money."

"Our money," she corrected.

"Your money," he insisted.

They sank deep into the bedding and held one another. "The time will go fast. You'll be busy. I'll be busy," Eric said.

Jenna instantly thought back to the summer, to what her husband had done to idle away his lonely hours. "I'm sure your *friend* will keep you from being lonely…maybe host some more parties here."

The feathery brush of his fingers against her skin stopped. "My *friend*? I know you don't like Mark, but you can at least say his name."

Sitting up, Jenna hugged her knees. "Okay, Mark. And you're right. There's something about him I don't like."

"Something?" The word was delivered as a question but coated in derision. "There's *nothing* about your P.R. rep I like, *nothing* about any of the lackeys from your talent agency that I *like.*" Eric grunted as if bothered by a dull and persistent pain. He steeled his eyes, the rich blue dulling pewter as he snapped off the lamp. "And there is absolutely nothing about Alan Stark that I like."

"They're business associates. I'm not asking you to like them," Jenna said into the haze of darkness.

"And I'm not asking you to like Mark. I'm just asking you suck it up and not complain if I feed him a burger once in a while."

Jenna slowly closed her eyes glad for the darkness. She couldn't look at her husband because he was going to hate what she said next. "I think his being here isn't just about bumming a meal. I think he's using you because of me."

Rising from the bed, Eric grabbed a pillow and coverlet. He spoke into a void of black. "I know your time is more valuable than mine. Your job is certainly more important. But I never imagined you thought my friends only hung out with me because of you." Shaking his head, he walked steadily through the double doorway of the main suite. "I guess I was really stupid to think there was anything at all about me that mattered."

Jenna sucked back the swell of misery building beneath her eyelids. After hearing the door click shut and Eric's footsteps fade, she let the tears cascade down her cheeks. She cried herself to sleep and when she woke the next morning, he had already gone to work, having left for the first time without kissing her goodbye. Maybe she had been wrong to share her feelings about Mark but there was something about him Jenna just couldn't get past.

****

Mark Chambers paid his dealer for the gram of coke even after tasting a sample and complaining it had been cut one too many times.

"What do you expect for a hundred bucks, pure rock?"

"At least something I can get high on."

"I can sell you a couple of vials of crack for forty. That ought to get you through the day if you're not happy with the blow."

Mark tossed his head, flaunting a wealth of expensive highlights then tugged at the collar of a designer shirt he'd bought on sale but still beyond the boundaries of his income. "Hitting a pipe is for low-lifes."

Grinning, the dealer made no attempt to stifle a forthcoming laugh. "Whatever, Chambers, you want the stuff or not?"

"I'll keep the coke."

Mark climbed behind the wheel of his vintage sports car and sped to one of his daytime haunts. In the parking lot he fed his nose sparingly, snorting meager doses of euphoria and confidence. He stepped inside the saloon, seedy by even Hollywood and Vine standards, and took a seat on a ripped vinyl stool. He slapped a ten on the bar and ordered a drink. A blonde in a skimpy tank top and cut offs sidled over. Rolling her tongue around the straw in her glass, she set it down and then fluffed her hair. It was a provocative but decidedly sloppy lifting of pale arms. Mark introduced himself with his stock lines and *the look* but made no offer to buy her a drink. When she excused herself to go to "the little girl's room" he had the bartender refresh his own.

"Why don't we get out of here, I've got some blow," he drawled once the girl returned. "We can have a little party."

"Sure." She slipped from the stool, almost losing her balance and causing her weighty breasts to sway under her shirt.

Mark followed her, her body listing as she wobbled out into the afternoon sunlight. He frowned. Lumpy ruts dimpled the backs of her thighs. The amber hue of the tavern had hidden recognizable flaws in the voluptuous swell of her body.

Her cheap clothing and brash swipes of makeup were an immensurable difference to what Mark had at one time enjoyed, but the slump in his finances had caused a slump in his love life. He had been collateral damage and fired along with Eric after the Meghan Morrissey mishap.

In his car, Mark sat in the leather bucket seat with his neck tilted back against the headrest. He reached over and began to stroke the woman's thigh, his fingers snaking close to her crotch. He closed his eyes and sighed. There'd been a time he'd had his pick of hot women—starlets who tired of fucking old men and hot forty-somethings tired of fucking their old husbands. Not long ago, he had enjoyed the cool perfection of satin sheets while the scents of expensive perfumes filled his nose.

He tore his hand away from the woman's spongy thigh.

"What's the matter, baby?" she asked. The tone was an octave as low as a man's.

He reached over to open the car door. "I changed my mind."

"Aw c'mon," she said, wheedling in her sandpaper voice. "I thought you wanted to party?"

She bent toward his lap, and Mark looked down at a snaggle of flyaway platinum that blended into brassy, dandruff speckled orange. Mark yanked her by the frizzled locks and slammed her into the passenger side door. "I said get the fuck out."

He grabbed the handle and shoved, and when the door opened, she bounced onto the pavement. "You asshole!" she screamed as he sped away.

Steering in the direction of the freeway, Mark's hand shook. "Fucking trashy cunt," he wailed, swiping at angry tears in his eyes.

He turned in the direction of Malibu and Eric's house. Eric Laine, a nobody from nowhere, living in a mansion with his famous and beautiful wife. Stuck in a bumper-to-bumper impasse Mark fed his nose one last time. He licked the tinfoil clean and let it flutter out the car window.

Chapter Eighteen

Laboring to stay awake and attentive, Jenna drank more coffee than her stomach wanted to tolerate. With her eyes dark rimmed and her hair in a loosely disheveled ponytail, she looked an intolerable mess compared to Bree Davis who was sitting next to her on the couch holding a portfolio. She handed Jenna sketches from it. They were finely rendered illustrations of the costumes she would be wearing in her new film, dresses of weighty velvets in sumptuous colors, detailed with beads, embroidery, and ribbon. *Beautifully insignificant*, Jenna thought as she studied them. Bobbing her head up and down, she nodded as if impressed. She and Eric were still treading lightly, arguing more and making up less.

"We need to set up a schedule for the fittings," Bree said.

"Alan knows my schedule better than I do."

"Oh of course." Bree grinned with a clipped arc of lips, her eyes uninvolved in the expression. Promptly moving on she retrieved folders from her briefcase and spread them out on Jenna's coffee table. "I have the names of women who would make good candidates for your personal assistant. It really is time you hired someone."

Jenna glanced with disinterest at the resumes of strangers, one of whom would end up sharing her home. "I'm not sure about this. I thought I'd wait for my friend Randi to graduate from college. She's smart and should finish early."

"You need someone now. Alan thinks you should consider a live-in housekeeper also, even hire a small staff."

"It's always what Alan thinks."

Home was the only place where Jenna found any sanctuary from the crowds and chaos her profession cultivated. Now even the house was to be occupied territory. Places where she enjoyed privacy washed away like dirt roads in a storm.

The front door opened, and Eric walked through. She felt her face warm, then cool as Mark followed. It was his first visit in a week, the first since Jenna and Eric fought over the constant intrusions. Her line of vision made a quick change of direction to the table where folios of potential "house-mates" were spread out like a losing poker hand. She could hardly complain.

Mark ambled over, his smile a wide crescent, his affect an air of pure charm. Jenna offered a reserved but polite hello. He kissed her cheek and she fought not to shrink away from the unctuous feel of his lips.

Mark turned his attention to Alan's assistant. "Bree, sweetheart, gorgeous as ever."

As Jenna was about to ask her how she and Mark Chambers knew one another other, Eric clamped a hand on his friend's shoulder and shunted him in the direction of the kitchen. "Looks like you're in the middle of business. We'll get out of your way."

****

In the kitchen, Mark burrowed in the refrigerator

and grabbed a beer, laughing as he popped it open. "I don't suppose you told your wife that her manager's assistant has the hots for you."

"Bree doesn't have the 'hots' for me," Eric said. "Don't run your mouth and start trouble." Nervous beads of sweat dampened the back of his neck, and he felt the tops of his ears flush red.

Mark laughed more and took a long swig. "Whatever you say."

"You hungry?" Eric was eager to change the subject of his acquaintance with Bree Davis.

"Nah, had a late lunch."

The rapid blinking of his eyes told Eric his friend had enough speed in his system to miss several meals before hunger revisited. As they stepped out to the patio, Mark's blissful energy put Eric more ill at ease. Mark was volatile when high. Downing his beer he stretched out on a lounge chair absently tapping his foot, while Eric, perched at the edge of an ottoman, glanced through the glass doors at his wife and Bree.

"Why so nervous, buddy? It's not like you bagged her. Of course you could have if you'd wanted to."

Glowering, Eric took a sip of his own beer. "I don't *bag* women. Even when I was single, I never chased after them like it was a sport."

"You're a noble man, my friend."

"And you can be a real asshole at times. Did you have to cruise over to Bree and act like you were old pals?"

Gauzy clouds on the horizon changed shape and water passed through the pool's filter in a gentle rush. Mark settled more comfortably on the chaise. "Should I have pretended *not* to know her? She practically lived at Crimson last summer."

Eric shook his head. "I just don't need the hassle of explaining to Jenna why I never mentioned Bree being at the club. We have enough to argue about these days."

"Just say she came there to see me," Mark said.

"I-I guess I could."

"You guess?" Lines creased Mark's mouth and his eyed darkened. "What the fuck does that mean?"

"Let it go, will you?"

Bounding from his seat, Mark played a piano overture on his thighs with his fingers. He sniffed at the air, his face puckered, eyes blinking chaotically. "You don't think I'm good enough for someone like Bree Davis, do you?"

Eric scrubbed at his hair and groaned. "Take another hit of whatever you're on, Mark. You're not quite paranoid enough yet."

"Paranoid?" Mark's eyes opened wide, his pupils dilated even though his face was bathed in sunlight. "Your wife treats me like I have a disease. Tell me that's all in my head."

He was spinning—a response to something—a response to nothing. It was the one constant of a drug high. Eric twined his fingers around his beer bottle and quietly watched his friend twitch, and jerk, and vent his anger.

"Wait till you've been in this town as long as I have, bro. One day you're riding high, the next you can't get fucking arrested."

Eric aimed his sight at the sun-bleached travertine tiles beneath his feet. From experience he knew it did no good to reason with someone crashing. He listened to Mark spew a pitiful dialogue about his past, the

181

unfairness of show business, the bar business, and life in general, jumping from one exhaustive subject to the next, and barely taking a breath.

His only thought at the moment was getting Mark out of the house before Jenna heard his drug induced ravings. "You're fucked up man. You're not making any sense."

"No shit. How could my fucking life make sense to *you*?" Mark did a dance around the patio, and then counted on his fingers, itemizing luxuries he felt he deserved but didn't have. "Beach house, view of the ocean, built in swimming pool. You didn't have any of this when I met you. You were sleeping on the beach like a withered fucking starfish." He stretched both arms wide as if making a declaration. "And now you're living in a palace with your fucking princess."

Eric's patience abandoned him. "That's enough. Have your fit somewhere else, not here."

"You throwing me out?" Mark paled, his body suddenly shaking. Teary-eyed, he folded back down onto the chaise.

Frustrated, Eric rubbed his temples. "No, but you're leaving. You're going to politely say good-bye to my wife and Bree, and I'm going to drive somewhere and stay with you until you reel it in. If not, then I will throw you out. The choice is yours."

****

Eric drove Mark away from exclusive Malibu to the Santa Monica Pier. Early evening the area was a mix of tourists and local residents who shared the same Pacific sunset night after night. Leaning on the railing, Eric studied the water, a dusky breeze drifting across his skin and ruffling his hair. Closing his eyes, he listened to the rush of the returning tide hoping it would wash away his misery, if even for just a moment. It didn't. The thought of Jenna leaving again was a steady ache and he didn't have the energy to take on Mark's baggage as well—Mark who stood staring beyond the sunset, giving more attention to his cigarette than the brilliant orange dipping below the horizon.

"You need to get yourself together," Eric stated flatly.

Mark sucked more smoke into his lungs and spat a mouthful of phlegm into the water. "Who are you, my mother?"

"I'm just trying to be a friend."

The sun's waning light became a white slice that disappeared, leaving in its place an indigo aura that shimmered and hung for just a breath.

"You're right. It's not my place to judge." Eric backed away from the railing and turned to leave. "See you around."

"Wait! Hold on." A gut punch of panic appeared to hit Mark as the last door to the "good life" shut at his back. "Y-you're right, things haven't been going so great since we got fired. I guess getting high is how I've been dealing with it." He lowered his head, shoulders slumped, hands in his pockets, and his feet shuffling remorsefully. "I acted like an asshole before. I'm sorry." The tone of his voice was humble, his eyes downcast. "I'm starving, man. I was too embarrassed to say so before, but I'm tapped out."

****

Eric treated Mark to a meal and several cups of coffee while he again rambled stories that made little or no sense. Eric listened, his expression fixed. Shoving his plate away, he rose from his seat and reached into his pocket for money to pay the tab.

He counted out the bills in his hand, laid them on the table, and spoke without looking at Mark. "I can't do this anymore."

"W-what do you mean," Mark stammered as an oily sweat dotted his skin.

Eric shook his head in resignation. "This. I've had to deal with junkies my whole life. I can't do it anymore."

"You prick," Mark rasped. "I found you on the fucking—"

"Beach," Eric finished. "You let me crash at your place and you introduced me around. How long am I supposed to pay you back before I'm off the hook?"

"C'mon." Mark's complexion dulled to the color of raw linen. Only his eyes indicated evidence of blood as scarlet capillaries crawled along the milky sclera. "We're the same you and me. We both had it tough, but we hang together, help each other out. We're like brothers."

Leaning in, Eric braced his palms flat on the table. "Did we both have it tough? When we first met, you told me you were from Chicago and your father was a lawyer. Ten minutes ago, you claimed you grew up in Palmdale, your parents on welfare. Hard to keep the stories straight when you're stoned, huh?"

Eric held a fist to a spot beneath his ribs where an ache grew. Experience had taught him to walk away even if it hurt—to recognize when it was time.

"I didn't want to believe it, but my wife was right about you all along."

Eric walked out of the café never looking back to

see Mark's fear give way to anger.

****

Eric stepped quietly into the house. Jenna was asleep on the couch oblivious to the noise coming from the titan-sized television. Sketches were scattered near her feet. Eric picked them up to study them and took a heavy breath. He was bone tired. Bending down he brushed a kiss to her cheek. She stirred and fluttered her eyelids. "Where have you been?"

"I'll tell you about it tomorrow."

He took Jenna's hand in his and led her up the grand staircase to their bedroom. He wrapped himself around her as he did most nights and fell into an unusually troubled sleep. A sleep plagued by dreams of losing her.

Chapter Nineteen

Mark had to cover his eyes to keep the white-hot glare of the sun from burning his retinas. Traffic whizzed by, and a dog's high-pitched yap pierced the air. He whispered to the near empty street, "Where the hell am I?"

He rubbed his eyes again and staggered about, eventually finding his car parked diagonally across two spots. A ticket flapped against the windshield. Moving at a crawl, he reached the car, opened the door and dropped onto the scorching leather seat.

The keys dangled from the ignition and burned his fingers as he grabbed them. "Fuck." He flipped open his cell phone and discovered there were only two bars of battery service. "Shit." The vintage car wasn't equipped with a cell phone charging port and the list of contacts was almost obliterated beneath the scuffed screen of the phone. "Think, think, think."

With trembling fingers, he punched a name on the keypad and a voice eventually buzzed through the phone's speaker. "Stark Management. How may I direct your call?"

"This is Mark Chambers. I need to speak to Alan."

"I'm sorry. Mr. Stark isn't available. Can I take a message?"

Mark cleared his throat. "Listen, I'm a client and it's important that I speak to him."

"I'm sorry." A series of polite and businesslike excuses hit Mark like slaps from a cold hand. He coughed again, then interrupted the voice on the phone with despairing pleas.

Begging eventually turned to threats as the cell's power slipped away. "Listen to me. I said I'm a client and I need to speak with Stark. Now! Tell him if he doesn't come to the phone, my next call is to Angel."

As Mark rattled off Jenna's home phone number, Stark's voice came on the line. "What is it? I'm busy."

"Too busy to take calls from clients, Mr. Stark?"

"Chambers, I'm an entertainment manager. You have to actually have a career for me to manage before you can be one of my clients."

Mark sat broiling in his car, his phone slick in his hand. "You said you'd hook me up with some agents. That was over a month ago. I did what you asked, and you said you'd represent me."

A breath of annoyance sputtered through the line before Stark answered. "I made an off the cuff comment about *maybe* being interested in representing you. We have no official arrangement."

"Don't fuck with me, Stark." Mark's voice was shrill, the excitable squeal of an animal in a snare. The air in his car was an acrid stink. Hot desert winds had made their way to the coast and newspapers tripped along the ground. The yellow hue of a faraway canyon fire hung over the horizon. "We had a deal. You called me and said if I kept Eric busy, you'd manage me. He and Angel have been fighting like cats and dogs. I *did* what you asked."

Silence filled the line before Alan answered. "I said Angel needed to focus more on her career and less on her marriage. You misunderstood."

"Bullshit." The shakes became more violent while sweat kept him plastered to the car seat. "I swear I'll go right to her house now and tell her how you're trying to fuck up her marriage."

After another pause, Alan Stark spoke, his tone dark and uncompromising. "Listen to me, you fucking crackhead. Say one word to Angel about this arrangement you *think* we had, and you'll never sell a candy bar at the movies, let alone star in one."

"But I-I—"

The iridescent blue numerals on the phone's keypad snapped to black. "No!" Mark wailed. "No! No! No!"

His body began to twitch as if bugs danced along the line of his backbone. He searched his wallet for money to buy something to stop the desperate shaking but there was nothing in it but a collection of credit cards extended beyond their limit. Frenzied, he slid his forefinger into every crevice and found a small plastic bag buried behind his license. In the bag were four tablets—Rohypnol, amped up, bootleg pills cooked in a boarded-up building in the Wholesale district.

Mark squeezed the plastic bag in his hand, breaking the tablets. "What the fuck am I supposed to do with these?"

A slow trickle of activity began as businesses opened, and people began to dot the streets. Awnings were rolled out, sandwich boards and racks of souvenir apparel were wheeled to the sidewalk. Mark took a calm and steady breath as he methodically continued to crush the little green tablets. His hands no longer shook as he slowly ground the crumbled pills into a fine powder. He scooped a small bit under one fingernail, brought it to his nose and snorted. Instantly, he smiled, cool and relaxed.

Turning the key in the ignition, he revved his car's engine and turned onto the 10th Street entrance ramp to Highway 1 and Malibu.

****

Jenna checked the clock on her cable box, calculating the amount of time she'd have to enjoy a hot shower and some privacy. There wasn't enough time. There never was. What she did have was the luxury of remaining swaddled in a towel instead of rushing to do her own hair and makeup before sprinting off to work. In an hour, her entourage would be in her bedroom to get her prepped for a photo layout of her home. *Celebrity Style* was doing a feature on her perfect house, her perfect homelife, and her perfect marriage.

Yes, girls. Leave your family at fifteen, and you too can live in lonely luxury while being told what to wear, where to go, and who to love. You too can live in a spectacle of public glamour as your personal life disintegrates.

She stepped into her walk-in shower and a perfect one-hundred-degree spray of water from a rainforest shower head rushed against her skin. Lathering up, the scents of the most expensive body wash and shampoo permeated the steam. Memories of the shallow tub in the bathroom she shared with her brother stung. Part of her longed for the minty bite of the deodorant soap her mom bought in a twelve-pack brick. She wished for the pounding on the door as Kyle demanded she get out so he could brush his teeth. Sighing, she let the water wash it all away.

Her shower done, Jenna sat, her hair wrapped in a towel, the Egyptian Pima as luxe as the carpeting beneath her feet. She slipped into a satin robe and waited for the party to begin.

****

The dusty convertible rolled through as the gate swung wide. Mark pulled close to the front door. There was no limo or SUV parked in the circular driveway. And more importantly, the hulking Lombardo wasn't there to defend the castle. Mark stepped to the front door. He had to squint to bring the lock into focus. Eric didn't have the imagination to put his keys in a better place than the kitchen drawer and Mark had pilfered a spare weeks ago.

Slowly, he opened the door and stepped inside. No creaks or groans of rusty hinges sounded from the expensive hardware, and the door shut behind him with a delicate click. He quickly disabled and reset the alarm just as he'd done with the gate. Eric had also been very careless about punching in codes with Mark standing close enough to catch sight of which numbers were pressed.

He padded about the living room, then stepped through the patio doors. No one was there. Eric was already gone and at work for the day. Mark's footsteps made no sound on the thick carpeting, but he tread lightly when he reached the kitchen's marble tiled floor. As was his habit, he helped himself to a drink, a few healthy shots of top shelf vodka which he poured into a heavy crystal tumbler. The sound of footsteps on the floor above caught his attention; he huffed the mirthless giggle of a bratty child used to getting away with bad behavior. Carrying his glass and the bottle of vodka, he made his way up the steps.

****

Jenna was sitting at her dressing table when the sound of knocking drew her attention to the open doorway. She angled her head, anticipating her husband's soft eyes and handsome grin reflected in the mirror. Instead, she saw the sunken contours of Mark Chambers' face.

"Knock, knock," he whispered, his tone the ragged chafe of an obscene phone caller.

She stood, instinctively pulling the belt of her robe tighter. "How did you get in here?"

He offered nothing more than a lazy shrug as he leaned into the door frame sipping from a glass. Jenna's heart hammered. Mark, normally well-groomed, listed idly, his clothing creased and dirty. His mane of hair was oily and snarled around his skull. Dark stubble covered his jaw. The most alarming aspect of his appearance was the liquid glow of his bloodshot eyes.

"I asked how you got in here." Jenna's eyes flitted from corner to corner, seeking a place of refuge. The main bath or the walk-in closet. Even a leap from the nearby window was preferable to being alone with Mark Chambers.

He took one loping shuffle, bringing him closer. "I came in through the front door, but maybe you'd prefer I use the back entrance…like the help."

Reaching for calm, Jenna swallowed the fiery acid leaping into her throat. "A reporter from *Celebrity Style* will here soon. You need to leave."

"After we talk. Have a drink." He lifted the bottle of vodka as if it were his to offer.

"I can't. I told you I have an interview."

Slowly, she sidled to her nightstand where her cell phone lay but Mark rushed forward and grabbed it. "Nuh-uh, no Lombardo and no Eric. Just you and me."

"People will be here any minute," Jenna said.

He sipped more of the vodka, and she watched his stubbled throat expand as he swallowed. He closed his eyes, and sighed, clearly enjoying the crisp tang of the liquor. But the moment didn't offer her enough time to slip past him.

He set the glass and bottle on the nightstand. "I want you to square things with me and Eric. He was my friend long before you came along." Mark took a step closer, his face relaxing into a leer. "Y'know, we used to share everything."

Fine hairs rose on Jenna's arms, and Mark's suggestion hung in the air like a fetid odor. Her gaze darted to a framed picture of her and Eric, taken at a premiere. The crystal frame was heavy enough to use as a weapon. Like her phone, Mark snagged it before she could grab for it.

He stared intently at the photograph. "Why Eric?" Mark's glassy eyes shifted from Jenna to the photo and back. "Why is it never me?" he repeated in a sad whisper. "Me and Eric are so much alike, but it's always him."

"You...are...nothing...alike." Jenna kept her words decisive, not one syllable open to even the slimmest of interpretations.

Like a sudden, unpredictable squall, Mark's temper flashed. He launched the frame into the wall. "You just don't want to see it!"

Crystal shattered into an explosion of glass and dust. Reflexively, Jenna blinked, covering her face to protect herself against the spray. She rushed to the doorway, but Mark lunged and grabbed her, painfully twisting her arm behind her back and pulling her to him. "Always Eric," he said yet again. "I think it's my fucking turn."

Jenna's heart boomed against her ribs; her pulse thundered in her throat, her ears, the soles of her feet. Her body became a collection of violent drumbeats. The stench of cigarettes and the metallic tang of drugs, alcohol, and perspiration wafted around her. Dregs of cologne added to the mix. She gagged.

"What's wrong? Am I making you sick?"

She struggled to escape his grip. "Let me go. You're hurting me."

"Am I?" Her pain seemed to enliven him, her fear the catalyst that made him appear to want more. "That's how I feel every single time you look at me and stick that prissy nose of yours in the air."

Increasing his hold, he dragged her closer to the bed then dumped the crumbled tablets into the glass of vodka. "This will make you feel better."

As he forced the tumbler to her lips Jenna tried to spit but the fiery liquid rushed into her throat. What felt like only moments later, her vision blurred, and her body became weightless.

****

Eric cut his morning's work short and returned home to pose as the dutiful husband for yet another magazine feature. He was halfway down the driveway when he spotted Mark's car parked near the front door. Icy hands teased the back of his neck. As the memory of his friend's irrational tirade replayed in his mind, he ran to the door, unlocked it and quickly shoved it open.

In his haste he never reset the alarm.

"Jen?" he called out. His gaze swept the room, settling on the couch where he had hoped to find Mark drinking a beer and begging apologies.

Eric looked again around the open space hoping to find his wife. "Jen? Babes, I'm home."

The pool. They were probably out by the pool.

When he found the lounge-chairs unoccupied, he raced back into the house and bounded the stairs to the second floor two at a time. He rushed through the doorway and into his bedroom.

A blow, like a bat to the stomach, made him stop. His lungs emptied and his body became a hollow space caving in upon itself. He gulped air and coughed, trying desperately to breathe.

Mark was in bed with Jenna, hammering away with steadfast speed. She put up no resistance, her body, buried beneath his, amid the tangled sheets. Unable to move, his feet weighted to the floor, Eric watched as Mark grunted, then stiffened and shuddered. Eric rubbed his eyes and blinked, trying desperately to prevent the scene from reaching his brain to settle forever as a memory.

Then the kaleidoscope of images meshed enough for him to understand what was really happening. Jenna's arms lay limp at her sides, her legs boneless and splayed wide. She wasn't moving or reacting.

Rushing to the bed, he wrapped one arm around Mark's throat, almost crushing it as he pulled him away. With the force of a wild animal snapping the neck of its prey, he launched Mark into the dresser. A howl of pain accompanied his landing. Eyes wide, he scrambled to his feet, but Eric reached out and slammed him into the nearest wall. Mark slid to the carpet, his body no more stable than a pour of water.

"Get up," Eric growled. "Get up, so I can kill you."

Cowering, Mark crawled into a corner between the dresser and the closet, holding up his hands, and begging forgiveness, only to be yanked upright and punched full in the face.

Coughing, spitting blood and teeth, Mark cried and screamed as Eric's fists smashed into him again and again, each punch accompanied by the sound of bones snapping.

****

Two deputies from The L.A. County Sheriff's department and private security guards arrived to find a cataclysm of broken glass, upended furniture, and a figure being thrashed around the room. They struggled to subdue Eric, who kicked and raged, violently punching anyone and anything within reach. One deputy suffered a bloody nose, and when Eric's elbow slammed into another's stomach, he used his nightsticks to restrain him.

"Don't move," a deputy ordered as he slapped handcuffs onto Eric's wrists and forced him to the floor. "Don't fucking move."

After another deputy radioed for an ambulance, he approached Jenna. "Miss, can you tell us what happened here?"

It was an obvious struggle for her to pull the sheet around her body. "M-ma…h-ushban." Her words were garbled as if they lay cemented to her tongue.

The two security guards rushed over. "Is she all right?"

"Seems pretty out of it." The cop padded to the

corner to tend to Mark. "Just lie still; the ambulance will be here any minute."

Curled on the floor, he whimpered as blood coursed from his mouth and nose, fanning scarlet around his face.

From the other side of the room Eric roared. "Let me go! I live here!" He strained and labored against the cuffs shackling his wrists and the knee digging into his spine.

"Shut up," the deputy said while holding a handkerchief to his nose.

Within minutes, an ambulance arrived along with another police cruiser. Paramedics rushed to Mark and a new set of law enforcement from the sheriff's department, a sergeant and a detective, entered the room.

"What do we have?" the sergeant asked.

"We're trying to get statements but…"

Mark was groaning, Eric still crushed into the carpet, and Jenna limp on the edge of the bed.

The detective flipped open a small notebook and stepped around upended furniture and broken glass. Walls were sprayed with blood. A scrap of lingerie, fine as spun sugar, lay on the floor. A man's shirt and trousers were neatly folded on a chair.

The uniformed officer spoke. "The guy in the cuffs says he lives here. He was beating the hell out of the one on the floor."

"Caught an intruder in the house?"

"And beat the clothes off of him, Sarge?"

"Ah." the sergeant nodded. "So what does the woman say?"

The deputy angled his head toward the nightstand

and the tumbler and bottle of vodka. "Not much. She's intoxicated."

Eric was pulled to his feet still struggling against the handcuffs. His chest rose and fell in a violent surge. "I came home from work and found that motherfucker. I found him on top…he was…he was…" Tears slowly rolled down Eric's cheeks. "Jesus let me out of these things. I need to go to her."

"Let's take this down to the station."

A deputy stepped over to Jenna and asked her to get dressed. Nodding, she made a feeble attempt to stand. Her body rebelled in a manifestation of sweat, her complexion faded to ash, and she collapsed onto the floor.

****

Flashing lights and the short, shrill whoop of sirens announced the arrival of another ambulance. Immediately behind it, a limo pulled in with Alan and the reporter and photographer from *Celebrity Style* magazine. Alan all but leaped from the car, rushing to the doorway, his suit jacket flapping behind him.

"What happened? What the hell is going on?"

"Sir, I'll have to ask you stay back," one of the uniforms said.

Alan bobbed his head frantically, still questioning the chaos of ambulances and police vehicles congesting Angel's driveway.

"You have to leave, sir," the deputy insisted.

Alan turned, flailing both arms at the limo driver, sending it back down the drive. "What happened?"

A gurney rushed past and disappeared through the front door of the mansion. As if on cue, a second gurney, carrying someone whose face was a ruined pulp of flesh, came out and was lifted into the waiting ambulance. A row of photographers and several news vans had already arrived and stationed themselves outside the gate abutting the driveway. The photographer from *Celebrity Style* was among them.

Alan spun around to take in the chaos. Nettles of ice stung his skin.

Just as the first ambulance took off in a blast of lights and sirens, a handcuffed Eric was led from the house, accompanied by someone Alan assumed to be a plain-clothes detective. Behind them a second gurney appeared.

Jenna—Angel—wrapped in heavy cotton blankets, her eyes closed and strands of her platinum hair falling loose, lay on the stretcher, still as death.

"Look, I'm Alan Stark, her manager. I need to know what happened!"

The deputy motioned for his sergeant who lumbered over. "Mr. Stark, I can't tell you much more than what we found. Mr. Laine had an altercation with someone inside the house and Mrs. Laine appears to have overdosed on something."

Alan felt more of a chill beat at his skin. Blood rushed from his head and dizziness assailed him. "No. That that's not possible."

The screaming of sirens pierced the air as the ambulances raced from the property. The cruiser with Eric caged in the back seat also took off in a whir of lights and sound.

"The man…who was the man on the stretcher?" Alan's voice, high and thin, cracked as he spoke.

"Chambers," the deputy answered. "Name's Mark Chambers."

Alan gasped, his heart drumming in rapid beats. He gulped air but it didn't stop the frenzied rhythm. He clutched his chest and collapsed to the pavement.

****

Eric sat on the cot in his cell. He leaned against the wall, one knee raised, his forearm resting on it. His other leg was stretched out in front of him. He worked the muscles in his jaw but didn't speak. He was out of words. His interrogation had lasted for hours. He had explained over, and over, and over, how he had come home to find his wife being attacked. Detectives seemed unconvinced. He should have known better than to resist.

Eric supposed they wanted him to make their lives easier and confess to assaulting Mark. To say he found his wife with another man and beat the crap out of him. He wouldn't. They advised him to call a lawyer. He tried several times to contact his boss, Tom Larity, but had no luck. That was hours ago.

A deputy approached the cell. "Last chance, pal. Your bail hearing is in half an hour. You're not getting out of here without an attorney."

"I already tried my boss. He wasn't home."

"Look, if you don't call a lawyer you'll be held over. Your wife's a rich movie star. There must be someone you can call."

Eric stared up at muddy green cinderblock. A stainless-steel toilet sink combo was in a corner. He'd been given a private "suite," a step up from the cage where the drunk drivers and snatch and grabs were crowded together down the hall. "I'm a carpenter. I make twenty bucks an hour. If you want me to call someone, get me the fucking yellow pages." Again, his attitude was his downfall.

"Talk like that in front of the judge and you'll be here all weekend."

Another deputy, the one Eric punched back at his house, lumbered over to his partner. "Holyfield over there's got visitors."

They opened the cell, led Eric back to the interrogation room, and pushed him down onto a chair, keeping both of his wrists shackled. Outside the door, a commotion erupted. Voices and what sounded like a dozen sets of footsteps marched purposefully to where he was under guard. With parade like fanfare, Jack Morrissey entered the room surrounded by deputy sheriffs. Accompanying him was a man impeccably dressed both in clothing and attitude. He carried a briefcase.

Jack signed autographs for the deputies and approached Eric. Resting one broad hand on his shoulder, he asked, "How are you, kid?"

Eric answered with a trembling sigh. "I need to get out of here, Mr. Morrissey. I need to see my wife. They won't even tell me how she is."

"This is David Coleman, the best criminal lawyer in California." Jack stared Eric in the eye. "He'll get all this straightened out."

"Mr. Morrissey I can't afford—"

"No arguments, kid. I owe you. This one's on me."

Chapter Twenty

It was sometime in the late evening before Eric was released from The Lost Hills Sheriff's station. He had to push his way through the chaos and clamber of reporters, first at the station house, then at the entrance to the hospital. It was like walking through lightning strikes as press and photographers descended.

Eric, Jack, and Dave Coleman were stopped as they approached Jenna's room. A young deputy with close-cropped hair and crisp uniform stood guard. "No one is allowed inside."

Jack glared at the deputy. "The boy is here to see his wife and he'll damned well see her."

A petite, dark haired woman carrying a tall paper cup of coffee sprinted down the hall. "Gentlemen, I'm Detective Alvarez. I'll be the one to decide when anyone can see her."

Coleman possessed the all-business brashness that came with an Ivy League diploma and corner office in Westwood. "I'm Mr. Laine's attorney. As next of kin, he has the right to see his wife."

The detective appeared unfazed. "You know the drill, Counselor. She's a witness. I talk to her first."

Eric, his clothing still dirty and blood-spattered, looked plaintively at the detective. He made a sound as pitiable as a wounded animal. Leaning back against the wall, his head hit the hard plaster with a thud. His words were a desolate whisper. "I need to tell her how sorry I am."

Alvarez, looking as if she wanted to wrap him in a blanket, softened. "I understand, but not until she's given her statement."

Eric was beyond anger or violence. On the other side of the door, his wife lay drugged and raped by a man he had brought into their lives. It was justice that he was not allowed to be with her. Guilt was a weight more onerous than anything he had ever felt.

"This is my fault, I did this to her."

Coleman cut him off. "Don't say another word."

****

Alan looked down to where hand-carved mother of pearl buttons once fastened his three-hundred-dollar shirt. His jacket was wrinkled, ruined by the paramedics who had examined him. Adding to his indignity, he still lay on a gurney, attached to a heart monitor, in a cubicle of the emergency room. A nurse occasionally padded over to tell him they were still waiting for the test results. If Alan wasn't still plagued by shortness of breath, he would have ripped the electrodes from his chest and removed the oxygen tube from his nose.

"Why haven't I been admitted to a private room," he demanded of the doctor who had examined him.

"Try and be patient, Mr. Stark. The lab is analyzing your blood enzymes, and you haven't been admitted to the cardiac wing because so far it doesn't look like you've suffered a heart attack."

"Then why the hell can't I leave?"

The resident's tight smile broadcast his annoyance. "We wouldn't want you to walk out of here and have you collapse on the street, now would we?"

Carrying a chart, a nurse rushed over. She handed it to the doctor and hurried away, shaking her head as she went.

"Looks like the paramedics were on the money, Mr. Stark," the doctor said as he flipped pages. "All your tests are negative. You had an anxiety attack, probably a little stomach acid, too, which could explain the pain in your chest. We could order an upper GI to see if anything is wrong with your stomach, but I think that's premature."

"Then am I finally being discharged?"

"Yes, sir. I imagine that stretch limo I saw cruising the parking lot is yours."

Alan rolled his eyes. "No, Doctor Einstein. It belongs to the wino singing in the next cubicle."

The doctor gave his head a tired looking shake. "You can sign out at the front desk."

Alan waited for the nurse to come back to detach the oxygen and give him back his jacket. He was leaving the ER, but he wasn't leaving the hospital until he'd seen Angel and gotten every detail of her condition.

Whatever happened at her home was sure to turn into a media feeding frenzy once the story hit the papers. He needed his phone, which was in the limo, and a change of clothes. This could be as bad a situation as one could get. He may just have that heart attack yet.

****

Jenna woke to the sound of voices. Something was off. The width of the room was too narrow and the window on the pastel-colored wall was in the wrong place. *Her* bed in the Malibu house was yards away from a span of creamy white Venetian plaster and a bank of French doors that led to a covered lanai. *Whose room is this? Where am I?*

Struggling against lingering fatigue, she sat up and realized an I.V. was inserted into her hand and something like a clothespin clipped to her finger. *Oh my God.* Panic swift as a slap roused her and she rubbed at her eyes to wipe the film blurring her vision. She was in a hospital.

Words tore from her throat. "Someone help me! What's going on? Why am I here?"

Voices coming from the doorway hushed and a woman in scrubs dashed into the room. She checked the monitor by Jenna's bed and smiled. "Your color is better and your oxygen saturation good. I'll get your doctor," she said as she rushed off.

Another woman stepped inside. She was dressed in black slacks and jacket with a snowy white button-down shirt. A six-point gold star was clipped to her belt.

"W-what's g-going on?" Jenna appealed to the woman dressed in the statement crime drama outfit. "Did I have a heart attack?"

"No." The cop spoke in the soft and unthreatening tone used by someone trying to coax a kitten from its hiding spot "I'm Detective Alvarez. Do you remember anything about what happened at your house earlier today?"

"M-my my house? No. Why am I here? Where's my husband?"

Alvarez pulled a chair close to the bed. "He's right outside, but I need to speak with you first."

Panic crept a fast path up Jenna's backbone. Her throat became instantly dry, and it hurt to talk. Her words barely scraped through. Alvarez handed her a paper cup filled with water.

"Please tell me what's going on?"

"There was an incident at your house. Can you remember anything about it?"

Shaking her head, she sipped more but the water offered only a moment's relief before her tongue turned back to sand. "What kind of incident? I want Eric. I want to see my husband."

"You will. I promise, you can see him in a little while." Alvarez again spoke softly. "I just need to know about your day. Anything could be important."

Jenna took a staggered breath. It hurt, hurt to breathe and it hurt to speak. She was sore all over. "I had an appointment for an interview with...I don't remember. My cleaning lady came over early. It was barely light out."

"That's great, Mrs. Laine. Do you know what time she left?"

"I think...I don't...don't know."

Jenna sank deeper into the bed, engulfed by the pillow and blankets, she drifted back to her house. "The house wasn't dirty. It just needed to be...to be dusted." She let her eyelids fall shut and saw the pristine creams of her walls and furniture. "My house is white. Always clean. Pure white."

"Mrs. Laine, stay with me. What happened after you sent your cleaning lady home?"

Jenna heard her name being called. The voice sounded tinny, echoing as if it were coming from far away. Then she realized the voice belonged to the woman sitting next to her, the police detective. She rubbed at her temples, trying to remember but there was nothing. Then ice touched her skin. Sounds like glass breaking and the smell of something putrid attacked her sinuses.

Sound blared, lights flashed then the images were gone. Something bitter seeped up from her stomach, burning the back of her throat. Her middle clenched and she brought her hand to cover her mouth. She leaned over the side of the bed and threw up.

****

Eric watched a nurse speed into Jenna's room. Helpless, he pressed his fingertips into his scalp and gulped back his fear. "Oh, God what's happening now?"

Doubling over he braced his hands on his thighs to prevent his legs from giving way. He wiped at his eyes with his sleeve, a sleeve stained with Mark Chambers' blood.

****

Eric's lawyer threatened to bring a lawsuit akin to the wrath of God against the hospital if his client was not immediately apprised of his wife's condition. A doctor, a slight figure who looked young enough to still be carded at a bar, clicked the ball-point pen in his hand in an anxious rhythm. "Mrs. Laine vomited, a probable result of the concussion."

Eric groaned. "He hit her."

"Uh, Mrs. Laine also has a contusion and small head lac." The doctor illustrated the location of the laceration by pointing to a spot on the back of his own head. "The EMTs said she collapsed; I'm assuming she hit her head."

"Go on," Coleman urged.

"Mr. Laine, does your wife have a prescription for

any anti-anxiety meds? Since she was unconscious when she was brought in, we ran a rapid drug test. She had a high concentration of benzodiazepine in her system."

Eric shook his head. "No, she barely takes an aspirin when she has a headache."

"Not to worry," the doctor said. "We'll narrow down exactly what she took when we have more precise results from the lab."

Eric's head snapped up. "She didn't *take* anything."

Both Jack Morrissey and Dave Coleman inched closer. Eric was strained beyond control, his body like a tight wire ready to snap. Jack laid a hand on his forearm. "Easy, kid," he said softly, but his expression also spoke of malice.

The doctor cleared his throat. "I should really discuss the rest of her condition with Mr. Laine and the police."

"I'll go grab some coffee, "Jack said, excusing himself.

Coleman stood firm. "I'm representing Mr. Laine."

The doctor nodded and said, "We were asked by the sheriff's department to do a rape kit. There was no vaginal tearing, no bruises on her thighs or wrists, none of the usual obvious indications of rape. She does have a bruise on her jaw and hematomas on her neck and right breast."

Coleman perked up. "That's evidence of force."

The doctor nodded. "The bruise on her jaw was definitely caused by a blow, but I'm afraid the other marks appear to be...um...hickeys."

Eric pressed his fist into his middle and groaned.

"F-fuck."

The doctor continued. "We did find the presence of semen. Mr. Laine, I'm going to have to ask you to give us a sample of your blood to use as comparison."

Eric squeezed his eyes shut as a thin line of tears trickled down his face.

****

The detective questioned Jenna again, but she was still adrift, her mind's eyes seeing everything through a haze. Whatever happened at her house had no weight or substance, and the memories of it dissipated like steam. She slept fitfully until the feeling of a steady draft of warm air, puffs of someone's breath drifting across her skin, woke her. She bolted upright, gasping. A hand clutched her arm, the pressure intensifying as she tried to pull away.

"Baby, it's me. It's okay. It's me."

Eric had been slumped forward, his upper body resting on the bed with his head cradled in his arms. One of his hands had been touching her shoulder. "Shh, honey, it's me. It's me."

Jenna threw her arms around his neck. He held on, rubbing his hands up and down her back. "I'm so sorry, so sorry. I'll never forgive myself, never."

****

Whether it was stomach acid or a heart about to rupture, as Alan read the morning papers, breathing became more of an effort. Major newspapers from coast to coast carried Angel's picture on their front pages. There were small photographs of her in skimpy tour costumes, cropped over larger, grainy pictures of the scene in her driveway—police cruisers, ambulances and her husband led away in handcuffs.

Alan slammed his hand down on the papers as his insides continued to roast. All outlets of the media reported the same blanket story. Eric Laine had come home to find his teenage wife in bed with his best friend. The articles were straightforward; nothing libelous or even disputable had been printed.

Close friend. Beaten. Bedroom.

No matter what was printed thereafter, those were the words the public would remember.

Chapter Twenty-One

Mark Chambers rang to summon the nurse for the fifth or sixth time that morning. With his jaw wired, his right wrist fractured, and several ribs broken, it was a burdensome process just to reach for the glass of water on the bedside stand, then bring the straw to his mouth.

An I.V. containing pain meds had been inserted into to his hand, but he refrained from pushing the button to send another dose into his blood stream. He'd been advised to be awake and alert for his appointment with the best personal injury attorney in So-Cal. He had a million dollars-worth of stitches and planned to sue Eric Laine for each one.

After the nurse arrived, Mark made grunting noises in the direction of the television. It was noon, and *Afternoon Buzz* was starting. Using the remote, she pressed the On button, and Mark came to attention as his image filled the screen. It was an early headshot, a glorious image of smoldering eyes and lustrous hair. Reporters recapped the story of how "actor" Mark Chambers had been the victim of an assault by his best friend.

"He's in guarded condition. Still not completely out of the woods," a toothy anchorwoman sang from the small TV suspended in the corner of the room. *"The L.A. County District Attorney's office maintains no special consideration will be given to Laine because of*

his wife's enormous popularity."

The wires attached to what little remained of Mark's teeth prevented him from stretching his mouth into anything resembling the smile from his headshot.

****

David Coleman and Los Angeles District Attorney Matteo Garza shook hands. Both men wore expensive suits and poker faces. They sat at a table, a long length of golden oak, and clicked open briefcases.

"I'm prepared to offer your client a deal," Garza started.

Coleman's expression remained as neutral as the colors in the generic conference room. "A deal for defending his wife from a rapist?"

"That's your client's story. The crime scene points in a whole different direction."

Coleman sat easy and calm in a high-backed leather chair, volumes of law journals in neat rows on shelves behind him. "C'mon, Garza. You know Cambers attacked that little girl as well as I do."

"What I think and what I can prove in court aren't always the same. You know *that* as well as I do."

Sighing, Coleman spoke around an effortless smile. "You never did have much of a backbone, Matt."

Garza slapped his hands onto the table, an indication that his mood was in swift decline. "Jesus Christ, Dave. America's teen sweetheart gets attacked in her own house and I can't gather enough evidence to bring her attacker to trial. It's a fucking election year. Do you think I need this shit?"

One of the high-hat fixtures rained light directly onto the thinning circle of hair on the top of Garza's head. Pink shone through a sparse fuzz of black and gray and the district attorney rubbed at it as if it suddenly itched. "I've had my guys from the B.O.I. overturning every rock in every club in L.A. All they came up with is that Chambers did well with the ladies. A lot of married women and actresses were in the mix and none of them are coming forward to say if he had any nasty habits in the bedroom."

Reaching into his briefcase, Coleman removed a folder. "My client was witness to the attack. I have his sworn deposition."

"Your client saw Chambers and his wife in bed together. Your client also has a juvie rap-sheet long enough to wallpaper this entire room."

Garza came out of his chair to pace the floor in front of the bookshelves, rubbing furiously at his balding pate. "Isn't it just possible Angel got caught cheating? Her memory loss might just be a convenient way for her to save that sterling reputation of hers."

Chambers shook his head. "No backbone, Matt."

Garza drummed stocky fingers against the grainy wood of the table. An expanse of blue, cloudless and too vibrant, glowed beyond the windows. "If I try Chambers with nothing but Laine's testimony, a first-year law student would get an acquittal."

The DA's reluctance to try Mark Chambers was the status quo in rape cases, especially in the world of show business where power players routinely twisted the arms of politicians. Violence against women was rampant.

Coleman took an easy breath. "Let's move on to the good news then."

"That I can give you." Garza said as his smile returned. "I'm prepared to recommend Laine do community service, no jail time."

Coleman didn't hesitate. "I told you he's not prepared to make a deal."

Calm once again abandoned Garza. "You haven't even heard it yet."

"I don't need to," Coleman stated flatly. "My client was defending his wife from an intruder in their home. No matter how you knock it down, if he pleads to anything it'll be as good as admitting he found his wife fooling around. He won't do it."

Throwing up his hands, the DA's tone was almost a lament. "I've got two cops and two security guards who witnessed Laine beating Chambers. They heard Laine repeatedly say he wanted to kill him. If this goes to trial, your client is going to prison."

Coleman closed his briefcase, stood, and walked toward the door. "We'll see."

****

Since Eric refused a plea bargain, a trial was on the court's docket two months to the day of his arrest. Celebrity trials were as engrossing as a serialized murder mystery, and when one ended, the public was eager for another to start. Tinsel Town didn't disappoint. The People v Laine was a glitter-dusted carnival of media coverage, one that took its toll on Jenna. Eric could do little more than watch, day after day, as the bright golden gleam in her eyes faded. He suggested she fly home to stay with her parents, but his attorney *insisted* she be present in court to show her support.

Opening day of the proceedings was like a red-carpet gala with a who's who of L.A. powerbrokers in the gallery. Nick Lombardo and a retinue of security shuttled Jenna and Eric through a steady clamber of reporters begging for a soundbite and battling each other for position near the besieged, young couple.

"No comment," Nick repeatedly shouted as they rushed through an offensive of camera flashes.

The art-deco building's marble floors and high ceilings exaggerated the resounding clatter of footsteps and the rustling sound of people shifting in their seats. Jenna sat behind the defense table, flanked by her parents who had flown west to be with her.

Columnists were in attendance, as well as Caz, Jon, Alan, and most of the staff from Crimson. In the back of the courtroom, Bree Davis sat looking cool and detached. Then as if a vacuum exhausted all of the air in the enormous room, eliminating all sound and movement, Mark Chambers made a grand entrance.

****

Day one was committed to the usual reading of charges and opening statements by both attorneys. Eric, standing with his hands clasped, offered a somber, "not guilty."

The People v Eric Laine commenced.

As the judge gave the jury their instructions, Eric wanted desperately to turn and glance at his wife. He didn't. He stared ahead, anchored in place, knowing if he caught even a glimpse of Mark, he'd pounce so hard, court officers would have to shoot to stop him.

****

At home later that evening, exhausted yet vibrating with anxious energy, Eric yanked at his tie and tore at the top button of his shirt. Stretching his neck from side to side and rolling his shoulders, he tried to release the buzzing inside his body. Jenna was upstairs and he thought to check on her but didn't want to wake her if she was asleep.

"Fucking coward," he whispered to the dark. He couldn't face her.

****

Days of testimony followed as the prosecution presented their case. District Attorney Mateo Garza called the security guards who'd rushed into the bedroom to find an enraged Eric Laine and a bleeding Mark Chambers. Though they denied hearing the defendant threaten the victim, the DA struck gold later, when he direct-examined police officers. The one whose nose Eric had broken seemed particularly eager to describe the violence that took place at the Malibu mansion.

"Yes, sir. I heard him say he wanted to kill Chambers."

"Nothing further."

David Coleman had few objections to any of the prosecution witness's testimonies. Coleman was a picture of calm confidence, each day in a different, perfectly tailored suit. Most spectators in the gallery were also in smart attire. It was joked by one of the television commentators that a best and worst dress list was going to be released.

Each day Jenna appeared in either demure navy or beige, her blouses buttoned to her throat. Her hair was plaited into a thick braid or bun at her nape. She sat composed showing no emotion. The only day she reacted was the day Mark Chambers was called to testify.

****

As he was sworn in, Mark appeared as a wide-eyed

and pained portrait of innocence. Trembling, he told the jury how devastated he was to be so cruelly disfigured, and to have no chance to pursue his dreams of acting. "Look. Look at me," he begged of the jury.

He cast an apologetic glance in Eric's direction and made a sucking sound that whistled past the chipped remnants of his teeth. "I-I know what Angel and I did was wrong...but we fought the attraction for so long, we just couldn't help ourselves."

His words prompted a buzzing of whispers, and as if pausing for a cue he waited and then lowered his head as tears poured from his eyes.

As Eric listened to his former friend lie, watched forced tears rolling down his face, he felt the courtroom walls narrow. Even the frigid air conditioning couldn't cool the blistering heat rising from his collar to his face.

"I want my wife out of here," he whispered to Coleman.

The lawyer jotted a note onto a yellow, legal pad. *Don't lose your composure.*

"My composure?" Eric's voice started to rise. "That scumbag just lied about having an affair with my wife and you said nothing!"

"I'll get him during rebuttal." Coleman urged Eric to lower his voice, but Eric slammed the side of his fist against the table hard enough to disturb the water glasses.

"Quiet your client, Mr. Coleman," the judge warned.

The room again filled with a drone of voices and the sound of shifting bodies. Despite earlier warnings, Eric stood and turned to see what was happening and saw Jenna, her hand pressed to her mouth, climbing past her father to get to the aisle. Her footsteps were steady against the marble as she ran for the exit. Eric instantly bolted from the defense table to follow, but bailiffs stopped him.

Banging his gavel against the sounding block, the judge demanded, "Leave your seat again, Mr. Laine, and you'll be remanded to a cell for the remainder of this trial."

"Calm the fuck down," Coleman whispered.

Still standing by the witness chair, the DA grinned as if Eric had just served him the victory. Red faced, and clearly angered by the melodrama, the judge pointed the gavel in Eric's direction. "Tell your wife her talent as an actress and her performance is not appreciated. Have her keep the theatrics out of my courtroom. Have I made myself clear?"

"Crystal," Eric said. He stared narrowly at the bench and at the man whose job rested on the ability to be fair. "Now let me make *myself* clear. She wasn't fucking performing."

As the judge stood, the sleeves his robe billowed over the podium. With one hard rap to the sounding block, he charged Eric with contempt of court and ordered bailiffs to take him away.

****

The trial continued for less than a week as there was little in the way of physical evidence presented. A victory hinged on who was telling the truth, the defendant or his one-time friend, the victim. Though attorney Dave Coleman sat, day after day, appearing unconcerned by the testimony of the ER doctors, police, and friends of both Mark Chambers and Eric Laine, when it was his turn to present the defense's argument he transformed into a lion—a powerful and steady predator intent upon devouring its prey.

He grilled Mark Chambers, tripping him up at every junction, snaring him in his own web, and catching every lie.

"You testified earlier, that you affair with Mrs. Laine began in the summer. How could that be if she was *away* on tour?"

"You testified earlier that you've seen Eric Laine fight and he's crazy-violent. Why would you sleep with the wife of the man you know to be…*crazy violent*?"

"You testified earlier that you love Jenna Laine, but you just signed a deal with *The Inquisitor* for a tell-all story about your supposed affair. Is that how you treat someone you love?"

Coleman's voice rose with every question and Mark squirmed in his seat as he pulled answers from the air. With each question, Coleman pivoted, purposefully directing the jurors' attention back and forth between defendant and victim—Eric, young, handsome, and despondent; Mark, fidgeting in the witness chair like a child wriggling not to pee his pants.

Coleman had one lone photo of Jenna, taken at the hospital, and enlarged onto a screen. Her head was turned to the side and her face was covered, but the angle showed a hematoma just below her ear. "Mr. Chambers, did you do that to Mrs. Laine?"

Mark stopped squirming and relaxed in his seat. He inhaled a slow breath as if a heady scent infused the air and gave him pleasure. "The hickey?"

He breathed again, shuttering his eyelids and smiling. Leaning forward, he folded languorously toward the microphone. "Yeah, I did that."

Twelve jurors witnessed Mark Chambers' scarred face settle into a rapacious leer.

"Nothing further."

Coleman's last witness was Detective Maya Alvarez who kept her statement simple. "I interviewed Mrs. Laine after she was brought to the hospital. As a detective who works in the sex crimes division, my professional opinion is that Jenna Laine was in no condition to consent."

Two days later, twelve jurors acquitted Eric Laine.

****

David Coleman made a concise statement on the steps of the courthouse, telling reporters justice had been served. Eric Laine had defended his wife from an intruder. Later, at their home, Jenna excused herself and retreated upstairs with her parents to rest while Eric played host to Coleman, Jack Morrissey, and Alan Stark.

"So what's next?" Jack asked Coleman. "I want that piece of dog shit, Chambers, nailed to the fucking wall!"

Coleman swirled the ice in his drink, then took a sip. "We still have investigators digging into his past. Something will turn up."

Jack paced, his feet stamping into the plush carpeting. "The kid was acquitted. Doesn't that mean the jury believed Chambers raped Jenna?"

"It means the jurors thought there was enough reasonable doubt to acquit Eric. Garza won't want to publicly admit he made a mistake by making a play against Chambers any time soon."

Coleman took another easy sip of his drink. Another victory had been added to his sterling record and his job was done. He finished his scotch, shook everyone's hand and left.

Jack reached for his smokes, then as if just remembering where he was, slipped them back into his jacket. "I've got a lot of friends in this town," he said, his voice a heated grumble. "I say we put some pressure on Garza, that spineless bastard."

"No," Eric said. He'd quietly lingered in the kitchen, waiting for his small celebration to end. "Jenna's been through enough. If the DA had the evidence to convict Mark, he wouldn't have gone after me. Just let it go."

"But, kid," Jack pleaded.

"Let it go," Eric begged. "For me and for Jenna."

Bringing his hand to his brow, Jack saluted his young friend. He nodded and left.

Eric fixed his attention on Alan, inviting him to also take his leave. Instead, the agent slid his empty glass over for a refill.

"You're kidding me, aren't you?" Eric said.

"So, you're not only a lousy husband, but a lousy host, too."

Eric swiped Alan's glass away to let him know there was no refill coming. "What do you want, Stark?"

"I want Angel to pull herself together and get back to work. She needs to put all this behind her and show the world she has nothing to be ashamed of."

Eric's fingers were knotted around the glass. He placed it gently in the sink before the temptation to smash it overcame him. Heat rose from his collar, and he felt his entire body burning hot and angry. "She *doesn't* have anything to be ashamed of. My trial is over. You and I can stop pretending to be on the same side. You know where the door is."

Stark's eyes were tapered thin and his voice a dark indictment. "I was right about you from the beginning. I knew you'd ruin her...drag her down to your level."

The words, so bitter and true, made Eric's heart pound with such intensity he imagined his ribs shattering from the force. He plunged his fingers through his hair and gripped his skull wishing he could stop the drumming inside his head, to mute the noise and expel the guilt. "Shut up, just shut up. I know what happened was my fault. If I could turn back the clock and never have met her, I would. As much as it would kill me, I'd walk away from her now if I thought it would be best but…"

"But what?" Alan challenged. "What?"

"It's too late. The damage has already been done. She's pregnant."

Chapter Twenty-Two

Jenna slept fitfully, tossing and lashing out at invisible hands. An early winter moon, full and luminous, streamed through the window, and she bolted upright with a gasp. Eric moved close to hold her, but she shrugged away from his touch.

"Are you okay?" he asked, resting his arms on his raised knees.

"I had a nightmare. I can't remember it." Jenna lay back down, rolling away from her husband, the man who, by her own calculations, couldn't have gotten her pregnant. She and Eric hadn't been intimate after her last period or Mark's assault.

Eric brought a gentle hand to her shoulder to comfort her. "Don't," she whispered, pulling the blankets tightly up to her neck. "Please don't."

"Okay. I'll sleep downstairs."

Jenna followed his departure with tired eyes as he stepped from the guest room. They'd begun sleeping there since the day of the attack—neither of them capable of entering the primary.

In the morning, just as the sun rose, the telephone chimed, startling her. She never reached for it. The insistent ring was the bleating of a lamb, the mewling of a kitten, the cry of an infant. Jenna equated every sound, every sight with babies. She rubbed her stomach, nothing more than a convexity that might result from a large meal. But it felt hard. The small swelling felt hard. Her breasts were tender and swollen to ripeness, her body already altered to accept the life inside it.

The phone rang again. *Why didn't she just turn it off, or unplug it?*

Because even basic ideas, the simplest of solutions escaped her. Since she'd scheduled the abortion, babies were all she thought about. She reached for the receiver to unclip the wire and break the connection when she saw the number was Randi's.

She picked up and cried her heart out to her friend.

****

During the next few days, an unusually hard rain pounded the California coast. Eric heard waves slapping the sand as he pulled into his driveway. Alan Stark's limousine blocked the spot by the mudroom entrance and Eric had to run through fat pelting drops to get to the door. He shucked sodden boots and stepped soundlessly into the kitchen. Treading barefoot, he grabbed a dishtowel to wipe the water pouring down his face and leaned into the doorway to watch the exchange between his wife and Alan.

Stark looked angry as he spoke to her, while she sat silently weaving her fingers together in her lap. Neither one of them noticed Eric enter. He removed his wet shirt, rolled it into a ball, and threw it into a corner by the door. It landed with a crisp clap onto the marble and both Jenna and Alan jerked at the sound.

"What's going on?" Eric asked.

Stark's reply was a tsking suck of air, and he cast a look of disapproving scrutiny at Eric, and the rivulets of water slowly trickling down his chest and stomach. "I would think after your recent escapade you might give some thought to turning the testosterone down a bit."

"It's pouring out. I had to park my car around your limo and run through the rain." He eyed Alan and snorted. "But you look nice and dry. Had your chauffeur walk you to the door with an umbrella?" The scarlet hue that immediately spread across Alan's cheeks told Eric he'd guessed correctly.

Alan recovered quickly from the barb. "Unlike you, my clothes aren't all wash and wear. I can't just wad my suit up into a ball and throw it on the floor."

Eric swiped at the droplets of water running from his hair and sent a spray in Alan's direction. "Yeah, well no one wants to see you without it."

After changing into dry clothes, Eric returned to the great room. Alan was gone and Jenna was in the same position on the sofa still staring at her clasped fingers. He approached carefully. She was fragile, a bloodless vestige of the beautiful and vibrant girl he adored. He took one of her cold hands in his and pressed it to his lips. It was a loving statement, and the best he could offer.

He knew he should take his wife into his arms and look into her eyes but he couldn't. Eric was too spineless to have to face the misery reflected in them, the misery he himself put there. "Did Alan say something to upset you?"

"No, but he was here when my doctor called."

The hair on Eric's nape rose. "And?"

"I told the doctor the date of conception. He said I'm too far along for an extraction in his office. I'll have to go into the hospital for a D&C." Jenna covered her face with both hands. "I should have paid attention to the signs and realized earlier."

Eric knelt at her feet. He patted her head as she wept silently, the low sniffling and quiet gulps tearing his heart to pieces.

She looked up, her golden eyes red rimmed and glossy. "It will be more invasive. They take a rod called a curette and—"

"Stop," Eric whispered. "I know what it means." He took her hand. It felt weightless and cold, dead.

Everything about Jenna was desensitized to the world around her. She rarely spoke, barely ate, and as Eric looked at her shadowed profile, he wondered if terminating the pregnancy would even be the remedy. Then he thought of how often he'd seen her unconsciously holding her hand to her stomach and swallowed back tears he longed to release.

"You don't have to go through with it if you don't want to," he said. "You've been through enough."

****

Jenna had no choice but to announce her pregnancy—a "happily anticipated" arrival due in the spring.

The tabloids, however, did the math and published reports which intimated Angel's husband wasn't the father of her unborn child.

Dropping the investigation against Mark had been the right thing. Reminding the public of the assault was akin to giving him license to hand out cigars.

Eric promised her, he'd love and care for her baby as his own but it was continual slips like saying "her baby" that made Jenna silently question his noble intentions.

How could he love a child that would be an

everlasting reminder of all that had happened, the rape, his trial, and the guilt she knew he wore like armor? How could her husband love the baby, Jenna wondered, when she wasn't sure she would be able to love it herself?

****

In mid-January Eric's boss Tom Larity suffered a mild heart attack. At the prodding of his family, he closed up shop and retired from the contracting business. At nineteen and twenty-one years of age, Jenna and Eric Laine found themselves unemployed while they awaited the birth of Mark Chambers' child.

Chapter Twenty-Three

Jenna heaved herself from bed, supporting the large mound of her stomach with one hand, using the other to maintain balance. Nausea and cravings had long ended but the beginning of her third trimester brought a new type of discomfort. The skin over her abdomen stretched uncomfortably, pulling and tugging when she moved too quickly. She slowly padded to the bathroom and, slower still, descended the stairs to the kitchen. She opened the refrigerator, ignoring the notes tacked to the door—prescriptions for prenatal vitamins she hadn't picked up and doctor's appointments she blew off.

When she did show up for the rare examination, her OB-GYN lectured her about the abnormally large amount of weight she had gained and scolded her over her diet. Her eating habits were abominable for an expectant mother; still, she reached past a container of low-fat yogurt to grab a donut.

She shuffled over to the counter where the house phone blinked rapidly. Pressing the voice mail code, she let the messages play out. Three were reminders for the ultrasound appointment she had later that day, the same one that had been rescheduled from a prior appointment which had been rescheduled from an even earlier one. She looked down at her hand. The skin was pink and shiny because it was so bloated. She pushed seven to delete all the messages.

"Screw it."

She had to bend over to see past her distended belly to her swollen ankles. The warnings about the dangers of pre-eclampsia and placenta previa sang in her head—again—but she'd fallen deep into a quarry of depression and simply didn't care. Once back upstairs she grabbed her hair and twined it into a sloppy bun, squeezed into sweatpants and left the house to meet with Alan.

****

After making it past the usual bombardment of press, Jenna entered Alan's office. The chair next to his desk seemed miles from the door and she was out of breath by the time she reached it. No longer able to make her body move with ease or grace, she let her bulk drop heavily into the chair. Alan's dark brows hung low over his eyes, his lips tightly puckered. By his expression, Jenna could tell if she ever wanted out of her contract, today would be the day to ask.

He glanced at his watch, something he had never before done in her company. She no longer rated his precious time. "I won't keep you," she said.

He laid one hand onto a pile of neatly arranged papers. "Everything you asked for is here." He spoke without looking at her. "I've made very sound investments for you, but quite a bit of your money is tied up in real estate. Now's not the time to sell anything. Petite-Belle Cosmetics backed out of the deal we were working on for the Angel line, and Castle Toys is hedging on the prototype for the Angel doll."

Jenna blew a weary breath, unintentionally making a small whistling sound. Her lips, like every other part of her body, were swollen beyond distortion. She rubbed her stomach. An unrelenting heartburn scalded her insides.

"Maybe I should lease the house and move to a smaller place?"

Alan shook his head. "You have a cash flow problem but you're far from broke. *Stalked* will be out on home video soon and your contract guarantees you a percentage of the gross. Royalties from album sales are down but when your live album is released, they'll come back up and it will cover reimbursing the sponsors for your cancelled tour dates."

His assurances offered little comfort. For the first time in her adult life, Jenna worried about her finances. Her mortgage was astronomical, and security, accountants, agents, and Alan, all took a chunk of her money. "My brother starts college next year. Will I still be able to pay his tuition?"

"I think the sooner you get back in shape and into the studio after the um…baby comes, the better."

****

Meghan Morrissey plopped another strawberry into the blender. After a six month stay at Malibu Healing Center, she was back home at the sprawling mansion she shared with her mother. Her father Jack, who'd taken a hiatus from films, was there all of the time. Meghan handed him a strawberry mango smoothie which he downed in one long gulp.

"I can say this much for these things, I can take a better crap now than I have in years."

"Gross, Daddy," Meghan said, then laughed.

It was a lighthearted, genuine sound. A positive image had finally developed from the darkness of a negative experience. Jack, Meghan, and Rachel Morrissey now sat around the dinner table like any typical American family—any typical American family who could afford a thirty-three-thousand-dollar hand painted antique from a 17th century Carmelite Mission.

They ate wholesome meals of lean meats and steamed vegetables and drank rounds upon rounds of fruit smoothies. They were the new and improved Morrissey's.

After dinner, they retired to the entertainment room to watch television. Meghan scrolled through the on-screen guide, reading the selections. "There's a sitcom on seven but the guy in it is one of the jerks I used to date."

Rachel Morrissey peered at the screen. "There's a movie on the Classic Network but the guy in *that* is a jerk I used to be married to." Female giggling chimed like the high notes of a piano roll.

"Very funny, ladies," Jack said. He grabbed the remote control. "I'm going to exercise my God-given right as a man and take charge of the television." He leaned back into the comfort of supple leather and began to leisurely surf the channels. He stopped dead. "What the fuck is this?"

Meghan and Rachel stared open mouthed at the screen and then both women turned to Jack whose face was variegated shades of red. "What the fuck *is* this," he roared.

"It's called *The Underground Comedy Hour,*" Meghan answered soberly.

On screen, Mark Chambers sat on a titan sized chair, its high back covered in purple velvet. The chair's wooden frame was intricately carved and painted gold. Mark smiled, his repaired teeth aglow, and a dozen brightly wrapped boxes at his feet. A maudlin country song with lyrics about an illegitimate baby played in the background. A pink and blue banner hung above Mark's head. It read: *Congratulations to the Father to Be*.

"I will kill him," Jack said. His voice rose and the mottled hue of his cheeks deepened to magenta. "How the fuck is this comedy?"

Rachel shook her head and pointed to the TV. "There is nothing funny about any of that."

Meghan sniffled and after wiping her eyes pressed her hands to her chest as if her heart ached. "That low-life fucker's been a regular guest on this show ever since he announced he was going to sue Jenna for joint custody of her baby."

"He what?" Jack exploded. "He can't! Why the hell didn't I know about this? Where the hell have I been while this was going on?"

Meghan hugged her father. "With me, Daddy. You've been taking care of me."

Jack pounded his fists into the cushions, glaring heatedly at the television. A gathering of obscenely attired cross-dressers handed Mark the gifts lying at his feet. They oohed and aahed as he opened each one. Items were so tacky they prompted snickers from the audience, others so vulgar, they drew thunderous laughter. The camera frequently cut to a woman, blonde, heavily made up, her stomach grossly padded to exaggerate pregnancy. She held a ridiculously large ball of wool and huge knitting needles. She smacked her lips together, blowing kisses at Mark.

"How the hell can they get away with this shit?"

Jack shouted. "This would never be happening if that spineless DA had put that bastard away where he belongs. I'll bury both of those scumbags, I swear…and the son of a bitch that produces this show."

"Daddy, calm down," Meghan begged. "You're going to have a heart attack."

****

As Jenna lumbered to the bathroom for the fourth or fifth time in an hour, she wondered how she would be able to walk at all in the month to come. She was five weeks away from her due date and felt so cramped and swollen, she could hardly breathe. Feelings of desperation and sadness had been replaced by such intense physical discomfort that grieving over a slowly dying career and quickly dying marriage was pointless.

Hemorrhoids, heartburn, swollen feet and fingers, and the persistent headache that made her vision blur were enough to agonize about. It would be over soon, she reminded herself daily, never letting her thoughts go beyond giving birth. Trying to imagine being a mother, the mother of Mark Chambers' child was too ponderous. As hard as she tried, she couldn't invoke the slightest bit of maternal feeling for the baby. The most she could manage was pity for the little infant whose mother might never love it.

She lay back on her bed, propped up on pillows and rubbing her stomach. The Braxton–Hicks contractions felt like the baby was going to blow right through the walls of her abdomen. Her back was so sore there was no longer a position by which she could achieve comfort. She regretted skipping her last two doctor's appointments and never having shown up for any of her ultrasounds.

She looked at the clock, 11:00 p.m. Eric would be home from work soon. She closed her eyes, hoping to fall asleep and avoid him and the concern that so quickly turned into brooding silence.

Chapter Twenty-Four

"I'm Eric, and I'll be your waiter," he said for the ninth time that evening.

He was working at Caz and Jon's newest venture, a posh restaurant on La Brea. As he walked away to order drinks for his customers, he saw them tilt heads close together and whisper.

Tourists. He'd become an attraction, like a star on the Walk of Fame. His customers would go home to *Bumfuck* and tell their friends they were waited on by superstar Angel's husband, the guy who tried to kill the father of her baby.

It didn't matter how often Jenna's PR firm denied the speculation, the tabloids continued to slip the phrase *Who's the Daddy* into each weekly edition. Eric envisioned reporters waiting in the maternity ward, syringes in hand to draw the baby's blood. He shook his head and went to the server's station to get his customers their seventeen-dollar gin and tonics.

Whispers that usually followed him through the rows of tables escalated into aggressive buzzes. His coworkers regarded him with such cautious expressions he quickly realized something was going on.

"What gives, Caz?" he asked, corralling his boss in the kitchen. "My customers are gawking at me more than usual and the guys on the line are looking at me like I'm going to explode."

Caz tapped his fingers together, stalling, while he called to one of the other waiters. "Be a love and cover Eric's tables will you."

"C'mon, Caz," Eric pleaded.

"All right, but first I want your promise that you won't do anything reckless."

"Caz!"

Eric's boss fanned himself with his hands fretfully. "Oh dear, all right…It's Mark, he was on that hideous show again."

Eric slowly nodded, familiar with Mark's insulting exploits on *The Underground Comedy Hour*. "Go on," he said, methodically curling and uncurling his fists.

"It was worse than usual. They…well…they threw him a baby shower."

Like a clap of summer thunder Eric kicked at a crate of empty beer bottles. "Christ. I should have killed him when I had the chance."

"There's more," Caz continued. "He's outside now with half the crew from the show. My guess is they want to give you your chance. They probably have someone planted at a table with a camcorder."

Eric felt his blood rush through his veins like a bullet, his anger so great his body shook.

"Don't go out there," Caz warned. "Jon won't let them in, and he's already called Mr. Lombardo to take you home. Just go out the back door and wait for him."

Seeing nothing but a red haze, Eric stormed through the restaurant and barreled through the front door. He made a lunge for Mark, but Nick rushed from his car and grabbed Eric around the waist before he could make contact.

"That bastard raped my wife, and you think it's

funny enough to put in a comedy skit?"

Mark cowered behind the producer's bodyguards, shivering while Eric continued his rampage. "You want material for your fucking show? C'mon, Mark, let's see how funny it looks when I kill you."

Coming from nowhere, someone aimed a video camera lens at Eric, but Nick had him contained in a Full Nelson. Nick's massive arms were firmly under Eric's and his hands braced at the back of his neck. "Stop it, kid, they're taping the whole thing."

"Eric, please." Caz's voice was a nervous flutter. "He's right. This isn't going to do you any good. Go back inside."

"You have no reservation here," Jon insisted. "Take your party and leave before I call the police."

The show's host grinned "That's all right," he said. "I got what I came here for. Now we can all go somewhere where we can get some *decent* food."

****

Nick held Eric firmly in place until after the cast and crew of *The Underground Comedy Hour* departed.

"Jesus, Nick, my fucking arms are asleep," Eric said. "Let me go."

Nick released him but Eric strode to the restaurant entrance and drew his arm back to punch the heavy wooden door.

"No, you don't," Nick said, grabbing him by the collar like a mama dog clutching a puppy.

Jon approached, both caution and sympathy in his voice. "Go home. I've got your tables covered and I'll hold your share of the tips in the office."

"Are you firing me?" Eric asked.

"No, of course not. But you're still snorting like a

wild Mustang, and as appealing as that is to Caz, I think it would be better if you knocked off for tonight."

A slow river of cars rolled by, and pedestrians walked along the avenue. A handful of photogs across the street clicked away.

Caz made a tsking sound and patted Eric on the chest. "Oh don't listen to him, love. He's positively evil. Have that nice big Mr. Lombardo drive you home and we'll see you tomorrow."

"I have my own car. Nick doesn't have to drive me home." But when Eric left, he could see Nick behind him, following.

****

At the house, Eric brushed by the rest of Jenna's security team in the driveway. Inside, he strode to the kitchen and grabbed a beer, downing it in three gulps. His heart was still bouncing off his rib cage, so he decided to make himself something stronger.

He reached for the bottle of scotch left over from his acquittal celebration, poured three fingers into a glass and threw the liquid down his throat. Even the most expensive single malt, no matter how smooth, becomes fire when downed so quickly and Eric coughed. Still, he repeated the process two more times.

The liquor eventually warmed him, making his skin flush but the sense of calm he had hoped to achieve was still an elusive goal. He filled the glass more than halfway, dropped a few ice cubes into it, and retreated to the living room. Sitting in the dark he nursed the drink along with his pride. Finally, after taking the last sip, the glass slipped from his hand and a weary sleep took over.

Sound from upstairs woke him. Disoriented, he had

no idea how long he had been out. Annoyed at being disturbed he squeezed his eyes tight but the thump of footsteps from above prevailed. "Fuck," he grumbled, rising from the sofa.

He made lopsided strides to the stairs. He was sleepy *and* drunk, stumbling as he climbed his way to the second floor. Jenna's rounded silhouette was a wavy blur in the bathroom doorway, and he veered clumsily around a chaise to avoid her. Finally reaching the bed, he fell backwards and lay there, swimming in alcohol and misery.

Padding over, she moved close to his sprawled form. "Are you okay?

Eric struggled to open eyelids that felt weighted shut, and mumbled sounds that didn't qualify as words. The short nap he'd taken only amplified the effects of the scotch.

Bending down, Jenna tapped him lightly on the shoulder. "Are you drunk?"

He leaned up on his elbows and scowled, bleary eyed and snappish. "What if I am?"

"Didn't you go to work tonight? Why are you in this condition?"

Eric snorted what was almost a laugh, his top lip curled lazily. "The same reason you're in *that* condition." He pointed a finger at her abdomen. "Mark was at the restaurant tonight."

Gasping, Jenna took an immediate step back. Her own eyes opened wide and pained, her fingers splayed wide against her stomach as if she were trying to disguise the distended swell.

"I-I'm sorry. I didn't mean that," Eric said.

"Yes, you did," she said quietly. "You've…you've

just never said it out loud."

He stood and swayed like a slow set metronome. "I said I was sorry, I didn't fucking mean it."

Jenna made to slip past him, but he loomed, arcing like something top heavy and in danger of falling. "You're drunk. I-I don't want to talk to you. I'm going back to bed."

"You never want to talk to me!" he shouted to her back. "You live in this house like a fucking hermit, shutting everything out, especially me."

His anger and humiliation, all the guilt-engendered self-loathing he kept so tightly contained grew inside and burst out at the one person who didn't deserve it.

"This sucks for me too y'know. Fucking tabloids. Fucking photographers following me everywhere I go. And Mark's out there, telling the entire world the kid is his. I never should have stopped you from getting an abortion."

****

Eric's words were like a hard slap, a stinging sensation that continued to radiate from its core and burn Jenna's skin. "But you did. You…you said you would love the baby."

Lowering his head, Eric took a shuddering breath, his shoulders and torso trembling from the effort. He dropped back down onto the bed and cried into his hands. "I'm trying…I'm r-really trying, but I can't. I hate Mark's baby being inside you. I hate the baby, I hate it."

Immobilized by his confession, Jenna stood quiet and still as death. A large fist gripped her throat from the inside. She couldn't speak, swallow, or exhale. She almost wished her heart would just stop so the pain would end. When she finally released her breath, it came out as a keening sob.

The cry, the pitiable lament spilling from her mouth jolted Eric and he lunged from the bed. He staggered heavily toward her grabbing her shoulders with clumsy fingers. "Jen, I'm sorry. I didn't mean it."

"Get away from me!"

She pounded at his chest, but he only grasped harder, more insistently. "Please, baby, please. I swear I didn't mean it."

"Get away from me!"

As she struggled, Eric's feet caught on the edge of the chaise and he fell, bringing her down as well. She slammed sideways onto the floor with Eric crashing squarely on top of her. Nick rushed in and pulled him from the floor, off of a dazed and groaning Jenna.

"Oh, God." Eric bent to reach for her.

"No. Stay away from her," Nick demanded. "I mean it, I heard you yelling at her from the driveway. You leave her alone now."

Eric started to speak, but Nick answered with a punch to the jaw and Eric toppled to the floor. Bending down, Nick gently supported Jenna to her feet only to have her moan in pain as a watery, pink stain spread across her nightgown.

Chapter Twenty-Five

Jenna woke up, her mouth dry as parchment. If not for the acute pain at her temples, the overhead light in the room would have made her think she'd died and was traveling to the other side. No one explained how severe a headache could be once the epidural wore off. Then again, she'd been less than a model patient and hadn't concerned herself with any of the options for giving birth. Her one and only plan had been to be here, sequestered away at the most exclusive maternity clinic in the Los Angeles area.

As hazy memories of the night cleared, she bolted upright in the bed. Frantic, she turned her aching head to search every corner of the beautifully appointed suite for the bassinette. It was nowhere in the room.

Jenna remembered the grueling hours of labor, the panting and crying out for painkillers. Then she remembered the numbness from the injection that packed the pain and pressure away. There was no pushing to assist the baby on its journey. She'd laid there like a sack as her unborn child struggled to escape the body of its uncaring mother.

"Why isn't it crying?" she'd said.

Why hadn't it cried?

Barbs of panic pricked her skin as she pressed the call button. The baby she was so convinced she could never love had been taken from the room in a rush.

Blue she'd heard someone say. "*The baby is blue.*"

She shook with fear, her hands a blur in front of her. The dryness of her mouth made her gag. She fought first to swallow, then to breathe. *Oh, God, please. Please.*

It was too early, the baby had come too early. Jenna envisioned a tiny creature alone in an incubator, struggling for breath, or worse. It might have died, died without ever having had anyone love it. She had never once crooned soothing words so the baby would know her voice. She'd never had so much as a single tender thought about holding it. Regret, fierce, and agonizing washed over her.

"Please God," she prayed again, "don't punish the baby because of me."

As she continued to urgently push the call button, her doctor entered. "Well. You woke up right on time to feed your daughter. That is if you're feeling up to it."

"Daughter." Jenna repeated the word in a whisper. *I have a daughter.* "I can feed her?"

"Somebody has to," the doctor answered with a smile. "She's a tiny little thing, five pounds on the nose. Gave us a moment there, but she pinked up nicely."

"She…she's okay?"

"Perfect. Ten fingers and ten toes. After we cleaned her up she let out a nice, loud cry. For a preemie she's remarkably healthy."

Moments later, a nurse wheeled in a Plexiglass bassinet. Inside was an infant swaddled in a white blanket and wearing a tiny knit cap. "She's a beauty," the nurse said. "Does she have a name yet?"

Guilt like a heavy weight pressed down. Jenna had never given a moment's thought about what she should name her child. Ashamed, she slowly shook her head.

The nurse smiled and patted Jenna's hand. "I think people try too hard to find the perfect names. I like the old standbys. I have a girl, Susan, and a boy, John." The nurse tittered and bent close to whisper. "Those are the most unusual names you'll find here in Southern California. The last three babies born in this room were named after fruit."

"Your children's names are beautiful," Jenna said, giving the nurse a teary smile.

Scooping the bundle from the bassinette the nurse handed the baby to Jenna. She peeled back the cotton coverlet for her to see the tiny face "You'll find a name for this little beauty. She won't be a plain-Jane that's for sure."

Holding her arms stiffly, Jenna made an awkward cradle for the newborn. Although wrapped tightly, the infant squirmed as if trying to find the perfect spot to nestle against. Her little head turned, she stretched her neck, and her mouth yawned open to a small *O* as if she might coo. Jenna marveled at how firm and warm the little body felt. The scent of baby drifted at her and she wondered if it was only something she could detect— the maternal essence that draws a mother to her own child.

She burrowed her nose in the baby's neck and breathed deeply. Gingerly, she placed one hand beneath the baby's head to support it as she drew her closer. With eyes glistening, Jenna studied her daughter's face. Curious blue eyes blinked back at her. Blue eyes, she thought, not hazel like her own. There were no flecks of green or gold in the baby's eyes. They were a pale shade of blue similar to Mark's.

Jenna dismissed the thought and brushed one fingertip across the baby's cheek. Nothing had ever felt so soft. She traced the shape of the baby's lips and nose, before running a fingertip across the pale indication of an eyebrow. This was her daughter's face, she thought. When Jenna looked into the pale blue of the baby's eyes, she would see her daughter's, no one else's.

Tiny fists struggled free of the blanket and the baby gave a shrill, startling wail. It was like music. Jenna picked up the bottle and brought it to the baby's lips while stroking the feathery tufts of pale hair curling around her ears. Bending her head close Jenna gave her daughter her first kiss. The nurse was right, not a plain Jane, but Jane, nevertheless. It was a beautiful name.

"Janie," she whispered tenderly, "Mommy is so sorry for everything. But I promise from now on, I will spend every moment taking care of you. I will love you and protect you, always."

****

Eric jumped from his chair in the hallway of The Oceana Hills Maternity Hospital. Almost an hour past, he'd watched the bassinette being rushed from Jenna's room and now it was slowly being wheeled back. He begged the nurse to stop so he could see his "daughter." Dewy-eyed he looked down at the bundle swathed in white. The card on the basket said Baby Girl Laine. Had the baby not been so tiny and hurried from Jenna's suite, he would not have had the chance to see the infant at all. A garrison of private security were at Jenna's door, and the men standing guard would not let him inside her room. He didn't give them any arguments.

Nick laid a hand on his shoulder. "Sorry I hit you so hard."

"I deserved it. I could cut my tongue out for the things I said."

Nick nodded, looking serious but sympathetic. "I called Jenna's parents. As soon as they can book a flight, they'll be here. I also called Stark. The press is camped out at the gate and they're waiting for an announcement. He'll know what to say."

Eric nodded, no expression belying his feelings. He'd paced for hours the night before, outside the labor room listening as Jenna moaned in pain. She'd refused to let him in—refused the warmth of his hand, refused his comfort. She hadn't wanted her husband, still half-drunk to be with her. If only she would forgive him now, he would take her and the baby away—away from the media, from Mark, from anything that dared to hurt them.

"Nick, do you think you can spare a couple of your guys to get me out of here? I need to go somewhere."

"Sure," Nick answered.

Nick's men cleared a path by the gate and Eric made his escape. He hopped a cab and managed to reach his destination without being followed. He wanted to make his purchases without the prying eyes of reporters. Contrary to what he had so callously said the night before, biology didn't matter to him. He was going to buy *his* child what she needed, and he was more than prepared to spend his last dime doing so.

He went to an upscale baby boutique on Rodeo Drive where a salesperson helped him pick out a collection of stretch terry cloth pajamas, an assortment of things called "onesies," and hats and sweaters. He moved on to the furniture department and ordered a bassinet with a lacy cover hoping Jenna would be pleased with the yards of frilly fabric that covered the wicker basket. He picked out the most expensive infant car seat, blankets, and crib sheets, then ended his expedition in the gift department.

Eric toyed with the idea of showing up at the hospital with a ridiculously large teddy bear, but only felt more ashamed of himself for thinking his wife could be coaxed into forgiving him because of a lame, grandstand gesture. She deserved better.

He continued perusing shelves packed with fuzzy animals wanting something the baby could wrap her small arms around, that one special stuffed animal that would make her feel safe and secure when she burrowed her face into the soft fur—the stuffed animal that would someday be threadbare from love.

Tucked behind the others on the shelf, Eric spotted a plain, white puppy dog with floppy ears. The material was velvety soft, and it had no ribbons or buttons that might injure or choke a baby. The little white puppy was just slightly larger than Eric's hand. He paid for his purchases, instructing the salesperson to have the bulk of the merchandise delivered, and left the store carrying the car seat with one hand and the puppy in the other. He went home and showered to make himself presentable for his wife and daughter.

An hour later he was stopped once again at Jenna's door, denied entry. Eric sat in the waiting room for hours, the white puppy in his lap. When visiting hours ended and the hallways and waiting room emptied, he gave the little white dog to one of the nurses and asked her to please give it to his wife.

****

At the hospital's gate Alan Stark met with reporters. The birth of Angel's baby was the story of the hour and members of the media crowded around, salivating like hungry cartoon wolves. He gave them the news that Angel, a.k.a. Jenna Laine, and her husband Eric, were the proud parents of a healthy baby girl.

"What about the rumors that the baby is really the love child of Angel and Mark Chambers?" one reporter wasted no time asking.

Alan stiffened but remained collected. "Mark Chambers is an opportunist, relying on his association with Angel's husband for his own personal gain. Chambers has no means of income other than what he's paid by the tabloids for his lies."

Another reporter signaled pen in hand for Alan's attention. "Didn't the police find Angel in bed with Mark Chambers? Isn't there some validity to his claim to be the baby's father?"

Alan once again cleared his throat knowing he had to delicately address the last part of the question. "The police never found Angel in bed with Chambers. What they found was her husband beating an intruder. There is no reason for anyone to take the man's claims seriously. He's a pathetic publicity hound who is at the moment making his living off of Angel's star status."

"Chambers says he'll order blood tests to confirm he's the baby's father. Is there any truth to that?" another reporter shouted, but before Alan could answer one question, he was hammered with another, and another.

"Will Angel take legal steps against Chambers?"

"Why hasn't Angel made any appearances since her pregnancy became public knowledge?"

Alan waved away the questions. "I've given you all the details you need to know."

He turned and walked away from the throng, knowing he had not satisfied their curiosity. Like the reporters themselves, the questions were not going to go away.

As they were about to disband, Mark Chambers and an entourage showed up at the gate. Alan watched the press descend on him as though he were a head of state, flocking to him. God only knew what kind of declaration Chambers would make and, short of killing him, there was no way to silence him.

Alan passed through the lobby and rode the elevator to Angel's floor. As he approached her door, a nurse stepped through. "Mr. Stark, Mrs. Laine says to go right in."

He tapped lightly, and slowly entered the room; sure he would find it dark, and her lying like a bloodless invalid awaiting the specter of death. Instead, the room was brightly lit, and she was up, looking out the window. The rigid set of her shoulders told him she was watching the commotion near the gated entrance. Her eyes, Alan imagined, would be red and swollen with tears, her lips quivering, and her face pale and telling of her desperate frailty. When she turned, he was stunned to see a steadfast mask of resolve.

"I want you to liquidate as many of my assets as possible, then set up an offshore account I can draw from. I'm through with all of this. "Everything. I'm leaving and I'm never coming back."

Chapter Twenty-Six

Six months later

Bree Davis strode into Alan's office, her gait, as always, confident. She neither bothered to knock nor asked his permission to enter. She walked immediately to the bar and fixed herself a martini. "Would you like something?"

Alan nodded. "Pour me a scotch. What are we celebrating?"

Bree sipped before answering. "My new job, my new man, and my new life. And I owe it all to you."

Intrigued, Alan studied her. Bree's hair hung loose and long enough to brush against her shoulders. It looked like she'd recently added highlights. Her face, usually pale, was imbued with a peachy glow.

"The new man seems to agree with you, but new job? If I'm not mistaken, don't you still work for me?"

"I'm branching out on my own." Her eyes sparkled and her lips curved into a coquettish grin.

Alan swallowed a mouthful of scotch and expelled a dry laugh. "I hope you don't think I'd let you get away with stealing any of my clients."

Pouting, as if hurt by the insinuation, Bree laid her hand against her chest. "No, no, Alan, I would never, especially now that you've lost what's her name."

"What's her name?" Alan felt an angry tic

pattering against his cheek as he downed the rest of his drink.

Grinning, Bree tapped her fingertips against her glass. "Be honest, Alan, If you thought Angel was ever coming back, you wouldn't have replaced her by signing that little Chrissy something or other."

A sudden weight settled in the center of Alan's chest. He eyed his favored single malt in its expensive crystal decanter, wanting to down every drop of the liquor so the pain would slip away. Losing Angel remained an intolerable ache. Losing her because of his own actions, crushing. Guilt was a burn so blistering even the cool assuredness of his own ego couldn't soothe it. He closed his eyes and sighed. "Angel is irreplaceable."

"Of course," Bree answered with a coy fluttering of lashes. "I do hope you'll miss me with the same…passion." She drained her martini and placed the glass on his desk. "I'll draw up an official letter of resignation and send it to you."

"Just a second." Alan blocked her path as she stepped to leave. "What the hell are you up to?"

Arms akimbo, she stared him down. "Like I said, I'm branching out on my own. I have someone in mind, someone who I think will go far. Grooming clients is something I learned from you, and as it turns out, I'm very good at it."

"You can't negotiate a new parking space in the garage without my say so," Alan sputtered. "If you've made a deal of your own while you still work for me, I'll see you in court."

Bree's expression was triumphant. "I don't think so, Alan, not unless you want everyone in this town to know about the arrangement you had with Mark Chambers or the argument you two had the day he attacked Angel. I was standing right outside your door when you were on the phone with him. I'd say it was that conversation that pushed him over the edge."

She leaned one hip against his desk and idly rolled her shoulders. "My client is going to be added to the cast of *Back Road to Paradise*. The producers have practically guaranteed him the part, and agencies are already fighting over him. I just have to work out a few minor details."

The bright Los Angeles sun breached a band of smog and reflected white against the window, momentarily bathing Bree in a vaporous glow. "You aren't going to interfere or use any of your influence to screw this up for me. In return I'm going to forget all about the sneaky little deal you had with Chambers."

Alan felt the air in the room turn weighty and thick, and breathing became an onerous chore. Bree had him. He couldn't risk anyone in the industry ever knowing how he betrayed Angel. Keeping it secret was the only reason he'd let her go. Spent, tired beyond belief, he folded into his chair.

"Fine," he said acquiescing to defeat. "If you're willing to gamble your career with some unknown on a prime-time soap that barely gets a two percent share, good luck to you."

Bree's ruby lips were a wide arc over perfect white teeth. "I'm confident it's all going to work out. My client is going to be playing a handsome, brooding, young drifter. The part was made for him. I'm sure he'll be a hit."

****

Eric folded a pair of his jeans, and absently dropped them into a cardboard box. A realtor found tenants for the Malibu house, and he was moving to a studio apartment in Inglewood. Bree had dropped by to help.

"You didn't need to come over. I don't really have all that much stuff to pack," he said flatly.

Bree's hips were an easy sway as she stepped across the freshly steamed carpet to one of the bare, white walls. She ran a hand along a knot of plaster where an obvious hole had been recently repaired. Other, similar fist-sized gaps pitted the wall. A bucket of compound and trowel sat on a tarp. "You're lucky you didn't break your hands. What were you thinking?"

He glanced down at his fingers, the knuckles scraped red. "Lay off, Bree. I'm not in the mood for another lecture."

She stomped over to his bed, grabbed a pile of T-shirts, and threw them in the box. "A major network offered you a once in a lifetime opportunity and you'd rather sit around drinking beer and punching walls. What the hell is wrong with you?"

With a lazy dip of his shoulders, Eric started toward her. "Nothing. This is the real me. My mistake was thinking I could be something else." He slid one arm around her waist and yanked her close, flattening her breasts against his chest. "The bad boy, isn't that what they want me to play on that stupid show?"

She made no attempt to pull away. "Yes, and you'd be crazy to turn it down."

Releasing her, he tossed more of his belongings into the box. "I'm not an actor. I'm a waiter."

"Well, that's a statement you don't hear very often

in this town."

Eric glared. He shied from cameras like a vampire the sun. Paparazzi interest in him had finally cooled and he wasn't about to reignite it. "I'm serious. I'm not an actor. Why would some producer offer me a part anyway?"

"Your face was splashed all over the papers. The producers think you have something."

"I'm not an actor," he repeated.

Rolling her eyes, Bree took a tired breath as if Eric's refusal was simply the petulance of a spoiled child. "You wouldn't even need to act. All you have to do is memorize dialogue and be your moody self."

"Oh I get it. Why get an actor to *play* a hood when they can get the real thing."

"Be serious. This could be a way for you to make a fresh start."

The words were like the lash of whip. Three months after Jenna disappeared from the hospital, he'd been served with divorce papers. A day later, he'd received her letter. In it she spoke of love, and forgiveness, and new beginnings. She wrote of her baby and how nothing was more important than keeping her safe.

I owe it to all of us to put the bad times in the past. In your heart I know you could never accept my daughter and I could never give her up, not even for you. I've signed the house over to you and paid as much of the mortgage as I could. When you're ready, sell it and use the money for a fresh start.

Be well, Jenna.

Fresh start—two words written on the pretty stationery Eric had crushed in his hand as he'd folded over onto himself.

Fresh start—two words, meant to be encouraging, had made him sit for hours weeping in the dark. *Fresh start*—two words now booming inside his head like cannon fire. His heartbreak and exhaustion made a sudden, sharp turn toward rage.

Hefting one of the boxes, he heaved it at the wall. "I don't want a fresh fucking start! I want what I had before!"

Bree moved close and laid her hands against his chest. "She isn't coming back, but I'm here, and I need a fresh start as much as you do. You know how intolerable Alan is. Please take the part, Eric. Do it for me. Let me represent you so we can both move on."

"No. The only thing I can even think about is finding my wife."

"Then take the part. Launching a search for her won't be cheap. Take the damned part."

****

Mark Chambers fished in near empty pockets for money for a pack of cigarettes. He was shy by a dollar. Candy and magazines were stacked on racks at the kiosk so he settled for a chocolate bar instead. It was the only thing he could afford.

With Angel gone *The Underground* had stopped calling, and the tabloids had no interest in his story. Even the sleazy bars on the Strip had no use for his services. He unwrapped his chocolate, and just as he was about to take a bite, the heading on *Trend Magazine* screamed up at him. *Ten Hot Newcomers to Keep an Eye on.*

"No, no, no."

Mark's eyes filled with tears. The weekly

periodical had nine thumbnail pictures set around one larger portrait. It was Eric, his smile and eyes aglow on the glossy cover. The candy bar slipped from Mark's hand and fell onto the grimy L.A. sidewalk.

Chapter Twenty-Seven

New York City, 2004

Jenna opened the largest of her trunks and placed Janie's sunsuits in a box destined for an area thrift store. Although she was well used to the chore of unpacking, this was the first time she was making her donations to a big-box reclamation center and not a rustic, village church. It was Autumn and they were back in the States—New York City—The Big Apple.

A little over two years ago, on a day not yet lit with sunlight, Jenna and her baby were secreted away from the hospital to an airstrip in Santa Ana. From there, she took a private jet to the *Chateau Thierry, Belleau Aerodrome* in France. Miles from the nearest town she'd rented a secluded countryside villa, employing the handyman and his wife who'd served the previous owners. Thirty pounds heavier and with cropped brown hair, no one in the small village had guessed the true identify of their famous neighbor.

For a while she and the baby lived an idyllic and isolated life, moving from one obscure town to another. She spoke to her parents frequently, flew them to Europe occasionally, but adamantly refused to listen to any news of Eric or of Hollywood. She tended to her small gardens, discovered she enjoyed cooking, and immersed herself in motherhood. It was a quiet and peaceful lifestyle of rose dawns, lavender fields, and wine. It was the quiet, easy lifestyle Jenna had needed to heal. Eventually, though, she yearned for home, deciding on New York and hoping the adage *hide in plain sight* was true.

She taped the box filled with baby paraphernalia shut and set it aside. She bundled Janie up in a red quilted jacket and white knit hat, but Janie immediately brought her chubby fingers to her throat and tugged at the strings. "No hat," she said, her bottom lip jutting stubbornly. Her daughter was well into the throes of the "no" phase.

Slipping into her own coat, Jenna took a glance into the mirror as she always did when she stepped outside. She brushed her hair with her fingertips to make the feathery bangs of her choppy auburn pixie sweep close to her eyes. Her baby weight had long dissolved, and she was thinner than she'd ever been because of her *laissez-faire* approach toward food while in France. Jenna swept her toddler in her arms, slipped on sunglasses large enough to mask most of her face, and left the apartment, looking every bit the chic European. And, if anyone were to recognize her as Angel she'd simply laugh and say, "Oh, I get that a lot."

Janie's attention immediately shifted to the bustle of activity in the street below. She had developed a particular fascination with taxicabs. "Ride," she squealed her delight.

"Maybe later," Jenna said. They went on an almost daily pilgrimage of cab rides to shops and their apartment was rapidly filling with artwork and knickknacks. Today, however, they were going to the bank. Once inside the Hudson Savings on Lexington

Avenue, Jenna filled out the appropriate paperwork to rent a safety deposit box. In it, she placed her rental agreement, two passports, and Janie's birth certificate, all with the legal name change of Black. Before returning to the U.S. Jenna had found an organization that helped women in abusive situations "disappear." The woman in charge, knowing Jenna's story, secured her documentation that gave her and Janie their new identities. Jenna in turn made a generous donation to the group, a small price to ensure there would be no paper trail leading to Jenna Welles Laine.

After closing the box and securing the lock, Jenna Black and her daughter walked out of the bank and into the crisp autumn air where they blended, unnoticed, into the hurried mass of pedestrians walking the bustling streets of New York.

By day's end, after more unpacking and tucking Janie in for the night, Jenna collapsed in a down-filled armchair. The cable service had finally been installed and she clicked on the television. "Let's see what's going on in this part of the world," she said aloud to no one.

The number of channels seemed to have increased from twenty to about a thousand in the last few years. Jenna imagined she could surf the options for an hour before she was back to the beginning. She surfed more, stretched languidly, and fell asleep wrapped in a knitted blanket.

A dreamy voice coaxed her awake. A shiver ran up her arms and she pulled the coverlet tight around her shoulders. She breathed her relief as she realized the television was still on. Relaxing back into the cushions, she yawned and closed her eyes when the voice beckoned again. It was deep, and seductively familiar. This time she snapped fully awake. Eyes wide, she stared unblinking at the images on the television.

An actor and actress, a perfect looking pair, were arguing. The scene was a fiery mix of anger and passion. The girl, pretty and pouting, slapped her companion. The man wore no shirt, his tall, wide shouldered frame lean but formed with cuts of muscle. His eyes blazed blue from his tanned face.

As Jenna watched, she brought her fingers to her lips to hold back a sigh. The man on screen pulled the young woman close. His hands pressed into her arms in an unyielding grip, until she began to submit, and then he brought his mouth down to cover hers.

Jenna's heart caught in her throat as she watched the scene play in her living room. Her breath came in a thready rasp and her eyes fluttered shut. She could almost taste the sweetness of the man's lips, smell the musk of his skin. She felt the hard muscles of his chest crushing her breasts and his breath a warm trail against her throat.

She knew everything the actress in the scene was experiencing because the man holding her was Eric.

****

Sitting at one of best tables at one of L.A.'s hottest spots, the star of *Back Road to Paradise* signed an autograph for the gamine-eyed girl who approached him. Bree tapped her fingernails impatiently on her menu. "The management is supposed to keep annoying fans away."

"I thought autograph collectors were a good sign."

"You've passed that point," she answered.

Eric smiled as another fan approached, pen, and

paper in hand. He quickly scribbled his name and passed it back. Bree waved for the manager who sent the remainder of the girls surrounding the table away. "We have more important things to discuss than your fans right now. Aren't you the least bit interested in knowing how my meeting with your agent went?"

"I'm on pins and needles."

Bree bit down on her lower lip, turning an angry grimace into a fragile looking pout. "This was a very difficult contract negotiation; you could show a little appreciation."

"I'm sorry." He covered Bree's hand with his own and rubbed gently. "Tell me how it went."

She brightened. "They've agreed to our terms. The producers will give you the salary increase, and instead of doing all twenty-two episodes next season, you only have to appear in twelve. That will leave you free to star in *Johnny Reb*."

Eric raised his water glass and lightly tapped Bree's in a toast but said nothing.

"I was hoping you'd look happier, starring in a feature is a huge career move."

"I'm happy," he said but presented no smile. He looked past Bree, past rows of tables covered in white linen and past an exposed brick wall where wine racks were bolted. As his gaze went to the greenery behind tall windows, he leaned back in his chair, still and pensive.

"Maybe it was premature of me to order champagne. This isn't the celebration I anticipated," Bree said.

"I spoke to the detective today."

Air left her lips in shallow puffs. "I thought you

gave up trying to find her, especially now that you and I have been…"

"I did. I just had him run her social security number one last time in a new public records data base."

"And?"

"And there's nothing. It's as if she doesn't exist. It's been almost three years and she's never contacted me." He raked his hands through his hair. "Mark isn't the only reason she ran away. It's me. She wanted to get away from me. I have to face the fact that it's time to let go."

Their waiter delivered the bottle of champagne, popped the cork and poured two flutes. Bree smiled and sipped, looking light and effervescent as the contents of her glass.

****

The following year the Civil War epic *Johnny Reb* premiered as one of the summer's biggest blockbusters. Fans of *Back Road to Paradise* flocked to see the big screen debut of their nighttime soap idol. Critics who presumed Eric Laine to be another television pretty-boy trying to make the jump to feature film were impressed with his acting ability. Offers for more work in film poured in for the handsome twenty-four-year-old, and by the end of the year Eric Laine was one of Hollywood's hottest properties, commanding a paycheck exceeding anything he could ever have imagined.

In a gesture of gratitude, lonely, on the rebound, and still hurting, he married Bree Davis.

Chapter Twenty-Eight

Greenwich, Connecticut, 2006

Janie Black stood on tiptoe reaching for the handle on the kitchen faucet.

"C'mon kiddo, we're going to be late," Jenna said. "It's almost twelve thirty."

"I'm just getting a drink of water, Mama."

"Here let me do that," Jenna offered, taking the glass and filling it. She assessed the appearance of her daughter and shook her head smiling. "You're quite a fashion-plate. Did you know that?"

"What's a fashion-plate, Mama?"

"Oh, it's someone who dresses *really* special."

A blur of colors bounced into Jenna's arms— purple and pink stripes, bright orange polka dots, and blue plaid. "Maybe we can stick to one color, just for today since it's picture day."

"But I like what I have on," Janie stepped back, and tugged at her orange vest. She moved her small hands to her waist and leaned on one hip—a small but firm mini fashion model, complete with the pouty assertiveness seen on a runway. "These are my favorite clothes."

Jenna couldn't halt the chuckle spilling from her mouth. Her daughter, a twenty-five-year-old trapped inside the body of a three and a half-year-old, never failed to impress her. "I'll make a deal with you. I'll let you wear your new dress. But you have to be extra careful at snack time."

"Okay." With that settled, Janie sped off in the direction of her bedroom to change while her mother wondered if she'd just been conned.

Later with a much toned-down child secured in her booster seat, Jenna drove past the uniform rows of condominiums in the development where she and her daughter lived. Greenwich Glens was their latest residence, the second in as many years. In the hallway of Leaping and Learning Pre-K, Jenna tried making order out of the impossible cowlick that made her daughter's bangs go askew. There wasn't enough spit on the planet.

She straightened the bow in her daughter's hair and chucked her small chin. "You smile real big when they take your picture. Okay, baby?" She kissed Janie good-bye and headed into town to do her grocery shopping.

Fiddling with the car radio, Jenna hummed along with an oldie from the sixties. The song was broken by static so she hit the scan button. An annoying advertisement screamed through the speakers so she hit the button again. The local news came on.

Television and film star Eric Laine was seriously injured in a freak accident on the set of his movie The Pirate. Location shots were being filmed before dawn in nearby coastal Rye, New York. A spokesman for the production company said Laine was performing his own stunt when he fell more than forty feet to the ground. He was immediately airlifted to Westchester Trauma Center where he is listed in critical condition. Production of the historical epic has been suspended.

The shrill blare of a horn jolted Jenna. She was firmly gripping the steering wheel, sitting at the green light unmoving. Sound from several other horns joined in as she sat swallowing bile and fighting the bitterness reaching up into her throat.

"Hey! Wake up," someone shouted.

Jenna's knees shook beneath the steering wheel and when she pressed down on the gas pedal, she sent the car pitching forward, fishtailing before screeching to a stop. More horns pealed and someone cursed as Jenna maneuvered her car back into the correct lane. The road ahead became a blur as tears filled her eyes.

"Critical condition."

She repeated the words with the solemnity of a prayer. A picture of Eric, broken and bleeding, started a new series of tremors to work on her system and Jenna had to clutch the wheel to control the shaking. Without consciously thinking, she pulled onto the southbound interstate that linked Connecticut and New York and headed toward the hospital. Hands shaking, she turned the radio dial searching for another news report and word on his condition. Each one she found related the same somber story, using phrases like clinging to life and near death.

In less than a half hour, she pulled into the hospital parking lot. Camera crews and news vans were already stationed near the entrance. Seized by the fits of trembling that accompany a great and sudden shock Jenna watched the commotion. Her stomach rebelled and she grabbed one of her green grocery bags and vomited.

"Oh, God," she whispered, swiping tissues from a box to dab at both her mouth and her eyes. She drove up and down the lanes of cars and parked. Walking on limbs with no more substance than water she approached the crowd not exactly sure what she was planning to do. Three and a half long years had passed and Eric, she reminded herself, was married to another woman. They were a regular presence in the tabloids and heralded as Hollywood's perfect couple.

Jenna's heart lurched and the pulse drumming in her throat came to a halt as she saw a sudden jostle of activity among the news crews. They shifted like one giant entity toward the hospital doors. Lights exploded, and microphones suspended from booms strained in the same direction like metal to a magnet. Head down, she hurried across the wide road and lingered at the edge. Two men in suits, another in a bright, white lab coat stepped through the doors. The press stilled, creating a hush more oppressive than any sound. When all was completely silent one of the men explained what had happened to Eric Laine.

A pyrotechnic device designed to simulate lightning had ignited too soon and thrown the actor from a tall prop built to look like an eighteenth-century ship's mainsail mast. Safety netting in place burned during the resulting fire and he fell more than forty feet onto smoldering ropes. The doctor followed with an account of the injuries, assuring the reporters that everything possible was being done to save the patient. Words swam in Jenna's head; "surgery, swelling, hemorrhaging, paralysis."

Her body pitched and swayed, tears trickling down her cheeks. Trembling, she fumbled in her purse for her sunglasses, thinking how careless she had been not to have put them on before. She needed to see him. Jenna knew with desperate certainty that she needed to get inside and see him—to see him even it was to say good-bye.

Slowly pushing her way through the swarm of reporters she listened as they called out more questions, impatient and dissatisfied with the vague bits of information and wanting more gory details. They waited, resolute, anxious competitors vying to be the first to report his death.

"Excuse me," a reporter from a local affiliate squawked as Jenna squeezed by her. "Where's your press pass?"

Ignoring her, Jenna edged closer to the front. The doctor was already on his way back inside, and hospital security was again ordering reporters to move back away from the doors. A man, tall, imposing, and somber, stepped close to the microphones. "The doctor has given his statement. Please clear the area. We'll let you know as soon as there's any change in his condition."

Thrusting through the horde of reporters, Jenna started after the man and was immediately halted by hospital security. "I need to speak with him," she begged, pointing at the burly man trudging away.

"Miss, you have to stay back," the guard demanded.

"Nick," Jenna shouted. "Nick, wait!"

The man slowly turned. He shook his head and rubbed pink-rimmed eyes. "Jesus, it can't be," he whispered. "It can't be."

As she felt herself being gobbled up by the curious press, Nick Lombardo pulled her from the crowd and swept her inside. He blinked, then his eyes became wide as if he were looking at a ghost. "Are my eyes playing tricks on me?"

"No, Nick, it's me."

"Oh my god, I can't believe it," he said, bringing massive arms around her and hugging tightly. "I'm so glad to see you, sweetheart, so glad."

"How bad is it?" she whispered resting her cheek against his chest.

Nick hugged tightly. "Bad…really bad."

****

Nick took Jenna upstairs to the intensive care unit. "He's awake but he's in a lot of pain. It'll help him to see you."

"What about…"

"She's in Switzerland having sheep piss or something injected into her wrinkles." Clearly, Nick Lombardo had no love for the current Mrs. Laine.

Behind a wall of glass in the ICU, Eric lay unmoving. Jenna gulped back a sob and hugged herself, moving in a slow, keening sway. Tubes and wires snaked around and into his body. Screens glared a dire visage of his vital signs, and she thought mournfully that the pumps and machines that blinked and flashed were the only things keeping him alive.

"Nick?" A man stepped toward them. "You can't bring anyone up here."

Again Jenna felt her knees weaken as the man neared. He was tall and well built; hard lines of worry were carved into an otherwise young and handsome face. His eyes were an intense shade of turquoise, troubled, deep, and familiar.

"Nick?" the man repeated, "Who is this?"

"Zach, this is Jenna, your brother's first wife."

Eric's brother took a step toward Jenna, took her hand and brought her into Eric's room. "He's almost too weak to speak but when he does, he calls your name."

They stepped quietly to Eric's bedside. "I can't even keep track of which bones the doctors told me he broke." Zach sniffled. "He's been through so much and come so far. This is so unfair, so…"

Jenna looked down. Eric, beautiful, vital Eric lay still, his face the pale gray of a polished stone. Purple stains outlined his eyes. Oxygen tubes were in his nose, but she could see the struggle it was for him to breathe, heard the pained rasp as he exhaled. His right leg was encased in an apparatus of rods and pins that looked like a torture device. One arm was in a cast, the rest of his body all but obscured by tubes.

"He had some internal bleeding, and they had to remove his spleen. Thankfully, he made it through surgery. Right now, he's paralyzed from the waist down." Zach cleared his throat. "If he lives, they're not sure he'll ever walk again. The doctor said the next twenty-four hours are the most critical."

Jenna's extremities went cold, hands and feet brittle as if long exposed to a winter wind. She was too numb to cry. Zach pulled a chair close to the bed. "I'm going to go donate blood. We're both AB-negative, not the most common blood type. He can have O, but I want him to have mine. He's real generous with me and my sisters and it's the least I can do for him." Zack cleared his throat again. "Thanks for being here. I didn't want to leave him alone in case…" He stepped from the room and never finished his statement.

Mechanically and in slow increments Jenna

lowered herself into the chair. Stunned, as if struck senseless, she stared down at her ex-husband, the man she'd fled from, the man she'd tried desperately to forget.

The man whose blood type was AB-negative, the same uncommon type as her daughter's.

Chapter Twenty-Nine

A slow, steady swell of pain became an unrelenting pressure in Jenna's chest. It left her as helpless as Eric, who lay quiet and broken. She watched his eyelids twitch, the dark lashes fluttering against waxy skin. Beneath those lids were her daughter's eyes. Jenna now knew it hadn't been just wistful longing. Janie, whose pale infant eyes had darkened to vivid turquoise, was Eric's child, conceived in San Francisco, and conceived in love. The light but uncomfortable period she'd experienced that long ago month had been her body's way of preparing to embrace his child.

"If only we realized," Jenna whispered.

Her stare drifted to the machine that recited the beating of his heart. Each jolt of light that skipped across the screen might be the last and she knew with desolate certainty if Eric's heart stopped beating, her own would break. "Please, you can't die, not now, now that I know."

He moaned and a weak cough shook his chest. The sound was liquid, a death rattle. The E.K.G. screamed shrill and rapid beats. Doctors and nurses rushed into the room in a furor of precise activity. For Jenna, the reality of time ceased. A nurse quickly ushered her outside where she could do no more than pray as doctors manipulated, urged, and begged the forces of life to remain inside the dying body.

"Please," Jenna begged, "please don't die, Eric. Please, God, don't let him die."

Torturous moments of uncertainty passed. Voices rang out, and blood was delivered by someone who barreled past. Nick appeared at her side, his eyes and nose red.

"I was in the chapel," he admitted. "I'm not ashamed to cry. He's a good guy and we've become best friends."

Jenna nodded and grasped his hand never taking her eyes away from the window. Activity on the other side of the glass slowed and for one horrific moment, Jenna thought Eric was gone. "No…Oh please no." She silently wept as a somber looking doctor came through the door.

"I need to speak with Mr. Laine's brother."

"He's giving blood," Nick answered. "What's happening in there? Is he… he…?"

"Very weak. But I really should be discussing this with family."

Nick who was still firmly holding Jenna's hand pulled her close and wrapped his arm around her shoulder. "We are family."

****

A chest tube had been inserted into Eric's side just below his armpit to keep his lung inflated and drain excess fluid. No blood had been found in the fluid which was an encouraging sign. As the hours passed, he miraculously gained a small fraction of strength. His blood pressure and heart rate improved, and the doctors offered a glimmer of hope when he displayed a minute reaction to a pin dragged along the arch of his foot. Except for the time it took to place the phone call to make arrangements for Janie, Jenna never left his side.

She rubbed her own ebbing warmth onto hands cold and almost lifeless. She stroked loving fingers lightly across his bruised cheeks while whispering words of comfort. There was so much more she wanted to say but the right was no longer hers. Jenna's eyes stayed locked onto the face of the man she had once loved; the man she knew deep down she would always love. Each moment passed in agonizing slowness, an excruciating wait for the next time Eric's eyes would open. All she could do was sit and pray and regret what might have been.

She dozed in a chair near his bed, waking each time he stirred. Throughout the night, he drifted between a deep state of slumber to a semiconscious state of anxiety. He groaned meager syllables Jenna strained to hear. His voice, nothing more than a whisper, was imbued with pain.

At one point, he cried out and Jenna saw his eyes rocking beneath the closed lids. She was sure he would have been thrashing his head from side to side if he were capable of doing so. He called her name more than once and it left his lips in a fragile whimper.

"I'm right here," she assured over and over, stroking his cheek. "I'm here."

As the first rays of morning sun bled through the blinds, the nurse who had periodically checked on Eric tapped Jenna on the shoulder. "Miss, I'm sorry but you're going to have to leave. Mrs. Laine has arrived."

Jenna turned at the sound of a commotion coming from the hallway.

"What the hell is she doing in there?" Bree shrieked. "Who let her in here?"

As Jenna attempted to stand, she felt the faint grasp of Eric's hand. "Please, Jen. Don't…go. Please."

Tears slipped down her cheeks at the feel of his hand. A hand she knew to be both strong and gentle, one that had touched her so many times, now almost incapable of maintaining the feeble grasp.

"Please." Eric's eyes, pained and pleading, were locked on to hers so intently that there were no nurses, no doctors, no power on Earth that could have made her leave his side in that moment.

****

In the hallway, Bree ranted at her brother-in-law. Her tone softened only when the doctors and nurses focused their attention upon her and suggested she continue her "discussion" in the lounge.

"How dare she show up here, and how dare you let her sit there holding his hand?" A blotchy streak of pale pink stretched from one cheek to another and across the bridge of Bree's nose like a winter sunset. "Well?" She tapped her foot on the tile. "Say something."

"Okay," Zach said, "If you're through with your jealous fit, do you want to know how he is?"

Bree Davis Laine sobbed into her hands. "I called the hospital from the plane every twenty minutes. I know how he is. This has been a nightmare for me. I've just traveled for fourteen hours, not knowing if my husband would even be alive when I got here, and when I do I find, that…*that woman* at his bedside?"

Zach rubbed at his temples then put one hand on Bree's back. "She just showed up, she lives in the area. It seems to help Eric having her here."

"No," Bree wailed. "She's the last person on Earth who should be here. She abandoned him. She's caused him nothing but pain." Bree clutched at Zach's shirt. "You have to know what she did to him. It was in all the papers. She cheated on him, had another man's baby for God's sake. I was the one who picked up the pieces. I want her out of here. Now."

Zach held Bree as she continued to cry. "Eric never told me anything about her. I asked him once, but he refused to talk about her."

Looking up, Bree was an appropriate picture of puffy eyes and quivering lips, her ashen pallor a portrait of sorrow. "He wouldn't. She hurt him. She was a spoiled brat who did whatever she pleased," Bree continued between hiccups and wet sobs. "A scandal destroyed her career, and she was finished. Trust me, now that Eric's rich and famous she'll try to worm her way back into his life and ruin it again. Don't be fooled by her sweetness. It's all an act."

"Okay, Bree. Okay. I'll make sure she leaves."

****

Jenna was in the ladies room, splashing water on her face when the door opened. She heard a clack of heels on the industrial tile. After wiping her face, she glanced up to see her former employee standing next to her. "Miss Davis."

"It's Mrs. Laine now."

"Of course," Jenna answered. Her exhaustion, both physical and mental collided and her stomach began to sour again. *Bree Laine*, *Eric's wife*. This woman, who once worked for her yet always seemed so in charge and so imposing, was no less so now.

"It isn't your place to be here," Bree said. "He's *my* husband now, and I'll take care of him."

Jenna returned one faint nod. She didn't have the

energy to spar with the woman and she wasn't interested in winning a battle of words. "Please, just let me say good-bye to him and I'll go."

Bree narrowed her eyes, eyes that looked to Jenna as though they contained bitterness instead of the fear and distress of a despairing wife.

"No."

Chapter Thirty

Jenna slipped into a stairwell and quickly took the steps to the ground floor of the hospital. After Eric's brother had "politely" asked that she leave, she'd brooked no argument.

Telling him Janie was Eric's daughter lay heavy on her tongue, but like everything that pertained to her daughter, Jenna made no snap decisions. She'd always kept Janie protected by carefully dissecting every choice she made—including what she and her daughter did, who they spoke to, and where they lived. This was no different.

On that day, Jenna snuck away like a fawn silently stepping through a forest glade. She never even said good-bye to Nick, for if she had, she would have let him hold her in his big embrace and she would have cried the truth.

****

Bergen County, New Jersey, 2007

Janie Black stared at her mother with a look of profound awe on her small angelic face. "Mommy, you look so pretty, just like a movie star."

Jenna smiled as she smoothed her hands along the delicate beadwork of the dress she was wearing. Her fingers shook a bit, and she hoped the slight tremble didn't reveal her anxiety. *If my five-year-old only knew.*

She had a date for opening night at the Met. The tickets had been a surprise from Warren Crandall, a man she'd been seeing for a few months. They were good seats but as much as Jenna loved Puccini, she would have preferred to enjoy the performance of *La Boheme* through opera glasses from the dress circle instead of the grand tier. The opening night of New York City's Metropolitan Opera was always attended by socialites, celebrities, and of course, the press. The grand tier was where they would be sitting.

Jenna leaned toward her mirror and threaded the posts of her smoky topaz earrings, also a gift from Warren, through her earlobes. He was one of the kindest and most considerate people she had ever met. He was also smart but shy in both his intelligence and attractiveness. He and Jenna were a good fit. Then again, she'd thought that about Jack, a rugged mechanic and Boyce, the English lit professor who taught at a local college two years and two towns ago. None of the places she'd lived in or the men she'd encountered had really "fit" enough and she'd always left before things could get too comfortable or too serious.

Jenna angled her head from side to side to determine how effectively her hair served as a disguise. It was tinted a deep ash and set into a mass of curls that fell wildly around her face. Time had passed, yet on occasion, someone still remarked about her resemblance to the once famous star. If tonight, in the opera lobby or restroom, someone should make the observation, Jenna would nod unconcerned and say what she always said. "Oh, I get that a lot."

She picked at one long lock of hair, pulling at the coil to let the wave drape over one eye and studied her reflection more closely. Her eyes were golden circles shining in contrast to dark shadow and charcoal liner. Her amber lipstick was a color she had never worn before and made her lips full and lush. Her dress was modestly high at the neckline but hugged her torso and hips so closely a plunging neckline wasn't necessary for it be drop-dead sexy.

It wasn't a sight Jenna was familiar with, a far cry from the neat conservative young mother who wore jeans or khaki trousers and man-tailored blouses. This sophisticated sensual look was also that of a woman, not the winsome, naive girl she had once been.

Warren picked her up promptly at five. He held one long stemmed red rose, its petals flawless and velvety soft. "You look beautiful," he said. But the compliment barely made it passed the breath of admiration that left his lips.

"Thank you." Jenna kissed him gently.

After Janie's sitter arrived, they rode to the city in Warren's late model, practical sedan.

He glanced quickly at her and then gave his attention back to the road. "I really it mean it Jenna, you look gorgeous. I'm a lucky man."

"I'm the one who's lucky. No one has ever treated me the way you do," she answered with a smile.

"Just say the word and you'll be treated like this forever."

Jenna cast her eyes away from the hopeful expression on his face. Although she enjoyed the comfort of being in his arms, and the subtle pleasure of his lovemaking, the sparks of passion weren't searing her skin. *Maybe in time.* "I'm not ready. I care for you so much, but I'm just not ready."

He smiled but she could see the disappointment sketched on his face even though she was looking at his profile.

"I can wait."

An hour later, they were dining at a small Manhattan bistro and later still, strolling arm and arm to the opera house. A modern collection of buildings was set far back from busy Columbus Avenue and taxis and busses whizzed by the open, tree lined plaza. Small white lights glittered on the trees and Jenna sighed contentedly as they climbed the steps to the entrance. Lincoln Center was one of her favorite places in New York, an elegant complex where the talented students of the famed Julliard learned their craft and the world's most renowned opera and ballet stars graced the stage.

An usher escorted them to their seats and Jenna eagerly perused the program. Huge chandeliers that looked like bursting stars retracted toward the ceiling, the orchestra warmed up, and the lights lowered as act one began. Warren's eyes frequently drifted from the stage to Jenna. He patted her hand when tears welled up in her eyes during Mimi and Rodolfo's duet and applauded with her as the curtain descended for intermission.

"Let's have some champagne," he said.

"Oh, I'm fine right here," Jenna answered.

"C'mon, we're at the Met. We have to have champagne at intermission. It's tradition."

Warren held out his hand and offered such a pleading look she could hardly refuse. They entered the orchestra-level lobby where a throng of patrons in formal attire milled about. Tenderly holding her hand, Warren led her to the bar.

"Thank you," she said, as he handed her a flute of champagne. Jenna drew the coils of hair falling against her shoulders toward her face.

"The pleasure is mine." Warren smiled, and with one finger brushed a ringlet away from her eye. He dipped his head close to hers. "I have a confession to make. This is the fanciest bunch of people I've ever been around."

Jenna glanced out at the crowd. Some of the women were resplendent, dressed in couture and dripping with jewels. It was funny how, no longer part of the spectacle, she found she could be impressed by it. "I guess we're just a couple of country bumpkins."

"Country bumpkins having drinks in the same room as celebrities…look who's standing over there."

Jenna turned and a fist squeezed her heart.

Eric, standing tall, his tux perfectly fitted to his wide shoulders, sipped casually from an amber colored bottle.

Jenna shuddered. "Oh my god."

"Oh, so I've got competition," Warren said on a laugh. "You're an Eric Laine fan." He pointed and lowered his voice. "Hey, look at that. He's drinking a beer straight from the bottle. He's at the opera, all decked out in a tux, and drinking a beer. Go figure."

As though Warren's words filtered through the crowd, Eric lowered the bottle and stared. Unblinking, unmoving, he stared. His lips parted as if he might call to her from across the room.

Jenna felt unseen hands suddenly at her back, pushing, urging her to go to him. *Tell him about Janie. Now's your chance. You have to tell him.*

She'd barely lifted one foot from the floor when

Bree appeared and looped one gloved arm around Eric's bicep. Scarlet velvet hugged her body, and her dark hair was swept high into an elaborate twist. A ruby surrounded by diamonds rested above very deep décolletage. The necklace was blinding even from a distance. Angling her lips, she broadcast a smug and triumphant smile.

Eric continued to stare while a red-faced Warren tugged at his tie. "I think he heard me. Good God I really am a country bumpkin."

The lobby lights flashed twice signaling the end of intermission. Jenna, her heart pounding frenetically, turned and she and Warren walked back to their seats.

****

Eric watched in pained breathlessness as the man with Jenna caressed her back and led her away. Bree yanked at his arm to rouse him from his stupor. Before facing her, he downed the rest of his beer.

They walked back to their theater box, a yardstick's space between them and silent. Eric drew long, hot breaths through his nose. It was torture to sit quiet in his seat knowing Jenna was so close. The moment he saw her, the air seemed to be charged with static and he felt his skin tingle. Only she could make every cell in his body respond like that. The sight of her was exhilarating. The sight of her devastating.

Memories of a girl with golden skin and hair as lustrous as the moon in a midnight sky swallowed him whole. Eric took another shaky sniff of air remembering the feel of that same hair caressing his body as they made love. He sat in the expensive box seat, oblivious to the music, oblivious to Bree's nails angrily tapping against her program, oblivious to everything save the sight of Jenna, a picture that would stay in his heart forever.

****

As Mimi lay dying in Rodolfo's arms and the last strains of *Done Leita Usci* faded, the curtain descended. Warren held Jenna's hand and rubbed her knuckles as she swiped at her tears with her other hand. "Does the opera always do this to you?"

"Yes," Jenna answered.

But it was a lie.

Chapter Thirty-One

Cromline, NY, six months later

Jenna signed her name on a dozen papers. After the formality of the walk-through, she'd sign the final note that would make the adorable little Cape Cod on Redbud Lane hers.

The realtor led her through the rooms—clean, the walls painted a standard off-white, the floors gleaming. The kitchen and bathrooms had recent remodels but everything else was original craftsman construction popular in the 1920's. Moldings, chair rails, and mantles were an artisan's gift to her. Jenna breathed deeply, lemon polish infusing the air in her new home, the one she'd hoped would be permanent. No more tramping about like gypsies. Stability for Janie was important. She would *not* be one of those kids yanked out of school every year. It was time to settle down.

Once the final paper was signed and the realtor gone, Jenna stretched arms wide and spun in a circle. She had a good feeling about the little house. It hadn't been bought in a convenient hurry, a space Jenna knew would be vacated before curtains could be properly hung. She'd bought the house after careful research. Less than an hour from her hometown of Pinehill, she and Janie would be an easy drive to her parents. But unlike Pinehill, a community of PTA and clothesline busybodies, Cromline was a reserved enclave with most of its residents living behind gates in homes stationed far from the next. The town was private…perfect.

Bundled in down jacket and boots, Janie came blustering through the French doors after exploring the yard. "Which is my room?" she asked breathlessly. "Are you really going to hang a canopy over my bed with sparkly stars?"

Jenna smiled down at the five-year-old. "I am, but until our stuff arrives from our old house in New Jersey, we're sleeping on the blow-up mattress."

A bag with clothes and toiletries, a small television, and linens were the only other items Jenna had packed. She glanced at her phone for the time. "Ready to do a little more exploring?"

Janie hopped up and down, her cerulean eyes wide and animated.

"I guess that's a yes then. Let's go *hunting* for a place to get something to eat."

Mother and daughter went to the main drag in town, a tree lined thoroughfare with specialty shops, and walked from block to block. *Hmm*, Jenna paused as she looked at the small sign in the window of an empty storefront. It read "To Let."

Hmm. She peered through the glass as an idea took root.

"Mama, I'm starving!" Janie tugged her hand and interrupted her musings.

"Starving? I am the worst mother ever."

Another block over they found a café, the sandwich board advertising the evening's specials. The regular menu was also balanced on the hostess' podium. They had a nice wine list and Jenna knew her search for an early dinner was over.

Two hours later, and back at the house, she settled Janie on the blowup bed and read her a story. After the long day's travel the sleepy child fluttered her eyelids and drifted off. Jenna made her way downstairs and grabbed the bottle of white she'd bought at the cafe. She'd neglected to pack any stemware and sat, feet crossed, leaning against a wall drinking what was left over from her lone glass at dinner. She picked up the remote control and turned on the small TV resting on the floor among cable wires and boxes. Jenna brought the bottle of wine to her lips and took a long pull. An easy heat warmed her face. She clicked till she found the correct channel, the channel broadcasting The Academy Awards.

It had been six long years since she'd concerned herself with The Oscars. Six years since she'd given any care to who wore what, who presented, who performed, and who got an Academy nod. Jenna had long detached herself from the world of bright lights and glitter. But this year was different. Eric had been nominated for best actor.

Jenna sipped as she watched the red-carpet entrance of celebrities, listening with half an ear to the interviews. Soft but thready air filled her as Eric stepped into the brilliance. A reporter asked him if he was excited at the prospect of winning and he simply shrugged and smiled in answer. *Was he*? Was gathering awards and accolades how he measured his life now?

A beaming Bree stood at his side. She was an image of perfection, stunning in a way Jenna didn't remember. Had wealth molded Bree Davis into startling beauty? Or had years of being loved by Eric given her the flawless glow?

"Stop it," Jenna whispered as she sipped more of the wine.

The night lingered on and the February cold stole through the curtainless windows. She wrapped a blanket around her shoulders and watched more. She'd been drinking a small amount of wine spread over the course of too many hours to feel really drunk, still a pleasant headiness lingered.

He was going to win, Jenna knew. He'd acted in the movie on the heels of his horrific accident, twenty-five pounds lighter, hollow-eyed and gaunt. He played a man who struggled with addiction, a role he perfected by channeling the desperation of his own childhood. That was something else Jenna knew. *Yes, he was going to win.*

The best actor announcement came toward the end of the program, but the camera periodically panned to him sitting front and center with his wife. They weren't holding hands, their heads not tilted toward each other's. *Could it be they weren't really as in love as the press reported?*

If Jenna were to somehow contact her famous ex, would telling him about Janie be news he would welcome? *Someday.* Someday, she'd tell him. The day would come when Jenna would have to once again look into his eyes. Her own fluttered shut and she pushed a tender ache away. *Someday.*

The category of best actor was announced, and Jenna straightened, her back flat against the plaster.

"And the Oscar goes to…"

Eric's name was called. An eruption of applause sounded, and the camera settled on him as an ecstatic

Bree leapt into his arms. After kissing her he sprinted to the stage. Jenna didn't hear his acceptance speech. The thumping of her heart drowned out all sound. She stared at him on her small television, watching as he smiled, holding the slender statuette in his hand. It was then she clicked off the set.

Sighing, she slid a bit lower down the wall pulling the blanket tight around her shoulders. She felt an odd mix of regret and pride. She also felt surprisingly happy for him as he still held a piece of her heart. A tear slipped from each eye. They weren't tears of sorrow, but the sweet pinch of emotion she'd feel if she were reading a beautiful poem. She remained sitting on the floor, eyes shut, as a time both joyous and heartbreaking flowed in a slow stream through her mind. As always, she let the memories come, breathing in and out until she was able to pack them away. Her time with Eric were love letters tied with a delicate ribbon—never to be thrown away but never to be read enough to wear away the ink.

She took a deep, cleansing breath and got up from the floor to put her empty bottle of wine in the sink.

Outside, landscape lights shone amber between scrubby bushes. Looking through the window and into the night she decided on a place for a swing set for Janie. Just off the patio would be the perfect spot. In the summer Jenna could sip lemonade and watch her daughter pump her small legs and reach for the sky.

Sighing contentedly, she switched on her phone and typed "stores to let, Cromline, New York." The little shop she'd wondered about popped up on the screen. It was a lovely space with glass plates set above molded panels of dark wood. The door in between was set back and a Victorian transom above was detailed with a flowery pattern of milky, stained glass.

"You're the perfect size for a little specialty shop. Maybe a children's store." Jenna stood in the kitchen studying more photos of the space on her phone. "Oh, what do you know about running a business?" What did she really know about anything? she mused. Maybe it was time to find out.

Jenna saved the realtor's webpage and turned off her phone. She'd call about the shop first thing in the morning. After five years it was time for a new life, a new career, and maybe even some friends—a new cast of characters. And if someone she met along the way should say she looked like the fallen star Angel, Jenna would smile brightly and say, "Oh, I get that a lot."

A word about the author…

Laura Liller scaled the steps of the elevated train trestle in her Bronx neighborhood at an early age. Her destination was New York City's High School of Art & Design – four short years later, The Fashion Institute of Technology. Laura hopes her art background and love of period clothing and architecture help her to "illustrate" her books as well as write them.

Laura currently lives in Upstate NY with her husband Mike and two cats. She has two daughters she lovingly refers to as "the girls who abandoned her." Laura is a typical romance fan and loves sipping wine outside by her fire pit with her husband.